PRAISE FOR WINTER RENSHAW

"Winter Renshaw crafts the best romances! She always delivers it all—angst, emotion, and humor. Her books are a true delight."
—Adriana Locke, *USA Today* bestselling author

"Passion. Drama. Angst. Renshaw nails the romance trifecta with her perfectly paced office love affair."
—Deanna Roy, *USA Today* bestselling romance author of the Forever series

"If you're looking for stories that are thought provoking, wildly sexy, and unputdownable, you'll never be disappointed with Winter Renshaw!"
—Jenika Snow, *USA Today* bestselling author

"The queen of contemporary angst knows how to curl toes while breaking hearts! A perfect romance for two imperfect lovers!"
—Sosie Frost, *Wall Street Journal* bestselling author

YOU OR SOMEONE LIKE YOU

OTHER TITLES BY WINTER RENSHAW

THE NEVER SERIES

Never Kiss a Stranger
Never Is a Promise
Never Say Never
Bitter Rivals

THE ARROGANT SERIES

Arrogant Bastard
Arrogant Master
Arrogant Playboy

THE RIXTON FALLS SERIES

Royal
Bachelor
Filthy
Priceless (an Amato Brothers crossover)

THE AMATO BROTHERS SERIES

Heartless
Reckless
Priceless

THE PS SERIES

P.S. I Hate You
P.S. I Miss You
P.S. I Dare You

THE MONTGOMERY BROTHERS DUET

Dark Paradise
Dark Promises

STAND-ALONES

Single Dad Next Door
Cold Hearted
The Perfect Illusion
Country Nights
Absinthe
The Rebound
Love and Other Lies

YOU OR SOMEONE LIKE YOU

winter renshaw

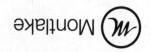

Montlake

Text copyright © 2023 by Winter Renshaw

Published by Montlake, Seattle

www.apub.com

Amazon, the Amazon logo, and Montlake are trademarks of Amazon.com, Inc., or its affiliates.

ISBN-13: 9781662513367 (paperback)
ISBN-13: 9781662513374 (digital)

Cover design by Hang Le
Cover photography by Michelle Lancaster
Cover image: @Andrius_Saz / Shutterstock

Printed in the United States of America

*To anyone who's found love in all the wrong places
when they weren't even looking for it in the first place.
And to T. W.*

CHAPTER ONE

SLOANE

"Can I just say . . . you make one hell of a *me*." My twin, Margaux, eyes my reflection from across the room before flinging her lavender velvet comforter off her legs. "Ugh."

Dashing to the hall bathroom, my sister's bare feet skitter and slide against the slick hardwood floors of our Midtown apartment. The clank of the toilet seat hitting the ceramic tank behind it sounds next, followed by god-awful retching that sends a flash of sympathy nausea to my middle. In the midst of everything, my stomach rumbles as if to remind me I haven't eaten since breakfast—not the wisest move when I'm about to go on a blind date with a total stranger on Margaux's behalf.

Dating—in and of itself—is hard enough.

Serving as someone's dating avatar? It's a whole new level of insanity that's going to require a substantial amount of liquid courage.

"I'm never eating leftover sushi again," Margaux says when she returns. Climbing beneath her blankets again, she rests her arm across her forehead like a sickly Victorian woman on a fainting couch. She's always been a glutton for sympathy, though. Anytime she has so much as a sniffle, you'd think she were dying of the Black Plague. Pointing across the room in my direction, she adds, "And I mean it this time."

"Sure you do." I wink and fix my attention on the pearl buttons on the cardigan I'm borrowing from her closet before running my palm along my fresh honey-blonde highlights.

"You should curl your hair," Margaux says. Food poisoning aside, she can't help but micromanage me. Despite being a mere two minutes older than me, she takes her big-sister role seriously, often wearing it like a badge of honor. At least that's what I tell myself. It very well could be that Margaux is just a control freak who lives to call all the shots.

"What? No." I wrinkle my nose and fasten the last button on my sweater. Despite it being June and an agreeable eighty degrees out, she insisted that this is what she had planned to wear.

"I literally curl mine every single day," she says. "You can't play the part without dressing the part, and that includes how I do my hair."

"But if he's never met you, how would he know you curl your hair every day?"

I was twelve the first time I attempted to wield a curling iron. It was an utter and complete failure of an ordeal, and I walked away smelling like singed hair and sporting a burnt spot the size of a postage stamp in the middle of my forehead. I've been curling iron celibate ever since, and I've vowed to embrace my stick-straight hair until my dying day. My sister can pry my flat iron from my cold, dead fingers.

"It's not about that," she says. "It's about authenticity. You're standing there in my heels, my skirt, and my cardigan. You're wearing my bracelet and my perfume and my lipstick. Your modern bob just looks low-key jarring with everything else going on."

She's not wrong about that last part. The lace and pearls on the sweater juxtaposed with the dainty gold tennis bracelet, hip-hugging wool pencil skirt, and classic red lip would be better served with loose, cascading waves, something romantic and feminine.

But there's no time.

And even if there were, I'd still give her a hard and resounding no.

"I thought you weren't trying to impress this guy? I thought you were just going on a date to appease your boss? I don't see how *any* of this matters." I bite my tongue to keep from pointing out that control-freak Margaux has entered the building, and she needs to take a back seat because she's knee deep in a bad case of food poisoning and I'm five minutes from climbing into an Uber, walking into a restaurant, and meeting some stranger as *her*.

She's not exactly in a position to be running the show.

"I just got my hair done this morning," I add, "which means I won't be curling a single strand."

The last time I pretended to be Margaux, I was twenty-one, and we were college seniors back in Ohio. She'd hit the frat parties a little too hard during finals week and all but promised me her firstborn child if I'd take her art history exam as her. Seeing how art history was (and still is) my favorite subject in the entire world, it was an easy yes. Hell, I'd have done it for fun because that's the kind of nose-in-a-book, head-in-the-clouds girl I was back then. I lived and breathed art in all its forms. Contemporary. Renaissance. Neoclassical. Cinematic. Literary. Undiscovered. Controversial. If it had a creative pulse, I couldn't get enough.

Meanwhile, Margaux lived and breathed boys, boss-girl besties, and being seen.

We may share facial features and a shoe size, but that's where our similarities end. Our personalities are night and day. If we didn't look undeniably identical, I might question our genetic relation.

"Fine, whatever," she says with a relenting sigh.

"Relax." I make my way to the side of her bed, adjust her blankets, and give her a reassuring smile before handing her the TV remote and her cell phone. "I've got this. Just rest, watch a funny movie, scroll TikTok, and try to refrain from puking your guts out again, okay?"

Sinking against her pillows, she nods. "I'll try."

"I'm going to grab you a ginger ale and some buttered saltines, and then I'm out." My watch vibrates on my wrist, letting me know my

Uber driver is almost here. My stomach somersaults. Even though this isn't *my* blind date, it's nerve racking all the same.

A first date is a first date is a first date.

I head to the kitchen and return with her drink and crackers and collect my phone, keys, and purse off her dresser where I'd left them earlier. She'd cornered me the second I got home from work—a mere fifty-two minutes ago—and begged me to go on her date tonight. Apparently she's gunning for a promotion, and her boss keeps dropping hints about setting her up with her single nephew. Coming from personal experience, I know what it feels like to not have the job you want, the job you've worked your entire life to have. I'd hate that for her.

"Sloane?" Margaux calls out before I leave for the night.

"Yeah?" I turn back, leaning against the doorjamb.

"Don't try too hard, okay?"

"What do you mean?"

"I don't want him to like you . . . I mean *me*," she says. "I don't exactly have the best track record with relationships."

It's true. All Margaux's romantic endeavors tend to go down in flames. The splits are rarely mutual and always accompanied by some dramatic fanfare. I love my sister, but I'd pity any man who attempts a relationship with her. There aren't a lot of men who can handle her larger-than-life persona and her boss-girl energy. She's not some diminutive wallflower with stay-at-home-wife ambitions. She has a personality, and she likes to call the shots. Most men tend to be more intimidated by her than anything. She's yet to find her equal, even in a city of millions.

"If I dated this guy . . . and if for some reason it didn't end well . . . Theodora could have me blacklisted from the industry." Sitting up, she adds, "Be nice. Be pleasant. But maybe don't flirt with him. Maybe . . . maybe just be boring."

Of all the things my sister has asked of me in our twenty-seven years on this planet, this one takes the cake.

"Can you do that?" Her round baby blues are filled with hope. "Can you be boring?"

"According to you, I already am, so it shouldn't be that hard," I say with a little more sarcasm lacing my voice than I intended. It's not easy being the introvert of our duo, to be made to feel like some kind of social pariah for not having twenty best friends on speed dial, for preferring a quiet Friday night in to an expensive blacked-out blur of a night out.

"Stop." Margaux rolls her eyes, her expression softening. "You're not boring. You're just . . ." I hold my breath, waiting for her to replace the word *boring* with some adjacent term that'll only serve as a backhanded compliment. Something like *quiet, reserved,* or *introverted.* "You know what I'm trying to say. Anyway, thank you for doing this. Truly. Thank you."

My watch vibrates, letting me know my ride is here.

"What's this guy's name?" I adjust my purse strap over my shoulder before tugging at the itchy lace sticking out from my collar. "I don't think you've told me yet."

"Roman Bellisario," she says. "Theodora showed me a picture of him once. Dark hair, dark eyes, razor-sharp jawline, tall . . ."

Margaux's voice grows distant as she continues to describe him, and the world around me fades away by the second.

I don't need to hear another word.

I know exactly who he is.

"My ride's downstairs." I swallow a hard lump that has suddenly formed in my throat. "Guess I'll . . . see you in a few."

Before I shut the door, my sister calls out a quick *good luck*—which is ironic because that's exactly what I'm going to need to get through tonight.

CHAPTER TWO

ROMAN

I trace a fingertip against the side of a perspiring crystal tumbler, focusing on the indentation on my left ring finger where my platinum wedding band has resided for the past ten years—three years too long, if you ask my aunt Theodora.

If it weren't for the mindless chatter of bar patrons around me, I could almost hear her voice gently scolding me for still wearing it, not mincing a single word as she reminds me I'll never find another woman with that *thing* on my finger, all but referring to it as deadweight.

But that's kind of the point.

I don't want another woman.

I want the one I had before she was heartlessly ripped from this world without warning by some spineless coward who hit her with their car and fled the scene before they could answer for what they did. The fact that the bastard is still out there, living life like nothing ever happened while our lives were permanently altered, is something I've yet to get over.

I don't know that I ever will.

Not even sure that I can.

"Another one, sir?" The young, overly friendly bartender points to my empty drink. He can't be much older than twenty-two or twenty-three, if I had to guess. Judging by the stars in his eyes, life hasn't screwed with him yet.

But it will.

Sooner or later, it always does.

I check the time on my phone—my blind date should be here any minute.

"Might as well." I slide the glass his way, and he uncaps a bottle of top-shelf Macallan, pouring two fingers' worth and then some, like he senses I'm on the cusp of something . . . *unnatural*. I've never been one to let nerves show, but I imagine I'm giving off the kind of vibe that tells everyone within a ten-foot radius that this is the last place I want to be tonight. "That's good. Thank you."

I take a sip and scan the restaurant portion of the bar in search of the poor woman my aunt sent to "save me from myself."

Her words, of course.

For the past few months, she hasn't stopped telling me about one of her employees at Lucerne Product Development, some blue-eyed, blonde-haired, bubbly "fun-time girl" who would "pull me out of my shell" and "usher me back into the world of the living."

I didn't waste my breath telling her blondes have never been my type.

And I love my shell—it's impenetrable.

It's Teflon and Kevlar and Fort Knox.

It's where my daughters are.

It's my entire world . . . what remains of it, anyway.

While I've no doubt been existing with one foot in the grave and the other one in the land of the living, there's no time stamp on grief. It takes however long it takes. I'm not going to hurry it up so my meddling-but-well-intentioned aunt has one less thing to worry about.

That's the thing about death—it's inconvenient as hell, and there's not a damn thing anyone can do about it.

Nevertheless, Theodora is the most persistent person on the face of the earth. She refuses to take no for an answer—which is how I ended up here . . . at the bar of some hotel restaurant in Gramercy Park, waiting for some poor stranger who's likely only doing this as a favor to her insistent boss.

Sliding my phone from my pocket, I pull up the Lucerne Product Development site, tap on the employee directory, and type in the name my aunt gave me: Margo.

Zero results.

Exhaling, I change the spelling, this time searching up *Margaux*.

The first result, Margaux Abbott, looks old enough to be my grandmother—white hair, chained glasses, librarian frown and all.

The second listing, Margaux Sheridan, matches Aunt Theodora's description of blonde and blue eyed. A blinding white smile that takes up the entire lower half of her face alludes to the bubbly part. I zoom in, examining her as if I'm looking for clues to some mystery—or a sign that tonight's not going to be an awkward, uncomfortable, complete waste of time.

Pale-pink earrings in the shape of large-petaled flowers hang from Margaux's ears in her company directory photo, and her lashes are much too long, dark, and thick to be natural. A triple-layer pearl necklace is fastened around her neck, and a diamond cameo brooch adorns her lapel. I can't be sure if she's going for a coastal grandma look or if this is some kind of a joke.

Darkening my screen, I return my phone to my pocket and my attention to my scotch.

"Mr. Bellisario?" A petite hostess dressed fittingly in head-to-toe black places a palm on my shoulder. "Your table is ready."

Drink in hand, I follow her to a corner booth with a single flickering candle, a pristine white tablecloth, and a small vase of three red roses in full bloom.

It's so romantically cliché it's almost laughable.

Once seated, I take a deep breath, get my shit together, and steal a glance around the room. All around me, silverware clinks against china and stemware. Voices drone on, conversations layered one on top of the other. The smell of expensive perfume and aftershave dances through the air, mixed with the savory scents of a five-star dining experience.

Everywhere I look are couples, their faces painted in soft candlelight as they gaze across the table at one another with stars for eyes. This restaurant gives a whole new meaning to the phrase "Love is in the air."

Theodora chose this place on purpose, I have no doubt.

I haven't been on a first date since Emma, and the day I married her, I promised she'd be my last date.

My *forever* date.

Death has a way of changing things, though, of making agreements null and void whether you like it or not.

I check the time, resisting the urge to roll my eyes at the fact that the allegedly effervescent Ms. Margaux Sheridan is eight minutes late. I'll give her seven more, and then I'm leaving. If there's anything I've learned in the past three years, it's that life is too short for the things that don't matter—like blind dates people agree to under duress.

For a moment, I visualize my life as sand falling through the center of an hourglass, each granule representing a second I'll never get back. When you lose something—or in my case someone—it forever alters your perspective on things.

All a person has, truly, is their time.

Everything else is inconsequential.

"I'm so sorry I'm late." A breathy voice pulls me from my muddling thoughts. Glancing up, I'm met with frosty Alaskan-blue eyes, a fringe of dark lashes, and hair the color of glazed honey and summer sunshine. "Traffic was terrible getting over here, and the Uber driver refused to take a different route and—never mind. I'm here. That's all that matters, right?" Her full lips pull into a nervous smile before she extends her hand like she's about to interview for a job. "Margaux. Margaux Sheridan. It's nice to meet you."

She's no Emma, but at least she has basic manners.

That and she's not the worst thing in the world to look at. Far from it. I'd have to be blind not to notice the subtle, radiant beauty emanating off her, quietly commanding my attention. Not that I have any intention of doing anything with said attention, but maybe tonight won't be the worst thing I've experienced in a while.

Could absolutely be worse.

"Roman." Rising, I meet her buttery-soft hand with mine and give it a firm shake better suited for a business meeting than a date, and then I wait like a proper gentleman as she takes the seat across from me.

Studying her in the quivering candlelight that filters the space between us, a strange twinge of familiarity hits me—like I've seen her somewhere before. I've never set foot in my aunt's building downtown, so it wouldn't be that.

"I'm sorry . . . Have we met before?" I ask.

She squints as if she's studying me. "Um, no? I don't believe so?"

"You look familiar." My gaze narrows as I try to place her, but my concentration is interrupted by our server.

"I get that a lot." She orders a cucumber gin and tonic before turning her attention to the food menu.

Sniffing, I say, "I took you as more of a rosé kind of girl."

"I would never." A flicker of a grin crosses her full lips before fading completely, like it was never there to begin with. Nerves, perhaps. I won't hold it against her. "There are rosé girls, then there are cucumber-gin-and-tonic girls. I can see how you might mix us up, but trust me, we're night and day."

Witty without being flirty.

I can respect that.

"Fascinating," I say with a gracious smile to compensate for my sarcasm. "So, Margaux, tell me about yourself."

I hate this.

I hate every damn second of this.

It's not who I am. It's not who I want to be. It's not *where* I want to be.

My muscles are riddled with tension, perhaps in an attempt to keep me from crawling out of my skin.

"Oh," she says, eyes sparking as if she's surprised by my question. That or she's nervous. I tend to have that effect on people—but tonight I'm doing my best to not come off like a giant prick allergic to happiness. It's the least I can do since she got dressed up and came all this way. "Um, what all has Theodora told you about me?"

"Very little, actually." I don't want to offend her with the fact that my aunt sold her as a *good-time girl*. To Theodora's generation, that sort of label has *other* connotations. I also don't want to offend her by confessing that I asked zero questions because I have zero interest in pursuing anything beyond this insufferable evening. "What has she told you about me?"

"Not a whole lot." She looks around the restaurant, though whether she's searching for our server and her drink or taking in the scenery is beyond me. It's all the same, I suppose. Tucking a strand of glossy hair behind one ear, she returns her serene gaze to mine.

"Okay, so on that note," I say as if I'm conducting a work interview, "let's start with you."

This is *excruciating*.

And it's clear I'm going to be doing the conversational heavy lifting tonight.

"What do you want to know?" She blinks at me with those baby doll eyes of hers, and I'm not sure if there's a single thought behind them.

My jaw tightens, and a dull ache floods the sides of my face as a tension headache forms in real time.

Margaux toys with her pearl necklace, tugging on it as if it's almost choking her. In the process, the top button of her cardigan has come undone, revealing a hint of creamy skin, but the rest of her is conservatively covered despite the early-summer heat wave we're having. When she's finished fussing with her necklace, she pulls at the itchy-looking lace collar of her sweater.

Nothing about her looks comfortable.

Nothing about her looks like she wants to be here either.

Perhaps we have something in common already.

CHAPTER THREE

SLOANE

This is painful.

Physically painful—all the way to the marrow of my bones.

I'm baking in this sweater and filtering every word that comes out of my mouth in an attempt to ensure that I'm dreadfully boring per Margaux's orders. My back hurts from sitting straight and proper and my face hurts from smiling and my head hurts from nodding.

It's taking everything I have not to wince and cringe my way through this clunky, flavorless conversation.

I take a generous swill of my gin and tonic, which isn't kicking in fast enough.

If Margaux were here—like she was meant to be—she'd breeze through all this small talk with a smile on her face and a witticism on the tip of her tongue. That woman has the art of conversation down to a science. She can talk to anyone, anywhere, about anything, and make it look like child's play. She can walk into a room full of strangers and walk out with five new best friends and an invitation to be in some stranger's wedding.

Me, on the other hand? I'd rather stick a rusty needle in my eye than talk about the weather, mayoral candidates, whatever new restaurant opened up in the East Village last week, or my favorite Hamptons hot spots. Superficial topics have never appealed to me.

At least I'm killing it in the uninteresting department, though I can't tell whether Roman's eyes are glazed over because of his half-empty glass of liquor or because I'm quite literally boring the man to tears.

"Food's taking a while, isn't it?" he asks only a few minutes after we order.

I get the sense he wants the evening to hurry along just as much as I do.

"Places like this aren't exactly known for their speed," I say in the most monotone voice I can muster in accordance with Margaux's rules. "Plus, I think it's only been five minutes."

Who knew three hundred seconds could feel like three hundred years?

He takes a substantial sip from his glass. I swear each drink that passes his lips is bigger than the one before it. The next time our server stops by, he'll be due for a refill, and the night is exhaustingly young.

I steal a look around the restaurant—it's all I can do to distract myself from the fact that I'm sitting across from Roman Bellisario . . . a notoriously elusive and demanding New York art collector whose reputation I'm far too familiar with, given my line of work. As the director of the Westfeldt International Art Gallery in SoHo, I've conversed and negotiated with his personal curator more times than I care to count, though this is the first time I've ever been face to face with the jerk himself.

Only so far, he's yet to be a jerk.

Bland, maybe.

But not an asshole.

Certainly not the arrogant dumpster fire of a man I was anticipating.

I imagine he's on his best behavior, given that this is a first date. Fortunately for him, he won't need to maintain the illusion that he's actually some kind of decent person because this first date will be our last date too.

Our paths first crossed three years ago, and in one of the worst ways.

"So did you grow up in the city or . . . ?" His voice tapers into nothing, like he doesn't have the energy to finish his sentence. The lack of excitement in his tone tells me this small talk is just as painful for him as it is for me. There's no twinkle in his eye that hints he's enjoying a single second of our evening so far.

"Ohio," I say. "A small town about forty miles north of Columbus. You?"

I keep the details to a minimum to avoid the risk of diving into any kind of conversation with meaning. This needs to be bare bones, dry, stilted, and forgettable.

"Born and raised here," he says. I can't be sure, but I swear he's stifling a yawn. He dips his head down and checks his phone.

I do the same.

"Sorry—it's my sitter," he says a moment later. "If you'll excuse me, I'll be right back."

With that, he leaves me alone at the table, disappearing into some hallway behind the hostess stand. Pressing my lips together, I wrap my head around the fact that Roman Bellisario is a dad.

There isn't a fatherly thing about this man.

He's a ruthless negotiator, a nepotism trust-fund type—the last kind of person I can picture tucking in a child at night or reading bed-time stories or doing the whole tooth fairy, Easter bunny, Santa Claus thing.

Though I imagine he has paid help who do that for him.

Most people like him leave the child-rearing to the salaried, résuméd professionals.

They outsource.

I nurse my drink as I wait for his return, and I take the opportunity to check a few work emails.

Our food arrives in his absence, and for a moment I contemplate whether he made the phone call up so he could bail. You never know with people, and to be completely honest, it would be a bold but fair move.

No one should have to suffer through this a minute longer than necessary.

From the corner of my eye, I watch the couple to my right. His hand brushes hers from across the table. She reaches to catch a drip of red wine from the corner of his mouth. In the midst of it all, he can't seem to take his eyes off her for a single second. They're connected, entranced, infatuated with one another.

It's been years since I've had that, and 99 percent of the time I don't think twice about it. Dating . . . sex . . . relationships . . . it's all taken a back seat these days while I focus on my career. The art-collector world is intricate, strategic, and all about who you know. Any spare time I have is spent on fostering my professional connections. I'm on an elevator to the top, and I have no plans to disembark anytime soon.

"Apologies," Roman says when he (shockingly) returns. "It's the first time in years that I've left the girls alone for more . . . they wanted to tell me good night before they went to bed."

Nearly choking on my drink, I clear my throat. "Girls? You have daughters?"

Being a father is one thing.

But being a girl dad? Completely different ball game.

"Two," he says. His dark eyes illuminate for the first time tonight. "Adeline's five and Marabel's four."

I've never been one to fawn over children and babies—to be honest, sometimes they scare me. They seem so delicate, so unpredictable, so fueled with unbridled emotion. But the idea of this tall, dark, and grumpy megawatt millionaire melting over his two little girls is . . . kind of sweet.

Immediately I picture two little darlings with velvet ribbons in their hair, patent leather Mary Janes, and dimpled grins. Like two little Eloises living at the Plaza.

And their names . . . I could *melt*.

Straightening my shoulders and clearing my throat, I remind myself I'm on a very simple mission. No need to complicate it or get off track. Besides, he could be the best dad in the entire world to them, but it doesn't change the way he treats other people—especially in my industry.

There's no excuse for being a grade-A asshole.

Ever.

Biting my tongue, I swallow my curiosity away to keep from asking about his ex. Even if this *were* a real date, the question would be completely out of pocket.

"So what brought you all the way here from Ohio?" he asks.

"A—" I stop myself before I blurt out the word *art*. "*All* the things the city has to offer."

I give myself an invisible pat on the back for that save.

"Right, but why Manhattan? Why not Chicago? Los Angeles? London? What brought you *here*?" he asks.

Bless his heart—he's making an effort now.

Though there's still a lack of enthusiasm in his dark-brown eyes or a hint of genuine interest in his monotone Bruce Wayne voice.

Roman slices into his filet mignon, forks it, and lifts it to his full lips. Two dimples flank his mouth as he chews, and his jaw muscles divot. There's no denying the man is attractive. Some might even argue he's hotter than sin. Broad shoulders, a permanent poker face, and Big Dick Energy tend to do that to a man.

Fortunately I'm not the shallow sort—and even more fortunately, I'm not here for myself.

"Came here in high school for a school trip." I leave out the part about the trip being an Alice Calhoun High Art Club trip. "Fell in love and instantly knew it's where I wanted to live after college."

"Where'd you go to school?" he asks. "And what'd you study?"

Again, there's very little interest being conveyed beyond his actual words, but since he asked, I'll answer. Each question, each bite only brings us closer to the inevitable end of the evening.

"The Ohio State University," I say, which is the truth. But I give him Margaux's major. "I studied marketing with a minor in communications."

"That's how you ended up in product development, I take it?" He forks another bite of his steak, and I deduce he'd much rather be putting a fork in this date.

It's funny—as much as Theodora was pushing for Margaux to go out with her nephew, I'd have assumed he at least wanted to take her out. Now I get the sense that he's merely doing her a favor.

"Exactly." The fewer words I utter tonight, the better. No need to wax poetic about the brand deals Margaux brokers—specifically the ones with social media influencers wanting to start a skin-care line or branch into athleisure or whatever "merch" is trending at the moment. I don't pretend to know half of what she does on a daily basis. All I know is she's really good at it. One of the best. "You?"

"Beg your pardon?" he asks, though I'm quite certain he heard me clear as a bell.

"You?" I repeat.

"What about me?" His eyes glint, as if he's keen to the fact that I'm using as few words as possible, as if he finds amusement in making me ask a proper, fully formed question.

"Where did you go to school and what did you study?" I ask. While I'm well aware of this man's reputation in the art-collecting underworld of the city, I don't know much about him otherwise.

There's no Wikipedia page on Roman Bellisario.

No website.

No red carpet charity gala photos.

Nothing.

At least there wasn't anything when I googled him years ago after he had me fired from my dream job over an honest mix-up.

I'd seen him at my old gallery a handful of times, walking around like he owned the place. Negotiating prices on nonnegotiable pieces.

Demanding private showings before or after hours. No one ever told him no. He was one of their biggest clients.

"NYU," he says, washing down his answer with a sip of amber-colored liquor. "I studied art history. Had every intention of advancing my degree and pursuing a career in higher education. Teaching, to be specific." He pauses, his attention flicking down for a beat. "Still think I'd have made one hell of an art history professor, but I guess things don't always work out the way we plan them."

"What stopped you?" I can't help myself.

I also can't help myself from imagining him commanding an auditorium full of young minds, his broad shoulders and generous biceps straining inside a tweed jacket, his messy hair and tortoise-framed glasses giving him that dark-academia edge that's all the rage right now. The front row would be filled with girls, all taking notes, all raising their hands for a chance to be in his hot seat, if only long enough to ask a single question.

As much as I hate it, the man is speaking my language. My skin is on fire, sparked with the electric urge to wax poetic on favorite painters, periods, and Picasso pieces. No doubt he's a man who knows his stuff, and I'm sure he could teach me a thing or two.

But *Margaux* wouldn't know a Picasso if it hit her in the face.

Margaux would talk about a Taylor Swift or Bruno Mars concert she attended at Madison Square Garden last month or some trendy, hard-to-find candle she hunted down in a boutique on Bleecker.

Still, I'm pleasantly surprised by the fact that he's not just some old-moneyed jerk trying to pad his portfolio with priceless works of art he can use for tax-evasion purposes down the road (it's a thing).

"My father." A hint of a wince colors his handsome face, and a divot forms along his jaw. "It wasn't the Bellisario way, or something along those lines. Feels like a lifetime ago. I try not to think about it too much."

"What's stopping you now?" I ask. If I had to guess, he looks to be somewhere in his midthirties . . . surely he's not still living under his father's thumb? If he's got enough cash to drop millions on Stefan DuMonde paintings and Ophelia Finnegan sculptures, he's got enough cash to pursue his PhD.

"Between running my father's company and raising my daughters, my spare time is limited these days."

"Do you have help?" I ask before clarifying. "Raising them?"

I shouldn't be engaging in this conversation, taking it to deeper levels and veering off the small-talk beaten path, but surely a question or two won't hurt.

"I have hired help, if that's what you're asking," he says.

His lips press flat like he wants to say more but changes his mind.

"I'm sorry. That must be difficult," I say.

"It's not the way we planned it, but it is what it is."

I would love to know what exactly "it" is.

Did they divorce?

Did she suddenly decide motherhood and marriage weren't for her and fly the coop?

Did she somehow tragically pass away?

What was her name?

What was she like?

And most importantly, what kind of woman can turn Roman Bellisario from a bona fide heartless bastard into a doting girl dad?

A hundred other questions flood my mind, but I wash them down, one after another, with my cucumber gin and tonic.

"Anyway." He tosses back the remainder of his drink before placing his fork and knife at the bottom of his plate.

He's done with dinner.

Probably done with this conversation too.

I don't say another word. I simply work on finishing my duck à l'orange and cauliflower mash.

"I'm sorry." I point at my still-full plate between bites. I've always been a slow eater, but tonight it seems especially that way.

"Take your time," he says, though I can't tell if he means it, if he's being sarcastic or gracious or all of that or none of that. All his mixed signals make him impossible to read.

Roman checks his phone . . . again.

Taking one more bite, I place my napkin over my plate to signal that I, too, am done. I'm still hungry. Famished, actually, given that I accidentally skipped lunch today. But no need to drag this date on longer than necessary. I'll hoover a bowl of Reese's Puffs over the sink like a heathen the second I get home if it means cutting out of this early.

Roman drags in a long, slow breath, pinches the bridge of his nose, and turns his attention back to me. I brace myself, preparing for some uncomfortable speech or phony excuse that'll put us both out of our miseries.

"I'm sorry," he says. "I haven't done this in a long time . . . the dating thing . . ." He begins to say something again, only to stop and pause. "Look, you seem nice and all, and I know my aunt meant well when she set this up, but I'm just not—"

His speech is cut short by the server, who presents a leather folder with tonight's bill. Lifting his finger, he motions for the man to wait, and then he retrieves three crisp hundred-dollar bills.

"Keep the change," he tells the guy, who walks off with raised eyebrows and a subdued smile on his face. Turning back to me, he continues, "My wife died, Margaux. Three years ago. To say it's been difficult would be the understatement of the century. I'm not really looking to move on. Not anytime soon, anyway. I'm focusing on my business and my daughters, and I don't really know how someone new would fit into any of that."

"You don't have to explain yourself." I stop him before he can continue since it isn't necessary.

Exhaling, he leans back, as if he's relieved, as if all the pressure has been released from the room.

"I'm pretty career focused myself," I say. "I'm flattered Theodora thought of me in this way, but I think we can both agree we're not a match."

Roman tosses back the final few drops of his drink before giving a nod, and he even flashes some semblance of a smile. While he doesn't seem like a happy man, there's no denying he's happy about this.

"I'm sorry about your wife," I say. And I mean it. He might be a colossal asshole who had me fired, but he's still a human being sporting a gaping hole where his heart should be. "Your daughters are lucky to have a dad who puts them first."

I would know.

Our father always put us first, even after my mother left him. We were his everything, his reason for existing. He made that crystal clear. He was hurting, but he still kept room in his heart for us. He never did get over my mother, but it wasn't for a lack of trying. She was it for him. Everyone else paled in comparison.

Roman returns his wallet to his pocket, an official signal that this date is over.

Reaching for my purse, I rise from the table. "Thank you for dinner."

"My pleasure," he says, though he doesn't mean it, I'm sure. It's just one of those things you say without thinking.

We leave the dining room together, head past the hostess, and weave through pockets of waiting patrons before hitting the sidewalk.

Stopping next to a newspaper rack, we give each other one final awkward smile and nod. No *goodbye, good luck,* or words of formality necessary. A moment later, he checks his phone for the millionth time tonight. If we were on a real date, it'd be a red flag, and I'd take it personally.

"Hm," he says, though he doesn't elaborate.

His mouth turns down at the sides.

I don't ask.

It's not my business, and it doesn't matter.

"All right then . . . ," I say to myself before turning to leave. Starting my walk home, I feel almost weightless as the stress of the evening evaporates into the city air. I Ubered here out of necessity earlier, given that time was of the essence, but nothing beats a Friday-night walk in an emptied-out Manhattan. The smells. The sights. The sounds. The people-watching. It's like being a fly on the wall of the most interesting place in existence. It's one of my favorite little pastimes, if one can call it that. Margaux always teases that I absorb my surroundings as if by osmosis. "See you around, I guess."

He lifts his phone to his ear, his dark brows knit. I don't think he heard me, nor is he aware that I'm walking away.

As he said earlier, it is what it is.

It's an expression I've always found banal yet somehow applicable to every situation in existence. Growing up, my father always taught us that we can't always change a situation, but we can always change our attitude toward that situation. Sometimes the best attitude a person can have is simply acceptance.

Chuckling to myself as I leave, I accept that this was the strangest date I've ever had in my life.

I'm four blocks into my journey when I bump into Roman at a crosswalk. Had I noticed him any sooner, I'd have kept my eyes down, only now it's too late. We're staring at each other, separated by four people and a restless standard poodle with a Louis Vuitton collar.

"Hi . . . ," I say, though it comes out as more of a question than a greeting.

"My driver had a family emergency," he says with a slight air of annoyance.

"You didn't want to Uber or . . . ?" I ask. There's always the subway. Or a yellow cab. Buses, of course. He has options. Trekking home in those expensive-looking leather loafers seems like it should be the last of them.

A brunette woman between us looks at him, then me, then rolls her eyes, as if our conversation inconveniences her. She pops a white earbud into her ear and steps aside, leaving a gap where she once stood.

"You headed uptown?" he asks, ignoring my question.

"Midtown," I say. The crosswalk light changes, indicating it's safe to walk. "You?"

"Upper East Side," he says.

Somehow in the process of making our way across the street, we wind up behind the four people and the poodle, the two of us walking side by side.

A block later and we're still walking . . . together.

It's strange, even stranger than the date we just ended, but I'm not going to be rude and suddenly veer off onto some side street only to risk bumping into him again.

My goal tonight was to be boring, not weird.

Huge difference.

Soon, though, that one block becomes two, which then becomes three, then four, and before I know it, we're approaching my street, and we still haven't breathed a single additional word to one another.

The second my building comes into view, I nonchalantly dig my keys out of my purse, jangling them as if to wordlessly let him know I've reached my destination. I'd thank him for walking me home, but I don't know if that's what he did? We simply happened to be going in the same direction on the same route at the same time.

"This is your place?" He breaks the silence.

I point toward the front door of my building. "This is me."

He stops in his tracks. His Italian shoes look out of place on this humble stretch of Midtown street.

"This building," he says, scratching at his temple. He points at the brown structure with matching front steps and the black iron railings and a sign that says THE MAYBERRY—ESTABLISHED 1912. "This one right here?"

My gaze narrows as I attempt to wrap my head around what he's getting at. Does he want me to invite him up for a nightcap? Or god forbid, a one-night stand? I don't care how disarmingly attractive this man is, I could never let him into my home *or* my pants.

He stands frozen beside me, contemplative, lost in thought, staring at the steps like he's seen a ghost. Snapping out of it, his gaze lowers. He runs his hands through his dark hair before blowing a hard breath between his full lips.

"I'm, um, going to head up now . . ." I jingle my keys once again. He looks straight at them as he rakes his hand along his jaw. "Have a good rest of your night."

His eyes drift toward my hand before settling on a cracked section of sidewalk.

"Jesus Christ," he mutters under his breath.

He's visibly upset about something.

Meanwhile, I've never been more confused about anything in my entire life.

"Everything okay?" I can't, in good conscience, leave him like this.

Is he diabetic? Is he having an episode?

His lips press together as our eyes meet. The streetlight above paints harsh shadows on his chiseled face, so I'm unable to accurately gauge his expression.

"Where did you get that key chain?" he asks.

I lift my keys, isolating the canary-yellow enameled *H* with the red leather lover's knot—a limited edition Halcyon key chain I happened to get during my tenure at the very gallery he got me fired from.

Years ago, we were attempting to broker a deal with an up-and-coming artist who went by the pseudonym Halcyon. Much like Banksy, Halcyon preferred to be faceless and nameless. An enigma known only for what they created and not what (or who) they were. Only Halcyon hasn't reached near the notoriety that Banksy has over the years. The average person wouldn't have the faintest clue who Halcyon is.

And to this day, no one knows.

They only worked through a third-party representative who kept their identity anonymous, and they haven't produced anything in years.

A cold flush of panic sears through me, and heat creeps along the back of my neck. It was a mix-up over a Halcyon piece three years ago that cost me my job. I'd sold a piece entitled *You or Someone like You* to a local collector for a sizable sum—the biggest sale my gallery had made that entire year—only to learn Roman had reserved it with another staff member. It was an honest communication mix-up. We didn't find out until it was too late.

It was a whole thing that I'd sooner wipe from my memory if I could.

"This one?" I ask.

"Yes." His reply is impatient, pressing. "Where did you get that?"

The yellow key chains with the lover's knots were made in a limited batch for promotional purposes, and I managed to nab one of only ten in existence. Being that it's a collector's item, it's slightly frivolous of me to use it as an everyday item, but its sunny yellow color makes me happy every time I see it, and it'd be a shame to let it sit in some box in some drawer collecting dust. Besides, it's a symbol of resilience to me. Mix-up or not, the sale of that piece was (and still is) my biggest to date.

To me, this key chain represents strength and perseverance.

I didn't let that firing get the best of me. If anything, it only made me tougher and more determined than ever to make it in my industry. I know how it feels to love your career more than anything in the entire world. As different as Margaux and I are, we're both dedicated, loyal, hardworking professionals. If being on this date tonight helps my sister get that much closer to her promotion, it's a small price to pay.

"Someone gave it to me a few years back," I say, feigning a foggy memory in hopes he won't pry any further. Then again, Halcyon is a popular topic among those in the art-world know. That said, Halcyon hasn't produced any work in years. Word on the street is that it was some PR stunt or get-rich-quick scheme, and that Halcyon (whoever they are) went back to their day job. I don't want to believe that, seeing how the paintings Halcyon made were visually stunning and original masterpieces. Guess we'll have no way of knowing until the faceless, nameless person behind the paintbrush steps forward.

If they ever do . . .

"You like Halcyon?" I ask. It's a stupid question, I'm sure. Every art collector loves Halcyon. Even if they don't like their work, they like how much their work is worth. Art that has only appreciated in value sevenfold since Halcyon quit painting.

I stop myself before asking if he owns any Halcyon pieces.

He never revealed during dinner that he collects art—only that he wanted to teach art history once upon a time—and it's a tidbit I only know because of my profession.

Margaux wouldn't know any of this.

"How do you know who Halcyon is?" he asks. But before I can answer, he adds, "I told you I was an art history major at NYU, that I wanted to be a professor, and you didn't mention you were a fan of one of the most obscure artists in the city? Someone only those in the know would . . ."

He stops talking.

I wrinkle my nose. I'm not sure what he's getting at.

"I'm sorry—I'm terrible at small talk," I say, hoping that's an acceptable answer. "I guess I should've worked that into the conversation, huh?"

His piercing stare burns into me. I shudder, worried he's somehow piecing everything together. I should have said my sister is an art dealer and gave me the key chain as a gift. Maybe that would've sufficed? Maybe he wouldn't have thought anything of it and let it go instead of pinning me into place with the weight of his scrutinizing glower.

I'm seconds from accepting the fact that the jig is up when his expression softens, and he waves his hand.

"I'm sorry," Roman says. "Forget I said anything. Just . . . forget all of this."

Before I get the chance to reply, he's making his way up the block. And to think, *I* was worried about being the weird one tonight.

Halcyon key chain in hand, I traipse up the steps and head to my apartment, grateful that this night is over and that I'll never have to deal with Roman Bellisario ever again.

CHAPTER FOUR

ROMAN

"They're out cold," my babysitter, Harper, says when I get home. The living room is dim, save for a lamp on the console table behind the sofa. She darkens her phone screen, peels a throw blanket off her lap, and meets me by the kitchen island.

"Were they good for you?" I ask, digging cash from my wallet.

"Perfect little angels," she says. "Though Adeline insisted that I read her two extra bedtime stories. She said it would help her fall asleep faster, and she was right. She was out before I even got to the second one."

Adeline can be quite persistent sometimes, not unlike her aunt Theodora.

"How was your date?" she asks, brows lifted. At nineteen, Harper's still just a kid herself, but she's known my family, as well as our circumstances, for years. She lives in the brownstone next door, and her mother used to invite Emma over for bunco and wine every Thursday with a few of her friends. Emma had no idea how to play, but she learned quickly, and it soon became one of her favorite things.

Every Monday for the first year after Emma's passing, Harper's mom would bring us dinner. In a city where most people are swept up in their own schedules and busyness, the Crawfords are a genuine breath of fresh air.

"Food was decent," I say, not wanting to get into the details. There's no point.

Harper looks at me with heavy, sad eyes—the way most people look at me these days.

I hand her a hundred-dollar bill from my wallet. "Thanks for watching the girls."

"Anytime, Mr. Bellisario." She offers a wistful smile before showing herself out. "Have a good one."

"You too, kid."

On my way to retire for the evening, I poke my head into the girls' shared room, lingering to watch my sleeping daughters long enough to see the rise and fall of their chests and hear the soft lull of their snores. Ever since Emma passed, I can't go to bed without checking to make sure Adeline and Marabel are breathing.

As always, death changes a person.

If anything ever happened to my girls, I don't know what I'd do.

A minute later, I'm changing out of my suit and climbing into my empty bed. The spot beside me is pristine, untouched, and ice cold. Emma's pillowcase hasn't been washed since she passed. My housekeeper knows not to touch it when she changes the sheets. Maybe I'm in denial about the way it still smells like her sunflower-scented shampoo, maybe it's all in my head, but I can't bring myself to wash it just yet.

Turning to my side, I reach to switch off the bedside lamp, only I stop to stare at the framed wedding photo on my nightstand.

I've spent hours, perhaps days, staring at this photo. Every square inch of it is forever embedded in my memory to the point where I could see it with my eyes closed if I tried hard enough.

Sometimes I swear I can still hear her gentle, infectious laugh. It tends to happen in those serene, quiet moments between waking and sleep.

I'd give anything to run my fingers through her sandy-blonde curls one more time, to have one more lazy Sunday morning with her, stealing kisses while the girls watch *Sesame Street* and the scent of her famous cinnamon rolls fills the air.

A man could have all things money can buy, but it's the small, priceless moments that make him truly rich. By my own definition, I'd be dirt poor if it weren't for my girls.

Shortly after Emma and I married, she suffered a bout of insomnia. It came out of the blue, with seemingly no explanation, but she'd work herself up into anxious fits she couldn't get out of. She hated taking medications for it because they'd only sedate her and never fully address the issue. Whenever she would take something, her insomnia seemed to come back tenfold the following night. She decided she couldn't go around it, so she was simply going to go through it.

Countless nights I'd lie awake with her, all but forcing my eyelids open with toothpicks so I could keep her company. Some nights she'd entertain us both by asking silly questions—*would you rather have Chiclets for teeth or chicken drumsticks for arms?* That sort of thing. We'd be rolling in laughter, imagining these absurd little scenarios.

Other times, her questions would take a somber turn.

For a while, she'd get caught up on topics related to death and dying. I'm not sure if it was a premonition of some kind or just her anxiety getting the best of her, but I'll never forget the time she made me promise that if I ever died, I'd visit her as a blue jay.

"Why a blue jay?" I'd asked. "Of *all* the birds? I'd much rather be a peregrine falcon or a hawk."

Rolling to her side, she peered up at me with a tender expression on her beautiful face, and she traced her thumb along my brow as she cupped the side of my cheek.

"Because," she said, "blue jays are intelligent. And complex. And they can get kind of mean when they feel threatened, but it's only because they're fiercely protective. You're absolutely a blue jay. One hundred percent. End of story. Period."

I laughed at the time, imagining myself as a little blue bird with a pointy crest on its head.

"What do you want me to come back as?" she asked me next.

"Nothing," I say, "because I'm going to die first. Husbands always die before their wives. Men don't live as long as women. It's science."

Emma rolled her eyes. "No denying you're a smart man, but you can't predict the future. If I die first, how do you want me to visit you?"

"I don't know," I told her. But it wasn't that I didn't know—it was that I didn't want to think about it.

"Maybe a flower or a number or a color or an animal . . ." She rattled off a dozen options.

"If you tell me you're going to come back as a marigold or the number twelve, then that's all I'm going to see. It's confirmation bias. I don't want you to tell me what you're going to be, and I don't want to choose what you're going to be. Surprise me. Make it unmistakably, undeniably you."

"Hm," she said as she rolled to her back and stared at the ceiling in deep contemplation. "Okay, then."

It was the last time we ever discussed that topic.

Not long after, her insomnia passed, and we got pregnant with Adeline. Everything changed after that. Emma practically glowed with happiness, like it was radiating from the inside out, pouring out of her fingertips. She'd wake with a smile on her face, obsessively talk about baby names and family traditions she wanted to implement, and every facet of her being was drenched in sweet contentedness. She hadn't even had the baby, and already motherhood was suiting her.

Anyone can reproduce, but not everyone appreciates what it means to be a parent.

Pulling out of my pensive reverie, I turn off my bedside lamp and recline against my pillow.

I never knew it was possible to feel numb and to feel everything at the same time, yet here I am. Feeling nothing. Feeling it all. Or maybe

I'm somewhere in between those two things, if that even makes sense. Though nothing has really made sense since I lost my wife.

I suppose this is par for the course.

All I know is there's no denying the fact that Margaux lives in the exact same building Emma lived in when I first met her. The steps outside her apartment—the ones with the black railing—that's where we had our first kiss. And the streetlamp Margaux and I stood under tonight was where Emma and I had our first fight (which was over almost as soon as it started).

But it isn't just the building.

It's the key chain too.

One of only ten in existence . . . What are the odds Margaux has one?

If that wasn't a sign from Emma, I don't know what is.

I only wish I knew what it meant.

CHAPTER FIVE

SLOANE

"You survived," I say when I find Margaux camped out in her bed, right where I left her.

She pauses her TV show, adjusts her blankets, and gifts me her full attention. A plate of half-eaten saltines rests on her nightstand alongside a mostly empty glass of ginger ale.

"I should say the same about you. How was it? Please tell me you bored him to tears." She checks the time on her phone before tossing it on the bed beside her. "I'm going to assume yes because you're home way earlier than I expected."

"I don't know if *boring* is the right word to describe tonight," I say.

Margaux frowns.

"But I think it's safe to say he won't be asking for a second date." I chuckle, rolling my eyes.

"Why are you laughing?" she asks, one brow lifted higher than the other.

"Because he's weird," I say. "The whole thing was a shit show. He's still very much in love with his wife . . . who died years ago, by the way . . . he's still in mourning. The poor thing had no desire to be out on a date. He was just trying to make his aunt happy. So you guys have that in common, I guess. But it was just . . ."

I struggle to find the right words to convey the incongruity of the evening, from the moment I sat down, to the clunky conversation, to the inadvertent walk home, to the bizarre exchange we shared outside my front steps.

"Do you remember when I worked at Brickhouse Gallery a few years back, and some jerk had me fired?" I ask.

Margaux scrunches her brows. "Yeah. It was a whole ordeal. You came home in tears that day and called out sick the next morning—which you never do. It was traumatic."

I lift a hand. "Okay, you're making me sound dramatic, which I'm not, but it was a horrible situation that I have no desire to relive in any way, shape, or form, but *anyway* . . . Roman Bellisario was the jerk who had me fired."

Margaux's jaw falls loose. "No way."

"Way." I cross my arms, leaning against her doorframe.

"I'm so sorry. Why didn't you say something when I told you his name earlier?"

"What would it have mattered? You needed me to go on this date so you can get that promotion . . . I wasn't going to screw you over last minute."

Margaux exhales, her head tilting. "I owe you big."

"Yes," I say. "Yes, you do. Still waiting on that firstborn child you promised me back in college . . ." Gifting her a wink, I yawn. "I'm going to bed. The sooner this night is over with, the better."

"It's barely nine o'clock . . ."

Nine o'clock to me is the equivalent of 1:00 a.m. to my sister.

I can't remember the last time Margaux was home on a Friday night. For someone who knows everything about me, who shared a womb with me for nine months and a bedroom with me for eighteen years, she seems to have forgotten that I *live* for my quiet Friday nights. It's how I unwind after a whirlwind week in a fast-paced city working alongside art hustlers who never sleep. I'm all about balance, and that requires making time to be alone with myself. My biggest fear is burning out doing something I love. I don't know what I'd do if I didn't have my love of art keeping my soul ablaze.

"Well aware," I say. "It's what us boring people do on the weekends."

With that, I make my way to the hall bath, strip out of Margaux's frilly fashion, and wash up for bed.

It's only when I'm lying wide awake a half hour later, replaying the strangeness that was my evening, that I decide to search up Roman's late wife online. After a fruitless twenty minutes on Google, I run through my contacts and shoot out a dozen text messages to my art-world friends, asking if they know anything about the infamous Roman Bellisario's late wife.

Almost all the responses I receive are to the tune of *I had no idea that guy was ever married.*

Except for one.

Her name was Emma, my friend Carina writes. Emma Whitfield. I don't believe she ever took his last name. She was cousins with my college roommate, believe it or not. I met her a couple of times. So sad about her passing. She was super sweet. Gave me her shoes once when we all went out for New Year's Eve one year. Mine were giving me blisters, so she traded with me.

No wonder the man can't get over her.

She sounds like a damn saint.

With that, I run a search on Emma Whitfield + NYC + obituary, and I click on the top result.

Emma Whitfield of Manhattan passed away Sunday, June 28, 2020. Emma was born in Boston, Massachusetts, the only child of Warren and Laurel Whitfield, on January 2, 1990. Growing up, Emma excelled in language arts and broke several girls' lacrosse records at her high school. She went on to attend the University of Massachusetts on a full lacrosse scholarship, where she majored in English literature with a minor in printmaking. Upon graduation, Emma moved to New York City, where she worked as a private tutor and freelance copywriter. Soon after her move, she met her future husband and soulmate, Roman. They bonded over their love of all things fine art and were inseparable from the moment they met.

Emma and Roman were united in marriage August 15, 2015, in a beautiful ceremony at her grandmother's summer home off the coast of Narragansett. They exchanged vows in front of over four hundred beloved friends and family members before spending three weeks touring much of Europe for their honeymoon.

Emma is survived by her husband, Roman, and their daughters, Adeline and Marabel, her parents, grandparents, and countless loved ones. She is preceded in death by a cousin, Deirdre Allison, and her beloved rescue cat, Karma.

Please join us in celebrating Emma's life at the Saint Paul Memorial Center at 2:00 p.m. Wednesday, July 1.

I scroll down to a video at the bottom of her obituary, one filled with assorted photos of a beautiful existence cut short. Every image of her bears three things in common—she looks happy, beautiful, and overflowing with life. A bittersweet song plays along with the slideshow, one that's somehow both uplifting and sorrowful at the same time.

I watch the whole thing.

Twice.

By the time it's over, my cheeks are damp with tears, and my heart is full of something that wasn't there before—compassion for Roman Bellisario.

Darkening my screen, I put my phone aside and close my eyes.

His wife's death coincides almost perfectly with his campaign to have me fired. Could it be he was simply having a bad time? Grief stricken? Angry at the world? They say hurt people hurt people.

All these years, I thought he was heartless.

Maybe I was wrong.

Perhaps all he was . . . was heartbroken.

CHAPTER SIX

ROMAN

"Who wants fresh doughnuts?" Aunt Theodora lets herself into my apartment Saturday morning, a giant pink box in hand. "Get them while they're still warm . . ."

Come hell or high water, this has been our weekly tradition since Emma passed. At eight thirty sharp each and every Saturday, she shows up with breakfast—always something from a renowned bakery or local restaurant—and then she takes the girls for a couple of hours. I know she thinks she's doing me a favor, but I always find myself watching the clock to see how much time is left before they come home or checking my phone for any texted photos or updates.

I know it's good for the girls to have some "girl time," but I miss them just the same.

Some weekends they go to a museum. Other weekends they go to a park or a toy store. Today Theodora's taking them for manicures and pedicures. It's all the girls have been talking about all week, and they already have their colors picked out.

Sparkly teal for Marabel.

Hot purple with white polka dots for Adeline.

Matching Barbie pink for their toes.

In the early days after our loss, Emma's mother visited every month. But as time went by, she found it harder to get away from work and carve out a long weekend in New York. Or so she said.

We used to go to Boston, but the last time we went, Emma's father and I had words over my so-called coddling of the girls. He had the audacity to call me a helicopter parent—whatever the hell that is. I had some choice words for him myself, though I don't quite remember what I said exactly.

It wasn't my finest hour.

And we haven't been back since.

Neither he nor I has picked up the phone and apologized, and I don't foresee that happening anytime in the near future.

Emma once told me that her parents were always hands off with her. All her accomplishments, all her accolades, she earned them on her own merit. They never pushed her to be an overachiever, and they never went out of their way to help her chase her dreams in any capacity. Despite all that, they never hesitated to take credit for any of her achievements.

Emma told me that a drunken aunt once let it slip that Emma was an "accident," that her parents were career focused and never wanted to be parents, but they were doing the best they could playing the hand they were dealt. She said everything made sense from then on out.

"Auntie Dora!" Adeline squeals from the next room, and the sound of little feet padding across the hardwood follows. "What did you bring us?"

"I brought you a lovely assortment of pastries," she says. "Doughnuts, croissants, scones. As the oldest Bellisario daughter, you'll get first pick."

Adeline claps her little hands and does a jump.

Sometimes I'm tempted to take an adorable photo or two and send them to Emma's parents without any explanation or description. Just a little snapshot of what they're missing. It comes as no surprise to me, now, that two people who didn't want to be parents also have very little desire to be grandparents. Emma would be heartbroken if she were around to see this. If she were still here, she'd be taking the girls to Boston on a regular basis, no doubt. Not for herself or for her parents but for our daughters. Everything she ever did was for their benefit.

If my father were still around, I have no doubt he'd be involved in their lives, though I'm not sure what kind of a role he'd play. His love language was money. The man couldn't shed a tear or utter a simple *I love you* to save his life, but when I came home with a good report card, he never hesitated to slap down his black Amex or schedule some epic vacation filled with unforgettable experiences.

He wasn't around by the time we had our first child, but I like to imagine grandfather-hood would have softened him a bit. The girls have cracked my ironclad heart wide open, that's for sure.

My mother visits from France twice a year—Christmas and then the middle of April, during the week between the girls' birthdays. Occasionally her new husband joins her, though the last few visits he's stayed back for various convenient reasons.

I'll never beg someone to be in our life.

If they want to, they will.

It's that simple.

"And where is Mademoiselle Marabel?" Theodora asks Adeline.

Adeline places a hand on her hip, tucking her chin and leaning in. "Don't tell Daddy, but she's watching YouTube."

Theodora glances up at me, and I shake my head. I blocked YouTube months ago, after I found her watching some questionable content better suited for someone thrice her age. The internet is a mine-field of crap, and policing the content my kids have access to feels like a full-time job sometimes.

"She's watching YouTube *Kids*," I say. "Adeline, go get your sister. Tell her it's time for breakfast."

Theodora places the box of doughnuts on the kitchen island before rummaging through the cabinets to retrieve plates and juice glasses. I grab a container of freshly cut fruit from the fridge. If she's going to load them up on pure sugar, I'd at least like them to have some type of real food to go with it. Even if they ignore it, at least it's there. It's an option. And it makes me feel like I'm doing something right as a parent.

Marabel meanders in—always a girl operating on her own schedule—gives Theodora a hug, then takes her spot at the head of the table, where she's insisted on sitting ever since she outgrew her high chair a couple of years ago.

"So, Roman," Theodora says a few minutes later, when we're all seated. Peering at me from behind a pair of cherry-red Chanel glasses, she adds, "How was your evening last night?"

I stare at my untouched blueberry scone.

"It was . . . interesting," I say.

She lifts a single eyebrow. "Interesting good? Or interesting bad?"

"Interesting neither." I take a bite to save myself from having to answer another question.

"Why do you guys keep saying *interesting*?" Marabel asks, swiping her finger through some pink frosting. "Interesting, interesting, inter-esting . . ."

"Hm." Aunt Theodora studies me with her trademark discernment. "You're still getting warmed up. You've been out of the game for far too long. I'm sure you felt a little out of your element."

I take another bite, again deferring any opportunity to speak.

"I hope you didn't scare her away," she continues. "First impressions are everything. And we all know how you can be."

I nod, chewing. Then I rise from my chair and pour myself a coffee, taking my time with the cream and sugar.

"Want one?" I ask, holding up an empty mug.

Theodora shakes her head.

"Did she talk your ear off?" She continues her line of questioning. "Sometimes I can't get a word in edgewise around her. In a good way, of course. I always tell her she has the gift of gab, she just has to learn when to rein it in sometimes."

I shake my head, taking yet another bite.

The Margaux I met last night hardly "gabbed" at all.

"Hm." Theodora frowns. "She must have been nervous."

I don't tell her it was like pulling teeth all night just to get her to give me more than a one-word response. But in her defense, our conversation wasn't exactly enthralling, and I wasn't doing us any favors.

People can sense when you don't want to be around them, and I have no doubt she was picking up on some of that.

"Where did you leave things?" my aunt asks next. "Are you going to try for round two? Maybe she was nervous? Though that doesn't sound like the Margaux I know at all. She's one of my top marketing gals. It's between her and this young man I brought on last year, fresh out of college. A real go-getter. While I absolutely adore Margaux, Franklin is really giving her a run for her money. He's quickly growing into his role, and he's brokered some record-breaking deals. Really thinks outside the box, that Franklin."

"How do you think outside a box?" Adeline asks with a giggle.

Marabel giggles back, never missing a chance to parrot her older sister.

"Yeah, what's that mean?" Marabel asks.

"It's when you take a problem and you get creative with it," I say. "You solve it in a way that most people wouldn't think to solve it."

"Like when Marabel got gum in her hair and I cut it out with my safety scissors?" Adeline asks, wiping chocolate frosting off her mouth with the back of her hand.

Theodora hands her a napkin before I have a chance.

"Sort of," I say.

"Hurry up, girls," Theodora says as she eyes what's left of their doughnuts. "Our nail appointments are in thirty minutes, and we can't be late or we'll get bumped."

"What's bumped?" Marabel asks.

"You're just full of questions today, aren't you?" I clean her chubby cheeks with a napkin before grabbing a Wet One from a kitchen drawer to wipe off both of their sticky hands. Monday through Friday, I'm leading board meetings and taking international conference calls. Saturday mornings, I remove frosting from faces and fingers. It's called balance. "It's when they give your appointment to someone else."

"Go on now, girls. Put your shoes on. I'll meet you at the door," Theodora tells them. As soon as they're out of earshot, she gives me a squinted glance. "I really hope you and Margaux give it another go. I know you don't see what I see, and I know you don't want to move on, but at some point you're going to have to. If not for yourself, then for them."

She nods toward the hallway, where the girls are chatting about nail polish colors as they fasten their Velcro tennis shoes.

"You know . . . Margaux reminds me a lot of Emma." Theodora keeps her voice low as she toys with the infinity-shaped diamond pendant dangling from her neck. "Always smiling. A true people magnet. It's why I always assign her to all our new clients. Everyone just adores her. They're drawn to her like moths to flames. Just like they used to be with Emma. It's like she's never met a stranger." Tossing her hands in the air, she adds, "Well, *I* adore her."

I say nothing because I have nothing to say.

Comparing Margaux to Emma is insulting to both of them, but mostly to Emma.

I don't know Margaux well enough, but I don't think anyone wants to be set up with some widower simply because someone reminds them of a dead person.

"Oh, come on." She rubs my arm and gives me a tender half smile. "It's not healthy to always be so serious all the time. And I can't remember the last time I heard you laugh. *Really* laugh." Theodora studies me with her trademark dissecting gaze. "We all know there'll never be another Emma, but maybe you can find someone like her? No one should spend the rest of their life in mourning. She would hate that for you. Emma would want you to be happy."

Theodora is right.

That's exactly what Emma would want.

But it isn't what *I* want.

I'm not ready to be happy.

I'm not ready to find some Emma knockoff.

"You should get going." I check my watch.

"You're right, I should." Leaning in, she kisses my cheek and gives me the same melancholy smile she always does when she's around. "We'll be back in a couple of hours, painted piggies and all."

I see my daughters off, and then I retreat to my study to check a few work emails and occupy my time until they return.

It's all I can do to keep from looking at the clock every other minute—or thinking about Margaux, her apartment building, and that damn Halcyon key chain.

CHAPTER SEVEN

SLOANE

"Hey, hey," I call to my sister when she gets home from work Monday evening. "I'm thinking we should order Thai tonight. Saw an ad this morning and spent the rest of the day craving pad see ew. Thoughts?"

She hangs her classic Burberry mackintosh jacket on the hat tree by the door and drops her keys with a heavy clink in the bowl on the console before carefully slipping off her black Chanel ballet flats.

It's like I'm not even here.

"Hello?" I call out. It isn't like her to ignore me. Glancing up from my phone, I check to see if she's on a call.

She isn't.

Returning my attention to the magazine in my lap, it isn't until I feel the sinking weight of her pointed glare that I look up and find her shooting daggers my way. For a moment, I'm taken back to our childhood, when I used to borrow her favorite markers and forget to put them back. Those days are long gone, though. I can't remember the last time I ticked her off about anything.

"What's wrong?" I ask. "Did something happen at work?"

"Yeah, actually." She breaks her silence, straightening her blouse and heading toward the living room with sure-footed steps. Stopping short in front of the leather wingback chair we bought at an antiques flea market two summers ago, she folds her arms across her chest. "Theodora pulled me aside today."

"And?" I swallow a lump in my throat. Did her plan for me to bore Roman Bellisario to death backfire? Is she *losing* her promotion because the date didn't go well?

"Care to tell me why Roman wants to see me again?" she asks with a single, angry arched brow. "Supposedly he told her he had a wonderful time, and now he wants my phone number."

I clamp a hand over my mouth, though it's a futile move, seeing as I'm rendered speechless at this revelation.

"What did you tell her?" I finally ask after I have a second to process this.

"What do you think I told her?" Margaux's voice is raised, which is never a good thing. Once she loses her cool, it tends to only get exponentially worse. "I had to play along. I had to smile and tell her I felt the same. Next thing I knew, she was on her phone, texting him my number."

Margaux makes her way around the chair, collapsing in a crumpled heap like an exhausted southern belle in a heat wave.

"I don't want to date this man," she says, enunciating every syllable. "I don't want to risk losing my promotion or my job or my reputation in this industry if this thing blows up in my face—and you know it will. It always does."

"I don't understand . . ." I manage a handful of words. "The date was awful. We had zero chemistry. Neither one of us attempted to flirt. I don't even know if he smiled once the entire time. If that's his definition of a great time, then—"

"—you realize if he wants a second date, you're going to have to be the one to go on it, right? God forbid he brings up some teeny tiny detail from Friday night and I look like a deer in headlights."

Sinking into the sofa cushions, I have half a mind to pray they swallow me whole.

"This makes no sense," I say. "I was devoid of a personality that night."

Margaux blinks, like she doesn't believe me.

"Why would I *want* to hit it off with the guy who had me fired? Why would I jeopardize your promotion anyway?" I come to my defense again.

With a groan, she pushes herself up from the chair, treks to the kitchen, and uncorks a bottle of red wine. After filling a stemless glass nearly to the brim, she takes three generous sips before returning to the living room.

"Fine," she says. "I believe you, but I'm just . . . this isn't good. This isn't good at all."

"Has he texted you yet?" I ask.

"Yes, actually. About five minutes ago."

That explains her sour mood the second she walked in the door . . .

I'm not well versed in the art of modern dating, but a guy who texts within hours of getting your number rather than playing it cool and giving it a day or two must want to see her again.

Er, *me*.

He wants to see *me* again.

"Give him my number," I say. "Tell him the number he has is your work cell, and tell him my number is your personal cell."

"Yeah, because stacking lies on top of lies is always a good idea." She takes another substantial drink of wine.

"Do you have a better idea?"

Margaux answers with a delayed, hopeless shrug.

"That's what I thought," I say. "Nothing about this makes any kind of sense. Friday night he said he wasn't ready to move on, that he was still grieving his wife. I told him I was too career focused to have a dating life. We were on the same page . . . then he walked me home."

"He walked you home? You never mentioned that." Turning toward me, her eyes widen, bewildered almost. "You don't walk someone home after a boring date. No one does that. You go your separate ways like normal people."

"His driver was unavailable or something," I say. "And it wasn't like he meant to walk me home. We were walking in the same general direction and ran into each other at a crosswalk . . ."

"At any point did he say anything that made you think he wanted to see you again?"

"Never," I say. "But he did get kind of weird at the end of the night . . . when he saw my key chain. The Halcyon one."

Margaux scrunches her face. "What are you talking about? What key chain? What's Halcyon?"

"Halcyon is this obscure artist who had this flash-in-the-pan moment several years back . . . Roman was upset that I knew about Halcyon but didn't say anything when he talked about being an art major. I think, anyway. It was weird. Also it was a Halcyon piece that cost me my job."

"Do you think he's onto us? Do you think he knows you're my sister and you're the one he had fired all those years ago?"

"No. At least, I don't think so? And I never told him anything about having a sister, let alone being an identical twin. There's no way. But he did say I looked familiar. Has he ever been into the office?"

"Not that I'm aware of."

"This whole thing is such a mess. I'm screwed. It's all going to backfire, I know it is." She takes another drink before shaking her head. There's a far-off look in her eyes, but not the good kind. I imagine she's envisioning every worst-case scenario she can all at the same time. "This is really, *really* bad. Like I don't think you comprehend—"

"—no, it's not as bad as you're making it out to be. It's not ideal, but it's not the end of the world. We just have to think outside the box."

"Me thinking outside the box is what got us into this mess in the first place." Leaning against the arm of her chair, she rests her chin against the top of her hand. "For the record, I'm not upset with *you* . . .

I'm upset about the situation. I know you were just helping me out, and I adore you for that. I just . . ."

"If he texts me, I can always tell him I'm not interested in dating?"

"No," Margaux says without pause. "If he goes back to Theodora and tells her I turned him down after I gave her permission to contact me, it's going to make me look like a liar. And the last thing I need is to give Franklin a leg up on the whole promotion situation. He's such a kiss-ass."

I've listened to my sister rant and rave about this new guy more times than I can count over the past year. I've never met him, but I'm just as invested in him not getting promoted as she is. He's a schmoozer. A wheeler and dealer. I've worked with people like him before, and they're skilled manipulators, promotion thieves.

"Take a deep breath," I say. Trotting to the kitchen, I return with her bottle of pinot noir and top her glass off. "It's going to be fine. If I have to spend more time with him, I'll just be as boring as I was before, and he'll lose interest eventually."

Margaux looks a little green around the gills, only this time she can't blame it on leftover sushi. Shoving her glass aside, she says, "I can't drink any more of this. Just the smell of it is making me nauseous now."

I take her glass to the kitchen.

"I'm texting him your number," she declares when I return. "And I'm sending you his number as well, so you'll know it's him when he texts you."

"Got it," I say when my phone dings. "Just let me handle this whole thing. Don't you have a work trip or something coming up? Don't you have to pack soon? Aren't you leaving, like . . . tomorrow?"

"Yeah, damn it. How's this going to work? If he asks you on a second date, you can't go while I'm out of town. If he says something to Theodora about meeting up with me, she'll literally know something's up. He doesn't know I have an identical twin, but *she* does."

"I'll just wait until you're back from Salt Lake City," I say with a casual shrug. While I'm every bit panicking on the inside as much as she is on the outside, I can't let it show. If I'm worked up, it'll only make her even more worked up.

A worked up Margaux is a miserable Margaux.

Remaining calm is in both of our best interests.

"You're going to have to pretend you're in Utah when you text him," she reminds me, as if I'd forgotten.

"Obviously," I say. "Go pack. I'll order some takeout. We can hash everything out after we eat."

Not that there's anything left to hash out. All I have to do is be dull and pretend I'm going out of town on a work trip, but I know Margaux will sleep better knowing we've discussed this whole thing extensively.

A few minutes later, I'm in the midst of placing a take-out order from Top Thai when a text fills my screen: It's Roman. Can you talk?

This guy isn't wasting any time . . .

I text him back: I'm in the middle of something right now. I'll be around later though.

I don't want to seem overly eager about this on the off chance he interprets it as any kind of interest in dating him.

I prefer to talk on the phone rather than text. Okay to call you after I put my girls to bed? Around eight or so? he writes next.

I send him back a yellow thumbs-up emoji—an attempt to be casual, if not intentionally cringey. The more I can turn him off, the better. Though I'm still perplexed as to how he could possibly be into me after the forgettable night we shared?

Talk to you then, he sends back.

After his inexplicable send-off Friday night, I can't imagine what he could want to discuss over the phone. And speaking of that—what modern human being prefers phone calls to texting?

Nothing about any of this makes sense, but I'd be lying if I said I wasn't completely and utterly intrigued.

I check my watch and calculate that it'll be a little over two hours until I'll have some answers.

———

His call comes at exactly 8:04 p.m.

Heat creeps up my neck as I clear my throat and stare at his name on my screen, a name that looks as out of place as it feels.

As much as I'm sure Margaux would love to be sitting next to me, supervising every word that comes out of my mouth, it's probably better that she's not. Last I saw her, she was shuffling into the hall bath lugging a box of matches, a Diptyque Baies candle, her phone, and the June issue of *Vogue*. I heard the bathtub running next, which was soon followed by the faint scent of lavender bubble bath wafting out from beneath the door.

"Hello," I answer his call in my friendliest yet most neutral voice.

"Margaux," he says with a voice like velvet. I picture him sitting in a leather wingback chair in some dark room of his fancy home. Maybe a glass of scotch beside him. "It's Roman."

"Yes. Hi." I settle against my headboard and pull my knees to my chest.

"Hope you don't mind my calling," he says. "Not a fan of texting. Things tend to get lost in translation unless you use a million emojis, and that's never been my thing."

"Have to say I wasn't expecting to hear from you after Friday night . . ."

He sniffs into the phone. "Figured you'd say that."

"What, um . . . what brought all of this about?" I ask the million-dollar question.

"My aunt," he says. "She's like a dog with a bone sometimes. She's insisting that we give it another try."

My shoulders tense at the thought of relaying that tidbit to my sister.

I've only met Theodora twice—once in passing when I had to drop something off at Margaux's office and another time when Margaux made me her plus-one at a company holiday party. Although I've spent only a handful of minutes around the woman, there's no denying she gives off powerhouse vibes. Tall, lithe, white hair shaped into a classic bob, thick Chanel glasses, a commanding presence.

If Miranda Priestly had a slightly less intimidating sister, it would be Theodora.

Every time Margaux says she likes Theodora, I secretly wonder if she's simply afraid of not liking her.

"Anyway," Roman continues, "I meant what I said Friday night. I'm not looking to date anyone right now. But I'm aware I didn't leave the best impression that evening, and after noticing your key chain, I feel I'd be remiss if I didn't offer you a personal tour of Halcyon's studio as an apology. I'd like to make it up to you, if you'll let me."

If I had a drink in my mouth, I'd have spit it out by now.

"Wait, what?" I lean forward.

I thought he was going to ask me out to dinner again—not offer me the opportunity of a lifetime . . . an offer I couldn't turn down even if I wanted to.

Silently reminding myself I'm "Margaux" right now and not art fanatic Sloane, I collect my jaw off my lap and clear my throat.

"Wow," I say. "That's . . . how do you have access to Halcyon's studio? I didn't even know Halcyon was still around? Do you know who they are? Are they still painting? And how do you know them?"

"Yes. I know who Halcyon is, but I can't answer any of your other questions," he says. "You interested in my offer?"

"Absolutely. Oh my god. Yes," I say before wincing, biting my lip, and dialing it back. Margaux would never be this excited about seeing some artist's studio. She'd give a delayed and casual yes before backtracking and acting like she had to check her schedule, and then she'd take a day or two to confirm . . . not because she plays mind games, but because her social calendar tends to be insane. "When were you thinking?"

If I let this slip through my fingers, I'll spend the rest of my life regretting it.

I'll move heaven and earth to make this work.

"How does tomorrow work for you? Sometime before five? My nanny leaves for the day at six, so I have to be home by then."

I'm seconds from giving him a resounding yes when I remember Margaux's flying to Salt Lake City tomorrow.

"I actually have a work trip," I say. "I'll be back Friday, though."

"The girls have a dance recital Friday night. What about Saturday?"

"I have a—" I stop myself before accidentally mentioning the Javier Sosa exhibition I'm hosting this weekend at the gallery. "How's next week look for you?"

"Monday," he says. "Four o'clock. Can you make that work?"

For a chance to see where Halcyon works their magic? A hundred times yes. I'd cancel my own funeral if it meant stepping into that sacred space.

"Yeah. Sure. I'll move some things around and plan on that." I downplay the freight train of excitement speeding through my body and maintain a calm tone.

Thank goodness he's not here to see the enormous smile taking over my face right now.

"Monday it is. I'll swing by the office and pick you up around three forty-five," he says.

An icy flash of panic rushes through me.

"Oh, wait. I might be working from home that afternoon." I wince as I lie, nibbling on my thumbnail and praying he buys it. Though I don't know why he wouldn't. "I like to catch up on emails and phone calls from home after coming back from a work trip. Less distractions that way."

I make a mental note to tell Margaux she'll be working from home on Monday. On the off chance Roman were to mention something to Theodora, the jig would be up, Margaux's promotion would be officially off the table, and all this would be for nothing.

"All right. I'll see you next week," he says with the emotionless formality of someone scheduling an optometry appointment. I suppose it's fitting, seeing how this isn't a date. I'm not even sure what a person would categorize this as? *Hanging out* is too casual. It's not like we're friends. Doing something together in a nonromantic way? What even is that?

Everything about Roman Bellisario is a giant question mark. It's only fitting that this is too.

"Sounds good," I say, wrestling the eagerness from my voice with the might of ten thousand wild horses.

Ending the call, I flop backward onto my bed, staring at the lifeless ceiling fan and the crack in the plaster behind it. My stomach is filled with butterflies. Not the romantic kind, of course. More like the kind I get whenever we install a new collection at work or anytime I have the pleasure of meeting a personal favorite artist of mine.

Never in a million years could I have imagined I'd have the chance to visit Halcyon's private studio . . . or that Roman Bellisario would be my personal tour guide for such an occasion.

I'd say stranger things have happened, but I don't know that to be true. The last several days have been some of the oddest ones of my entire life.

Sitting up a minute later, I head to the hallway—feet light as air— and rap on the bathroom door.

"So . . . Roman just called," I say, tracing my fingertips along a worn indentation in the door.

The sound of swishing water comes from the other side, like Margaux's suddenly sitting up from a relaxed position.

"What'd you tell him?" she calls out.

I give her a quick rundown.

And I don't stick around to listen to her wax and wane about what all could go wrong.

It's a simple studio tour. It's not a date; it's an apology.

It's all going to be fine.

Returning to my room, I pull up an old photo album on my phone from several years back, when we were fortunate enough to host a small Halcyon exhibit at my previous gallery.

Swiping through the images, I get lost in the sea of their beauty. Their punchy colors juxtaposed with their melancholic beauty. Print and paint combined with stencil combined with mixed media and provocative titles such as *Trashy Ballerina, Missile to the Soul, Pretty Poison*, and of course my all-time favorite—*You or Someone like You.*

I'm not sure what winning the lottery is like, but I imagine it feels something like this.

CHAPTER EIGHT

ROMAN

"Up there is fine, just past that bench," I tell my driver, Antonio, when he drops Margaux and me off outside a former garment warehouse in the Lower East Side Monday afternoon.

It's a hole-in-the-wall, off-the-radar space that's been converted into lofts, rented by artists and the like for various creative endeavors. But with its plain gray facade and the mess of scaffolding along the sidewalk, it's the kind of place most people don't think twice about when they're strolling past—which is one of the best things about it.

Artists can be anonymous here.

They can create without judgment, without onlookers, without unwanted attention.

Antonio parks alongside a small stretch of curb before jumping out to get the passenger door. Margaux climbs out first, tugging on the hem of her curve-hugging black lace dress when she reaches the sidewalk. It's a little number that covers everything yet leaves little to the imagination at the same time. I can't help but wonder if she wore this while she worked from home today or if she has a date after this.

"Wow," she says as she peers up at the expanse of industrial windows, though I don't think she's being sarcastic. Going by the starstruck expression on her face, she's completely in awe already, and we haven't even made it inside.

I punch in a code on the exterior door. Margaux makes no attempt to look over my shoulder, a move I silently note and appreciate.

The lock beeps, and she follows me to the stairwell inside. We climb two floors before making our way to the lofts, trekking down a series of long, dimly lit hallways. The faint scent of paint thinner, sweat, time, and inspiration lingers in the air like a permanent fixture. Euro-techno music pumps from one of the spaces, and from another comes one-half of a stranger's heated conversation.

I type in another code when we get to loft number seven—Halcyon's studio.

The lock clicks open, and once inside, we're greeted with a mélange of familiar aromas: oil paint, ink, gesso, and paper.

I flick on a nearby light switch before heading for the wall of windows, pulling back curtains to let some natural light flood the space.

A paint-splattered Bluetooth speaker rests in the corner, next to a wooden stool and an unfinished canvas piece resting on an easel.

Everything in here is exactly as it was three years ago—the day the music died, so to speak.

Along the far wall is a small collection of works that has never left these expansive, hollow walls, works that I'm sure could fetch a pretty penny if those in the know were aware of their existence.

Hell, even the unfinished one could go for tens, if not hundreds, of thousands with the right buyer.

Anchored in the center of the loft, Margaux takes in her surroundings with wide, glimmering eyes. She's statue still. Lost for words.

Where was that "gift of gab" Theodora was talking about?

"You . . . okay?" I break the silence after a few beats.

Margaux's shoulders soften, and she turns to me, her eyes glassy as if she's struggling to keep from crying—not exactly the reaction I expected.

"No," she says. "I mean, yes. This is . . ."

She lets her words trail into nothing before gingerly making her way to the easel in the corner. Standing back, like a patron admiring a priceless work of art at a prestigious museum, she clasps her hand over her mouth and releases a slow exhale.

"This is stunning," she says. "Even unfinished . . . it's incredible . . . the concurrence of the soft, blurred sections and the harsh edges, the light and dark, the surrealism . . . it's like if Andrew Breithauer and Mona Kane collaborated, only this is ten times better. A hundred times. I'm just . . ."

"I've never heard anyone mention Andrew Breithauer and Mona Kane in the same sentence." Stepping closer, I add, "You know a lot more about art than you let on."

She turns to me, and her eyes search mine.

"It's just a little pet passion of mine, I guess," she says, brushing it off like it's nothing.

But it's not nothing.

"Why didn't you mention it during our date, when I told you I once wanted to teach art history?"

Lifting a single shoulder, she says, "I'm . . . not . . . sure?"

"I wish you would have." It would've made our date much less awkward than it was. "Would've been nice to have some common ground besides my aunt . . ."

"Would it have changed anything?" she asks, squinting. "You said you weren't ready to date."

Pressing my lips together, I contemplate it for a moment before shaking my head.

"No," I say. "Probably not."

"You're a good nephew," she says, "wanting to make your aunt happy."

"Nah. I'm just a shitty date trying to make things right," I say. "Someday you can tell your friends that you went on the most depressing blind date of your life, but it's okay because he took you to Halcyon's studio."

"Is Halcyon okay with me being here?" she asks. "Can I tell people about this?"

"I'd prefer you kept this between us."

"Of course."

Hands folded in front of her hips, she moves away from the easel toward a painting leaning against the west wall.

"I don't understand why Halcyon is letting all of these perfectly good pieces sit in this loft instead of on walls and in galleries and hanging in modern art museums where they belong, where people can love them and appreciate their beauty." She tilts her head to the side, transfixed on a gritty lime-green piece depicting a decaying Manhattan skyscraper—a piece aptly named *Sour Apple*. "It's unfortunate, you know? If someone has a gift like this, they're cosmically obligated to share it with the rest of the world."

"Is that so?"

She sniffs a laugh, peeling her eyes off the painting and directing them at me. Our stares hold for a second longer than I expected.

"It's absolutely so," she says before her smile fades. "I feel that way about all talents. Some people are good with words. Some are good with people or comedy or the theatrical arts or architecture or medicine. It's such a waste to keep your gifts to yourself."

"Theodora says you have the gift of gab."

She pauses, perhaps confused, though I'm not sure why.

When her expression clears, she shrugs. "Sounds like something Theodora would say."

"She speaks very highly of you. She once told me you're the daughter she wishes she could have had."

Margaux places her hand across her heart. "She said that? Really?"

"She did." Although Theodora undoubtedly has the gift of persuasion. She could've been saying that as a way to sell me on the idea of dating someone she hand chose for me.

"She's too kind," Margaux says before moving on to the next piece—a neon-colored streetlight painted over vintage newspaper articles. "This is amazing. I'm already obsessed. Do you know what it's called?"

"I don't believe that one has a title," I say. "What would you call it?"

"Hmm." She presses her full lips together before inching in to take a closer look. "*Lost after Midnight.*"

"Interesting."

"It makes me think of wandering the city at night, an old newspaper rolling by, the sky the blackest black, maybe there's a little alcohol coursing through your veins so everything looks blindingly bright, neon almost."

They say the artist creates for themselves, but a work's beauty, truth, and meaning lie in the eyes of the beholder.

"What about this one?" She ambles to the next canvas, a gessoed piece covered in ripped and torn letters and splattered in black and blue inkblots. "Does this one have a name?"

"I believe that one is called *Letters Unsent.*"

She leans in to inspect the piece closer. "Are these actual letters people wrote? The handwriting is different on every single one."

"I believe so."

Turning to face me, her brows knit. "Why won't Halcyon release these? They're incredible."

Slipping my hands in my pockets, I do my best to remain casual.

"I'm sure they have their reasons," I answer, leaving it at that.

Margaux rolls her eyes. "This is truly some of the best Halcyon work I've seen. Do you know, someone resold their *Blurred Edges of Darkness* piece last year for three times what it originally went for? These are hot-ticket items."

"What, do you have some kind of inside track to the art world or something?" I chuckle. "That's an oddly specific thing to know."

"People talk, that's all." Waving her hand, she brushes off my comment.

She isn't wrong. In a city of millions, it tends to feel like a small town some days. Everyone knows everyone, and if they don't, they know someone who does. The art world is even smaller, like a community within a community. A dysfunctional extended family of sorts.

Moving on, she steps over to a larger piece, one that spans at least ten feet tall by six feet wide. The perimeter is shaded in bright-blue watercolors, which transition to acrylics before morphing into oil paint in the center. In the middle of it all, there's an intentional gash, like the artist slashed some kind of knife through the heart of all its beauty.

"This one makes me sad," she says. Reaching her hand toward it, she quickly pulls it back when she thinks better of it. "The emotion . . . it's intense."

"That one's called *Cerulean's Ruin*," I say.

"That's a perfect name," she says with a sigh. Hand clutched at her heart, she steps over to a slew of smaller paintings, maybe twenty-four inches by thirty-six inches.

"Do you own any Halcyon pieces?" I ask.

She snorts. "Theodora doesn't pay me enough to afford even a scrap of a Halcyon piece."

"That's a shame."

While my aunt is an astute businesswoman with an enviable financial portfolio and one of the top branding agencies in the nation, she didn't get that way by blowing through her money like there's no tomorrow. She pays her employees fairly and competitively, but not generously. Enough to keep them wanting to update their LinkedIn profiles.

"Do you want one of those?" I point to the three smaller nine-by-twelve pieces in front of her.

Margaux laughs, like she thinks I'm kidding.

"It's not nice to tease," she says.

"Pick one and it's yours."

She tosses me a sideways glance. "I can't just *take* a Halcyon painting . . ."

"Sure you can."

"So you just . . . have permission to give away their art?"

I lift a shoulder and give a terse nod. "More or less."

Her eyes scan the length of me, studying me before she settles back on one high-heeled foot.

"What's the catch?" she asks.

"No catch," I say before checking my watch. We have to leave in about twenty minutes so I can get home to my girls. "Just pick one."

"I can't . . ." She turns back to the three works. "I love them all . . ."

"Then take all three."

She releases a sharp breath. "I can't. It wouldn't be right."

"Halcyon isn't painting anymore. These pieces are collecting dust in this loft. They should be with someone who appreciates them."

"The fact that Halcyon's no longer producing makes these priceless . . . I just . . . it doesn't seem . . ."

"Are you always this difficult to give gifts to?" I check my watch again when a text comes through from my assistant, only it's nothing that can't wait. "I'd hate to see you on Christmas morning."

"I'm just speechless is all," she says. "I mean, not literally. Mentally. I don't know what to say to this . . . wasn't expecting it, you know? When you invited me here the other day, it felt like someone had given me a winning lottery ticket. Like a once-in-a-lifetime thing. Now that you're giving me a Halcyon painting—"

"—three Halcyon paintings," I correct her. "You're taking the entire series."

Her jaw falls, parting her pretty pink lips, which dance into a sweet smile.

"They're a set. They should stay as a set," I say.

"Are you absolutely, positively sure Halcyon would be okay with this?"

"You think I'd be doing this if they weren't?" I follow her to the next piece—a realistic portrait of a canary-yellow sunflower against an impressionistic starry sky titled *When Van Gogh Met Monet*. It was meant to be tongue in cheek, a satire almost. "I'll have them framed, wrapped, and delivered to you later this week."

With her hand pressed against her heart once more, she steps closer to me. Her pale ocean eyes rest on mine. I get the sense she wants to hug me, but she's holding back.

It's for the best.

I don't need a hug.

Knowing these paintings are going to someone who will appreciate them is all the gratitude necessary.

"I don't know what else to say besides thank you, thank you, thank you," she says. Her mouth spreads into a gracious smile again. In fact, I don't think she's stopped smiling once. "This is the most generous thing anyone's ever done for me, and you don't even know me . . ."

She looks as if she wants to go on, as if she thinks she owes me some long, drawn-out, elaborate display of thankfulness, but she stops herself.

"What are they called?" she asks. "What are their titles?"

"*Fool's Gold*," I say. "*Fool's Gold One, Two,* and *Three*."

She takes them in, inspecting them closely. "Ah. The little flecks of gold flake mixed in with the paint. Fits perfectly."

"We have to get going soon." I nod toward the wall of unfinished paintings, the last bit of the collection she's yet to see.

"Why did Halcyon just . . . quit?" she asks. Her heels click against the concrete floor, echoing off the tall ceiling. She runs her hands along her hips, smoothing out the bunched lace fabric that hugs her curves.

I begin to answer but stop myself.

Margaux inspects the incomplete works, though there's not much to see. Just some penciled-in outlines and a handful of tested paint colors.

"I have so many questions," she says with a breathless sigh. "But I know you can't answer a single one."

"Correct."

Returning to the *Fool's Gold* series, she lingers before them for a few beats before facing me again.

"I'm truly at a complete and utter loss for words," she says with eyes lit like stars. "Again, thank you so much. And tell Halcyon thank you as well, will you?"

I would if I could, but the truth of the matter is . . . Halcyon no longer exists.

CHAPTER NINE

SLOANE

"Your daughters . . . how old are they again?" I ask when we're seated in the second row of his chauffeured Escalade. My skin is humming. Alive with excitement. Never in a million years did I think I'd ever own a single Halcyon piece, let alone three of them.

Three.

He shrugs out of his navy suit coat and drapes it across the third row of seats. His white dress shirt strains against his broad shoulders, and the scent of faded cologne wafts off his warm body, filling the close space between us.

"Adeline's five. Marabel is four going on fourteen," he says as we inch through an intersection.

We're in the midst of rush hour traffic, and while it might have been easier to walk home from here, I didn't come prepared for that. Margaux insisted I wear a lacy dress and heels because that's what she'd have worn for this . . . nondate.

"You have any pictures of them?" I'm not sure if I'm crossing any lines by asking this. It's a personal question, and Roman is notoriously private. But after spending an awkward Friday night together and

You or Someone Like You

bonding over Halcyon, I don't feel like it's completely out of the realm of things I can ask about.

I'd love to know how Roman knows Halcyon well enough to have full access to their studio. Sometimes artists and investor-collectors form friendships. It's not out of the realm of possibility. But he knew all the names of all the pieces and had no qualms gifting me three priceless works, which leads me to believe it's more complex than that.

"I have thousands." He pulls his phone out with his left hand, thumbs in his passcode, taps on his photo app, and pulls up an album called A+M. Handing me his phone, he says, "They love posing for pictures. Never met a camera they didn't like. Definitely didn't get it from me."

I swipe through a dozen or so images—intrigued enough to want to see more but not wanting to appear like some creeper.

The oldest daughter, Adeline, has pitch-black hair like Roman that spills to the middle of her back in gentle waves, and she seems to have an affinity for Disney princess costumes. Her big green eyes are almost hypnotic, giving her sweetness a bit of an edge. The younger daughter, Marabel, has sandy-blonde curls and Roman's intense chocolate-brown gaze. At first take, they look nothing alike but are inseparable in every photo, always holding on to one another or posing in some kind of choreographed way. Hands on their hips. Back to back. Holding hands. They remind me of Margaux and me when we were younger.

"They're adorable," I say, giving his phone back.

Our eyes catch for a moment.

"I know," he says with a wink, though the rest of his face remains serious and somber. I can't help but wonder if he ever smiles? I imagine it would light up his entire face.

That said, there's a hint of lightness about him that wasn't there before. Nothing drastic, nothing tangible, just an overall vibe I'm getting.

"Do you ever see yourself doing this?" he asks.

"You're going to have to be more specific." I feed him his own line from earlier.

"Having kids," he clarifies.

"Um, sometimes? I mean, I think about it from time to time. It's not my main priority right now. Work is pretty much my whole life," I say. And that's the truth whether I'm speaking for Margaux . . . or myself.

At twenty-seven, I've yet to feel the urgency to settle down and start a family. It's always been in the back of my mind as something I'd like to do someday, but the tick of my biological clock is merely faint, like soft ambient background noise.

Ask me in ten years, and maybe I'll have a different answer.

Only time will tell.

Roman frowns. "Does my aunt know that?"

Shoot.

For a moment, I almost forgot I was Margaux—and to be honest, I think I've forgotten more times this afternoon than I can count. Basking in the surreal magic of Halcyon's personal studio ignited my soul in a way that made me forget what was really going on. It made me forget that none of this is real.

"Theodora is aware that I love my job, yes," I say, crossing my fingers and hoping it never comes up in conversation between the two of them.

Theodora is notorious for her modernized work culture, for giving people the ability to flex their schedules and work from home and take as many mental health breaks as necessary. She wants her employees to be "allergic to burnout." While her personal values tend to border on old fashioned, her workplace values are as modern as they get.

"I mean . . . it's not a bad thing," I say. "When I'm not working, I'm thinking about work. I guess that makes it feel like it's a bigger part of my life than it is. I just love what I do."

I hold my breath and pray he buys it.

"I see," he says. We stop at a red light. Glancing out the window, I notice a middle-aged woman walking a chubby, snorty brindle-colored french bulldog with an Hermès-orange collar. She cuts off a man in a three-piece suit who's screaming, red faced, into his phone. The woman bristles at the man and takes two steps farther away from him, just enough space for a skinny teenager on a skateboard to squeeze between them, nearly knocking the fuming man over.

Never a dull moment in this city . . .

"So what is it you do, exactly?" I ask when the stoplight blinks to green. The less we talk about me-slash-Margaux, the less chances I have to biff this.

"International shipping logistics," he says. "My grandfather started the company in the fifties. My father took over for him in the eighties and nineties. I'd go into more details, but it tends to have an Ambien effect on people."

"Yeah . . . that sounds . . ." I stifle a yawn I can't contain, covering my mouth with the back of my hand.

Anticipating my Halcyon tour all day followed by the actual tour and being gifted those works has worn me out in a way I wasn't expecting. Suddenly a date with my bed sounds amazing. I have no doubt I'll hit the pillow with a grin on my face tonight.

"Told you it was boring," he says without missing a beat.

Without thinking, I playfully punch his arm. If someone had told me I'd be spending a Friday night with Roman Bellisario, that he'd walk me home after and then ask for my number over the weekend, that he'd invite me to Halcyon's studio and gift me not one but three priceless works of art, that we'd be riding in a car together discussing his daughters and his job—I'd have never believed them.

Yet here we are.

I steer my attention forward, to the back of the seat in front of me, and then I check the street signs as we pass through another intersection.

We're almost to Midtown.

Cinderella's stagecoach is about to turn back into a pumpkin . . . or something.

A couple more blocks and this whole thing will be over.

I won't have to pretend to be Margaux anymore.

Relief washes through me, but the tiniest niggle of sadness settles in the pit of my stomach.

"Thank you so much for everything," I say when his driver pulls up outside my building. Placing my hand over my heart, I add, "Truly an unforgettable afternoon."

His mouth forms some semblance of a smile that's gone before I have time to fully appreciate it.

"I'll let you know when the paintings will be delivered," he says.

The driver climbs out, trots around the back of the car, and gets my door. He extends his hand, helping me out of the tall SUV. I feel bad that I don't know his name. For the past hour or so, my mind was focused on all things Halcyon. Now it's too late.

I tug on the hem of my dress, straightening the tight fabric back into place, and then I give Roman a friendly wave before heading inside.

A couple minutes later, I'm changing out of Margaux's dress and into jersey pajama shorts and a white cotton tank when my sister knocks at my bedroom door. It's unusual seeing her in yoga pants and a faded T-shirt instead of her normal frilly frocks, but seeing how she had no choice but to work from home today, I don't blame her for dressing for comfort.

"So?" she asks with sky-high brows. "How'd it go?"

"It went really good," I say.

"Why are you smiling like you're on cloud nine or something?" Margaux frowns. "Sloane . . ."

I hadn't realized I was grinning.

"What did you do?" she asks before I can answer. "Oh, my god. Did you flirt with him? Did you kiss? Please tell me you didn't kiss him."

I roll my eyes. Of course she's jumping to conclusions. It's what she does.

"It was nothing like that," I say. "He took me to Halcyon's studio and gave me three paintings. He's having them framed and delivered later this week."

Her wrinkled expression isn't a good sign.

"What?" I ask.

"Guys don't usually give women gifts unless they like them . . . or if they want something in return." She cocks a hand on one hip. "What's his angle? What's he gunning for?"

I lift a single shoulder. "I don't know? I think he just saw that I was a big fan of Halcyon's and he wanted to do something nice?"

"Do you even hear yourself right now?"

"Do *you* hear *yourself*?" I shoot her question right back at her. "Even if he did want something—and he doesn't—he's not going to get it. I made it pretty clear that work is my priority, and when he dropped me off, he didn't say anything about seeing me later. He didn't even say bye. He just looked at me. And then the driver shut the door. Does that sound like a man who wants something from me?"

"No," she says with a sigh. I knew she'd see it my way. "He sounds like a guy with shitty social skills."

I sniff a chuckle. "I don't get that vibe from him. I think he's just . . . in a funk."

While I hardly know Roman, I get the sense that he has more layers than a glass onion. The person on the surface is hardly representative of the person underneath the cold, impenetrably hard, distant facade he projects.

I never thought I'd say that about a man who cost me my job once upon a time, but I'm catching glimpses of a different side of him.

In another lifetime—one where I'm Sloane and not Margaux, one where he's not still woefully in love with his late wife—maybe we could have lit a spark and fanned the flames. Maybe there could have been something between us . . . or at least the potential for something.

"So no more dates then?" Margaux asks.

"That wasn't a date today."

"No more seeing him then?" she rephrases her question.

"Right," I say.

"Ugh." She places her hand on her stomach.

"What's wrong?"

"Ever since that sushi two weekends ago, I've literally been so nauseous." She smacks her lips like she's about to throw up. "But I'm not getting sick, I just constantly feel like I'm about to be sick. And everything grosses me out. Like I'm so hungry sometimes, but just thinking about food makes me want to puke."

"Even in Utah?" I ask.

"Yeah," she says. "I was popping a Pepto Bismol tab every few hours just to get through the meetings. It kind of went away over the weekend, but now it's back. Damn sushi. Never again. I swear on my life."

"Babe, I don't think it's the sushi," I say. "It'd be out of your system by now. Are you running a fever or anything?"

"No," she says. "I checked. Thought maybe I had the flu or something, but it's not that. I'm just queasy, like, all the time. Even brushing my teeth makes me low-key gag."

"You should go to the doctor because that's definitely not normal. There's a walk-in urgent care place a couple blocks from here. I can go with you if you want?"

Brushing her loose curls away from her face, she leans against my door and exhales.

"Yeah, I probably should go and make sure it's nothing contagious since I'm going back to the office tomorrow," she says. "If I get anyone sick, I'll never hear the end of it. Marcel gave the entire accounting department the flu two years ago, and people *still* bring it up."

"Want me to go with you?"

"No, it's fine."

"Let me know what they say . . . ," I call as she heads down the hall to her room to freshen up.

Ten minutes later, Margaux is dashing out the door, leaving a cloud of Chanel perfume in her wake, and I'm heating up last night's leftovers for dinner. The ding of the microwave almost drowns out the chime of my phone when a text message comes through.

It's an image of an earring, a black-and-gold Gucci bee with diamond-covered wings. Margaux insisted I wear them earlier today after she dressed me in that lacy shift dress. She said I didn't have enough sparkle, and she reminded me that she always wore something that glinted or glimmered anytime she left the house.

ROMAN: Is this yours? Found it in the car a little bit ago.

Those earrings weren't cheap, and they're a set my sister wears almost weekly.

I reply with a quick, Yes, it is.

For a moment, my breath strangely catches in my throat at the idea of connecting with him again, though I have no business getting excited over such a thing.

ROMAN: I'm seeing Theodora later tonight. I'll make sure she brings it to the office tomorrow.

My stomach sinks, heavy with disappointment that has no right to exist.

I reply with a simple Appreciate it. Thank you. Then I darken my screen, retrieve my dinner from the microwave, and spend the next twenty minutes trying to peel my thoughts off Roman Bellisario, what is, what isn't, and what can never be, no matter what.

Settling on the sofa when I'm done, I zone out with some salacious reality TV to keep my mind from wandering down streets it has no business stepping foot onto.

I've never considered myself a lonely person. I very much enjoy my own company. And I've never been one of those whose entire self-worth is wrapped up in whether they're currently in a relationship. I have no need for a boyfriend or even a friend with benefits.

My life is pretty amazing without the added complications a romance can bring.

But every few minutes, I catch myself picturing the two of us chatting all things art over wine and candlelight or waltzing into galleries and exhibits arm in arm, or sharing late-night conversations where he lets me peek through the cracks of his perfectly stoic facade.

In a different timeline, maybe that would've been us.

Could've been us.

I've dated off and on since moving to the city, and I've had a handful of boyfriends over the years, but not one of them had any interest in art, which always seemed to lead to an inevitable demise. I don't imagine filmmakers could date someone who doesn't like movies or musicians could be with someone who doesn't like similar music or athletes could be with someone who doesn't like sports. While I'm not an artist per se, it's the same sort of thing. Common ground is a powerful foundation for any relationship—romantic or otherwise.

The reality star on the TV screen sports a Day-Glo spray tan, shiny blonde extensions curled to perfection, and overlined lips as she talks to the camera about how rude another costar was at her charity dinner.

These are not the things that matter in life—other people's realities, other people's lives—but I'll be damned if they don't make for the perfect escape from my own.

Two hours later, I'm almost three episodes in and embracing my inner sloth when Margaux gets back.

"Hey," I call out, muting the TV. "What'd they say?"

The clunk of her keys dropping in the bowl by the door is followed by the soft skid of her designer sneakers against the hardwood floor.

With sluggish, steady steps she makes her way to the living room sporting a shell-shocked expression on her sheet-white face.

"What? What is it?" I ask.

"So, um." Margaux swallows, makes her way to the chair beside me, and slumps down. She looks like she's going to be sick again, but this time, she's making no effort to rush to the bathroom. "I'm pregnant."

CHAPTER TEN

ROMAN

I roll Margaux's black-and-gold bee earring between my fingertips. On the other side of the kitchen, Adeline and Marabel eat dinner. Between bits of grilled chicken, rice, and untouched steamed broccoli, they debate which of their million Barbie dolls is the kindest and which is the smartest.

"Skipper is the kindest," Adeline says. "She babysits. All babysitters have to be nice."

"Which Skipper? The brown-haired one or the yellow-haired one?" Marabel asks.

"That's a dumb question." Adeline rolls her eyes.

"Adeline," I say, keeping my tone stern. "No such thing as a dumb question. Apologize to your sister."

She presses her lips together before muttering an apology.

"Yeah, but which one?" Marabel asks, clearly stuck on the topic.

"The brown-haired one," Adeline answers. "The blonde one has the weird haircut, remember? It's spiky now. It makes her look mean."

"Oh, yeah," Marabel says, shoving her broccoli aside. "I forgot you cut her hair."

Adeline shoots me a look, as if she thinks she's going to be reprimanded. I ignore it, though. She's out of her scissor phase for the time being, and all household scissors have been placed far out of her little reach to avoid any future incidents.

"Girls, finish eating, and then it's time for your bath," I tell them before checking my phone. Theodora is supposed to stop by any minute. Last Saturday she took the girls to paint pottery, and she insisted on dropping off their kiln-fired finished products tonight on her way to dinner. "If you each have one bite of broccoli, I'll let you use your bath bombs and glow sticks in the tub."

The girls each release a little squeal before stabbing small pieces of broccoli with their forks.

Ten years ago, being a father was the furthest thing from my mind. After meeting and falling in love with Emma, it was the only thing I could think about. I wanted little versions of us, I wanted more of Emma to love, I wanted the whole package.

Never once did I imagine I'd be doing this alone.

"You go first," Adeline tells Marabel. "If you plug your nose, you won't taste it. That's what Noah Goldberg told me at school. Try it."

"Is that true, Daddy?" Marabel asks me.

"Sure," I say.

It's little moments like this—the ones that Emma would have loved—that send a painful squeeze to my chest.

It's hard not having anyone to share these with.

Of course there's Theodora, but I'm not going to blow her phone up fifty times a day with every little adorable thing my girls say or do. She already thinks I've lost all my marbles and then some. She doesn't need a constant stream of reminders about how isolated and narrowly focused I've become. I work. I come home. I do the dad thing. That's it. That's my life right now.

We're an island, the three of us.

"Hello, hello," Theodora calls from the front entry. Years ago, I gave her her own key—mostly for convenience but also because she insisted

77

that she should have access to the house in case of emergencies. "Special delivery for the Bellisario girls . . ."

Adeline and Marabel abandon their dinners, and I realize I wasn't paying attention and have no idea whether they tried their broccoli.

"Careful, careful," Theodora tells them as they wrap her long legs in a joint hug. She makes her way to the kitchen island, placing two small paper bags on the countertop. She retrieves the first ceramic item—a teddy bear painted at least a hundred different colors. "This one is Miss Marabel's stunning masterpiece." Slipping her hand into the second bag, she pulls out a pineapple piggy bank glazed in a bold combination of sunflower yellow and army green. "And one breathtakingly gorgeous piece of fruit for Miss Adeline."

The girls fawn over their creations, and Theodora watches with a twinkle in her steely gaze.

"Little artists," she says before giving me a wink. "It clearly runs in the family. You should think about enrolling them in classes at the Manhattan Children's Art Academy. They have pottery and ceramics, sketching, watercolors, mixed media . . . I have an in there. One of the founders is an old colleague of mine. I know they have a wait list, but I'm sure they'd make room for the girls if I asked."

While I could if I wanted to, I'm not going to bump anyone else from the wait list. When Emma and I first became parents, we both agreed our main goal was to not raise spoiled, entitled little brats. I could easily afford to enroll them in the best schools, hire them each their own nannies and drivers, and buy them every last Barbie or American Girl doll in existence, but I've been around long enough to see what kind of women little girls like that grow up to become.

The world already has an abundance of those types.

No need to add two more to the mix.

"Oh, no. Would you look at the time? I'm going to be late for dinner," Theodora says as she walks around the island. She wraps me in a hug before cupping my cheeks. "You need anything else before I take off?"

I'm about to shake my head when I remember the bee earring.

"Yes, actually." I swipe it off the countertop and hand it to her. "Can you give this to Margaux for me tomorrow?"

Inspecting the earring for a moment, her gaze flicks to mine. Curiosity washes over her expression, and I realize she's probably assuming Margaux slept over and left those here.

"I spent some time with her earlier today. Briefly," I tell her. "This must have fallen off in my car on the way home."

"Mm-hmm," she says, as if she half doesn't believe me, and then a sly smile spreads across the side of her red lips. Placing the earring in a small compartment of her purse, she adds, "All right then. Girls, give me hugs. I'm off to stuff my face with the most delicious lobster bisque in all of Manhattan. Someday I'll take you there too. Until then, you'll simply have to take my word for it."

The girls pile onto my aunt, who gives them what I can only describe as a skinny version of a bear hug. She's always been a natural beanpole, much to my fad-diet-addicted mother's dismay.

A half an hour later, the girls are in their tub—bath bombs, glow sticks, and all because they both swore up, down, and sideways that they did, in fact, try their broccoli.

In this sliver of a moment, I think about Margaux. Her enthusiasm for Halcyon was almost contagious. The way her eyes lit at the sight of each piece. The way she'd clasp at her heart as if it was thundering hard and it was all she could do to still it. The way she would gasp and exhale as if she was taking in the most otherworldly paintings she'd ever seen.

Her reactions appeared genuine.

I don't think she was oohing and aahing for my sake—she was truly in awe.

But while she was taking in the sights, I found myself taking in *her* . . .

The way her dress hugged every arch and camber of her body, the way her satin blonde hair skimmed the tops of her delicate shoulders when she walked, the subtle yet feminine way her hips swayed with each step she took. The way my car smelled faintly like her floral-musk perfume the entire ride home.

There was something different about being with Margaux this time. Maybe it was the lack of pressure since it wasn't a date and neither one of us was attempting to impress one another, or maybe it was the fact that we were just a couple of people bonding over our appreciation of art. But being in her presence tonight was almost a tranquil experience.

Natural in a way.

It wasn't forced or awkward.

I wasn't calculating the minutes until it was over.

Not to mention it was nice having an adult conversation with someone that didn't revolve around work or kids' activities.

For the first time in years, I felt a familiar piece of my old self coming back to me.

Tomorrow I'll pick up those three paintings from the Halcyon studio, and I'll have my assistant take them to be professionally framed. While I could easily find someone to deliver the works to Margaux on my behalf, I'm thinking it might not be the worst thing . . . if I did it myself.

CHAPTER ELEVEN

SLOANE

"Mr. Henwell, thank you so much for coming in this morning," I say when I greet my first client of the day on Tuesday. "I appreciate you moving our appointment. I have a little bit of a family emergency going on."

I'm tired but wired. I spent most of last night consoling Margaux, who was beside herself over learning about her pregnancy, and as a result, I downed not one but two Americanos this morning before I even set foot in the gallery.

Motherhood is the farthest thing from Margaux's radar right now (though to be honest, I don't believe it's ever been on her radar). On top of that, since she has an IUD, the doctors need to remove it as soon as possible, or else it could lead to a miscarriage or infection.

I'm taking this afternoon off so I can accompany her to the doctor for an ultrasound and the removal of the IUD.

Margaux is terrified, though I suspect her fear has more to do with none of this being in her grand plan than anything else. She has scheduled, designed, and crafted every detail of her ideal life for as long as I can remember. Unplanned motherhood was never on her vision board.

"Yes, yes, of course. Anything for you, love," he says in his posh British accent as he adjusts his wire-framed glasses. I first met Rupert Henwell when I worked at the Brickhouse Gallery years ago. We bonded over our mutual adoration of artist Melanie Biehle, and we haven't looked back since. "I hope everything's all right? It isn't anything with you, is it?"

He places his hand on my shoulder, his chin tucked and his voice low and thick with concern.

"No, no," I say. "It's my sister."

He lifts his hand and chuckles. "What kind of hot water has our Margaux landed herself in this time? Never mind. Don't answer that. Look at me—always sticking my nose where it doesn't belong. My mother would be horrified if she heard me . . . God rest her lovely soul."

"I'm sure she's going to be fine," I tell him without going into it. "She just needs my support right now."

"Tell her that everything always works out," he says, matter of fact. "It always, *always* does. Even when we don't believe that it can. It just does. Life is funny that way."

"I'll be sure to tell her that."

Rubbing his hands together, he scans the gallery. "Now where were those new Paula DeLang urns you were telling me about?"

"They're in back." I give him a wink and point to the door clearly marked **STAFF ONLY**. "We haven't put them on the floor yet. I told my boss you get first dibs."

"Have I told you lately how much I simply adore you?" he asks with a chuckle.

The last time I brought Rupert in for a private preview, he thanked me by sending an elaborate flower arrangement, gifting me a one-week stay at his vacation home in Nantucket, and writing a full one-page letter to my boss about what a talented, knowledgeable, and service-oriented art broker I am. He finished off with demanding I receive a raise immediately—which resulted in me receiving a generous onetime bonus.

I don't do this for the accolades or the gifts, but clients like Rupert are the maraschino cherry on top of an already decadent sundae. I only wish there were more like him in this industry, but alas, they can't all be diamonds in a sea of cubic zirconia.

"Oh, I wanted to thank you so much for that restaurant recommendation last month. You weren't lying when you said the scallops—quite literally—melt in your mouth," he says as we head to the back room. I usher him to a table covered in glazed urns of all silhouettes, shades, and sizes.

To anyone else, these items would be just vessels to hold cremains or flowers, but to someone in the know, they're sophisticated masterpieces. Paula's process is famously and painstakingly perfectionistic—down to the millimeter. She spends hours upon hours etching intricate patterns and designs into the clay before it so much as sees the inside of a kiln. On top of that, each piece comes with what she calls a "birth certificate" in the form of the date and time the piece was created and subsequently finished, along with a playlist of songs she listened to while making it and a detailed rundown of what inspired her, as well as what she ate and drank during the process.

Paula is notoriously famous for viewing her work as her children and treats each one as such. Her eccentricities might seem outlandish for the average collector, but they only serve to fuel demand for those in the know.

"Will Ms. Paula be making an appearance at the gallery anytime soon?" Rupert asks as he makes his way from vase to urn to vase before returning to the shiny onyx vessel that catches his eye.

"Not that I know of. From what I understand, she's mentoring some university students in Austria right now. If I find out when she'll be back in the city, you'll be the first to know," I say. "You like that one?"

I point to the black piece.

"The birth certificate is inside," I add.

Rupert carefully lifts the lid and dips his hand in to retrieve a piece of paper. Adjusting his glasses, he scans the details with utmost discernment.

As he reads, my phone vibrates in my pocket, sending a start to my heart.

My mind immediately goes to Margaux and her *predicament.*

"Rupert, I'm so sorry," I say when I pull my phone out to check my messages. Normally I wouldn't dream of interrupting a client meeting. "I need to make sure this—"

Only it isn't a text.

It's a call.

And it isn't Margaux calling me.

It's Roman.

As I hold my breath, the room starts to spin.

I silence the call and clear my throat.

"Everything all right, dear?" Rupert asks, blinking behind the pristine lenses of his expensive glasses.

Sliding my phone back into my pocket, I force a smile on my face. I wasn't expecting Roman to call. Quickly, I remember the paintings he's framing for me. He was probably calling to get a delivery address, though I can't imagine the paintings were framed this quickly? It hasn't even been twenty-four hours.

"Yes, sorry," I apologize again. "It was nothing. So, what do you think of this one?"

"I think this poor sweet little thing needs a home," he says as if he's about to adopt a pet from a shelter. "And I have just the place for it in my foyer niche."

"Perfect," I say. "I'll have it wrapped and delivered to you by the end of the week."

———

Margaux squeezes my hand so hard I worry she might crush it. A thin sheet of paper covers her lower body as she lies on an exam table in a small dark room.

"All right, are we ready?" The too-chipper ultrasound technician takes a seat in front of her machine. "Just going to squirt a little bit of this conducting gel on your lower belly, and then we can begin."

She grabs what looks like a clear ketchup bottle from a warmer, flips it upside down, gives it a couple of shakes, and spreads the goo on the lower half of Margaux's exposed stomach.

My sister sneaks a quick glance my way, and I offer a reassuring smile followed by an equally reassuring squeeze of her sweaty, trembling hand.

"We having a good day today, ladies?" the sonographer asks. Her eyes are glued to the screen, which is vaguely reminiscent of an abstract black, gray, and white piece by Harlow Hendriks I saw the other day. Harlow is fully color blind and paints only with those three tones, letting the shadows do all the work. "This weather is incredible, isn't it?"

Margaux doesn't answer. For the first time in modern history, the cat has her tongue. That and she's too focused on the screen, though I'm sure she has no idea what she's looking at.

The technician presses keys and buttons and moves the transducer around.

Everything's happening too fast for either of us to process.

"Ah," she says. "Here we go. Here's our little peanut."

She dials up the volume until a steady swishing sound fills the small room.

"Good strong heartbeat," the tech says. "One hundred fifty beats per minute. See this black space? That's the amniotic sac. And then see this flicker here? That's the baby's heart. You can even see baby's little arms and legs if you look closer."

Margaux's eyes are glued to the screen, but mine are glued to her.

She's as white as a ghost. Unblinking. I'm not even sure she's breathing.

Seeing the baby moving inside of her probably makes it much more real than two lines on a pregnancy test.

A single tear slides down her cheek, though it's impossible to know if it's a happy tear or something else. Now is not the time to ask.

"How . . . how far along am I?" Margaux breaks her silence. Her voice is small, a jarring contrast against her larger-than-life persona.

"Let's see here . . . ," the tech says. "You are measuring—wait. Wait a minute. Hold on here."

"What? What is it?" Margaux asks. She begins to sit up, then stops herself. "What's wrong?"

"Well, well, well." A lopsided grin fills the tech's face. "Looks like we've got ourselves a stowaway."

"What does that mean?" I ask.

My sister and I exchange confused looks.

"There are *two* babies in here," she says, moving the transducer until the screen shows two separate sacs and two distinct flickering heartbeats. "Twins."

Margaux wipes the tears from her face with the back of her hand. "I—I'm going to throw up, I think."

I grab the nearest trash can, and the tech scrambles to hand her a warm washcloth to wipe her belly with before flicking on the light.

Standing, I rub circles into Margaux's back while simultaneously holding the trash can close in case she vomits.

"You want some water, sweetheart?" the tech asks.

"No, thank you." Margaux closes her eyes and draws in a lungful of sterile air. "I . . . I think I'm going to be okay."

"You sure?" The tech hovers by the light switch, her steel-blue eyes heavy with concern. "I just need to measure baby B really quick, and then I can send the doctor in. Do you think you're feeling like you can lay back again so I can do that?"

Her voice is soft and comforting, like a preschool teacher convincing a scared child to cooperate.

Margaux nods, leaning back against the exam table.

A moment later, the room is dark, and the tech returns to her machine.

"Looks like they're both measuring twelve weeks and three days," she says before finishing up. She hands Margaux another damp washcloth before printing out a stream of photos longer than a CVS receipt. "These will go in your file. But these three are for you to keep."

She hands Margaux two grainy black-and-white images: one of baby A, one of baby B, and one showing the two of them together.

"Congratulations on the twins," she says with a genuine gleam in her eye. "I'll send Dr. Bitner in shortly."

The door closes with a heavy clunk, and a deafening silence falls over the room.

Margaux begins to speak, only instead of words, they're sobs. Hunched over, she buries her head in her hands. The thin paper covering her lower half crinkles, growing more speckled with tears by the second. Wrapping my arms around her, I squeeze her as hard as I can.

"It's going to be okay," I tell her.

"I was just starting to wrap my head around one baby," she says between sniffs. "But two? Two? Sloane, *two* babies . . ."

"I know, I know . . ." I hug her close.

"What am I going to do?" she asks.

"Do you know who the father is?" I'm guessing it's her friend with benefits, Ethan. They met on a dating app years ago and quickly realized they were a terrible match in all areas outside of the bedroom. He's a charismatic charmer with a blue-blooded pedigree, but he's not exactly fatherhood material.

"It's Ethan," she says without hesitation. I hand her a Kleenex from a nearby box, and she blows her nose. "Can you believe this? *Twins.* With *Ethan* of all people."

A knock at the door interrupts her pity party, and a moment later, a lanky woman with midnight-black hair pulled into a low bun enters.

"Hi, Margaux," she says with a warm smile as she heads to the sink to wash her hands. "Good to see you again."

Margaux mutters an emotional "Hello."

"Looks like we have ourselves a little surprise, don't we?" Dr. Bitner takes a seat on a rolling stool and scoots close to the exam table. "Or should I say, two little surprises."

"I don't understand how this happened . . . I have an IUD . . . I was getting my period. I mean, I think I was? Last time it was pretty light, but that's normal for me," Margaux rambles on as her doctor nods, listening intently, pitched forward like she's waiting for the perfect time to interject.

"Yes, these things are uncommon . . . typically occurring in less than one out of a hundred women using an IUD," Dr. Bitner says, "but they *can* and *do* happen. One thing to keep in mind is you have options, but regardless of what you decide, it's imperative that we remove the device immediately to prevent any potential infections or complications."

Margaux swallows hard before nodding.

I remain by my sister's side as Dr. Bitner completes her exam and the subsequent removal. When it's all over and we're checking out, I order an Uber so Margaux doesn't have to walk home in discomfort of any kind—emotional, physical, or otherwise.

Once back at our apartment, we spend the rest of the day watching reality TV and pretending like both of our lives aren't about to change in ways we never could have anticipated . . . more Margaux's life than mine, but there's no way I'd let her do any of this alone.

I think of Rupert's words from earlier today, about how everything always works out, even when you don't think that it will.

I want to believe him.

I *have* to believe him.

This is all going to work out, and everything's going to be fine.

It has to be.

CHAPTER TWELVE

ROMAN

"Be good, girls, and listen to Miss Grace." I drop the girls off at dance class Wednesday evening shortly after five o'clock, and then I linger for a few moments to watch them warm up in their little pink leotards and leg warmers. Their cheeks are rosy from smiling so big, and their eyes are lit as they cling to Grace's side.

I've noticed they do that lately—cling to people.

Women, to be specific.

While there are plenty of men raising kids on their own, many of them raising daughters, I can't help but worry if I'm giving my girls everything they need except the one thing they don't have . . . a mother figure. They have Theodora, of course, but she plays more of a "cool great-aunt" role in their lives. It's not the same.

I'd never date a woman for the sole purpose of having an extra set of hands or someone to relieve me of my parental responsibilities, but perhaps it wouldn't be the worst thing if someone came along who naturally fit into that role in our lives. Of course no one could ever fill Emma's place in our hearts, and there's no denying there's a deep, dark void where she used to reside. There's also no denying that the older the girls get, the more they're going to need the kind of guidance I'm not equipped to give them.

The idea of moving on—whatever that entails—sends a sour jolt of nausea down the back of my throat, like my body is rejecting the mere notion of such a concept.

I steal one last look at my girls before heading to my waiting car outside. They'll be here for the next two hours—first ballet, then jazz, then tap lessons. While I'd normally sit in the back seat of my idling SUV and check work emails to pass the time, I picked up those framed paintings for Margaux earlier today, and I might as well deliver them now.

My driver, Antonio, opens the passenger door the second he spots me strolling outside.

"Where to?" he asks a minute later.

"Just a second." I pull up Margaux's personal cell number and press the green button.

She answers on the third ring.

"Hey," she says, breathless. Was she running to the phone? Did she just finish a jog or fitness class? And why the hell do I care what she was doing anyway?

"Margaux." I collect myself. "I have those paintings. You home right now? Thought I could drop them off."

I'm met with dead silence—not exactly the response I was expecting given her reaction at the studio the other day.

"Um, yeah," she says. "I'm home."

"Is it okay if I bring them by?" I ask to confirm, seeing as though she's somewhat hesitant. "Unless you have other plans . . ."

My mind immediately wanders to a scenario in which she's going on a date with someone else or having another guy over. Not that it matters. She's free to date whomever she chooses. But the idea of her spending her Wednesday night with some faceless other man sends a twinge of . . . *something* . . . to my chest.

"Sure. Yes. Of course," she answers, a little less breathless than before. "Just, um, give me a little bit. Just got home from work."

Sinking into the buttery leather of my seat, I exhale, more relieved than I should be at this revelation.

"It's rush hour traffic, so it'll be a bit," I say.

"I'll be here. I'm in apartment 2C. I'll buzz you in when you get here."

I send her address to Antonio's phone, and he taps the navigation button. The guidance begins, though I doubt he needs it. He's been driving this city for the past thirty years and knows every corner and crevice like the back of his hand.

Eying the wrapped and framed paintings in the back seat, I think about her reactions at the Halcyon studio on Monday. I've been playing them on a loop in my head for two days now, though for what reason, I've yet to figure out.

Twenty excruciatingly slow minutes of bumper-to-bumper traffic later, Antonio pulls up in front of Margaux's building. Within seconds, I'm heading up the same familiar steps I've trod before—steps I never thought I'd trek again in this lifetime.

I press the buzzer for 2C and wait.

A few seconds later, the lock on the building door buzzes, and I head in.

After rapping on her door, I finger comb my hair into place and straighten my tie, which suddenly feels a couple of millimeters too tight. The door swings open a few seconds later, and standing before me is a dressed-down version of the woman I've spent all of a handful of hours with but can't seem to get out of my head lately.

"Hi." Her pale-pink lips arch at the sides, and she angles her head as she gazes up at me. Her sleek blonde hair is pulled back into a low ponytail, leaving a few strands to frame her heart-shaped face. There are no pearls on her tonight. No lace. No diamond earrings. No lipstick. Not even a hint of makeup at all. And yet here I am, staring at the natural beauty before me, losing my train of thought . . .

Margaux laughs a nervous chuckle before glancing down at her black leggings and gray Columbia University T-shirt.

"Spent the day in heels," she says. "I have this thing about being comfortable the second I walk through the door. You want to come in?"

She pulls the door open wider and steps aside. The faint scent of flowery candles and fabric softener wafts from inside, like she recently threw a load of clothes in and lit a candle. It's cozy and warm and welcoming in a way I wasn't expecting.

"I don't want to impose," I say.

Margaux waves me in. "Don't be ridiculous. You're hand delivering me three Halcyon paintings. The least I can do is offer you a drink."

Her apartment is classic and efficient yet homey—black-and-white checkerboard floors in the kitchen. Wood in the entry, hall, and living room. An old cast-stone fireplace filled with various shapes and sizes of ivory candles. Various works of art hung in strategic places along the white walls—one above a bar cart, another above the emerald-green velvet sofa, a small collage of various works in the hallway.

"You like whiskey, right?" she asks as she heads to the brass bar cart in the corner. "You seem like a whiskey kind of guy. I think that's what you drank the first night we met, anyway . . ."

"Whiskey's fine."

Whiskey, scotch, it all ends up in the same place.

I stand the three paintings carefully against the wall, just beyond the entry rug.

"Cheers," she says when she returns with a crystal tumbler in hand. One for me and one for her. "I don't normally drink this, but I'm drinking it in honor of you tonight and your generosity."

My mind immediately conjures up some scenario where we're drinking some ex-boyfriend's whiskey that was left behind and forgotten about, and I'm not exactly sure how I feel about that or why I even care.

"Cheers." I clink my glass against hers, holding her pale-blue gaze captive for what feels like forever and not nearly long enough at the same time.

I take a sip. Margaux follows suit, only she immediately breaks into a coughing fit. As soon as it clears, she heads to the kitchen sink for a glass of water.

"Pretend that didn't just happen," she says between substantial gulps. "Pretend I drank it in one smooth swallow and that I looked really cool doing it."

I let out a stifled laugh—something I probably don't do near enough of these days.

"Done and done," I say as I take her in. It's rare to find people who don't take themselves too seriously in this city.

Emma was the same way. Always self-effacing. Always making jokes at her own expense. It was one of the things I loved most about her. She was as authentic as they came. Unabashedly herself. Never afraid to look silly in front of anyone.

"Where are you going to hang these?" I nod toward the pieces resting against the wall.

"Oh," she says. "I was thinking of putting them above my bed."

She squeezes past me and reaches for the first painting, carrying it to the kitchen island and carefully peeling back the thick brown paper that protects it.

"*Fool's Gold*," she says before peeking at the back. "Number one."

Sipping my drink, I watch her do the same with the other two pieces, standing back in silence as she oohs and aahs over them as if she's seeing them for the first time all over again.

I set my drink on the counter, but in the process I accidentally place it on a small stack of mail. Moving it aside, it's then that I notice an unfamiliar name on a piece of correspondence: Sloane Sheridan.

Same last name.

Does she live with a family member?

An ex, perhaps?

Sloane could easily be a male or female name.

As I watch Margaux fawn over her gifts, I find my curiosity piquing by the second.

"What are you doing this Friday night?" I ask.

"What's that?" She glances my way, her smile fading.

My question was crystal clear. She had to have heard me.

"This Friday," I repeat myself. "Are you busy?"

Her pretty face twists slightly as she peers to the side, seemingly deep in thought. "Um, I don't think I have any plans . . . Why do you ask?"

Rolling my eyes, I offer her a playful smirk. "I want to take you to dinner."

She begins to speak, but I continue, feeling the need to offer an explanation, given my previous stance on not wanting to date anyone.

"I owe you a do-over," I say. "An actual do-over."

Her full lips press flat. This time I have no idea if her speechlessness is a good thing or a bad thing.

"I thought you said you weren't ready to date?" she asks.

"I *did* say that," I say. "And I'm not ready. I just . . . I like spending time with you."

Her mouth forms a slight circle, though no sound escapes.

My admission must have shocked the words from her lips, but it also shocks the air from my lungs. I release the breath I'd been holding. Who am I right now? All I wanted was to drop off some paintings. I never planned on asking her on a date. This was never my intention.

Now here we are.

Margaux eyes the paintings before returning her attention my way.

"I'm sorry," she says, placing her palm against her forehead as she releases a nervous laugh. "I'm just really . . . I wasn't expecting this. At all. You caught me by surprise, that's all."

"So is that a yes or a no?" I ask. "I promise you can't hurt my feelings. I'm basically Teflon at this point in my life."

Her lips tease into a charmed smile that soon turns conflicted, as if she's at war with herself on the inside. But the more she hesitates and delays her answer, the more I find myself silently willing her to say yes. They say you always want what you can't have, and maybe it's simple psychology at play here, but I want to see her again.

I don't want to drop off these paintings and carry on as if Margaux Sheridan no longer exists.

The key chain . . . the apartment building . . . the love of Halcyon . . . the way she finds her way into my thoughts at odd hours of the day . . .

It has to mean something.

"I want to . . . ," she finally answers, though the tone of her voice makes me think there's a *but* coming.

A disclaimer.

A reason.

An excuse.

While I can't remember the last time I was turned down for a date—it had to have been long before I met Emma—the sting of rejection is already coursing its way through my veins. Regardless, I maintain my best poker face.

"I'd love to get to know you better, Margaux," I say. "But I'll understand if the feeling isn't mutual."

Her shoulders deflate, and her pretty face tilts to one side as if to offer a silent apology.

"I'm sorry." She says the words I saw coming a mile away. "Can I think about it and let you know?"

In my book, a maybe is worse than a no.

If she gave me a no, I could lick my wounds and go back to business as usual. A maybe instills a sense of false hope, and there's nothing worse than wishing for something you know only has a 50 percent chance of coming true.

"Of course," I say. Tossing back the remains of my whiskey, I place the tumbler by the edge of her sink. "Enjoy the rest of your evening."

CHAPTER THIRTEEN

SLOANE

"How do I look?" I do a spin in front of my sister Friday night, finishing the move with jazz hands and a cheesy smile because I feel like an actress playing a part in an off-Broadway production.

Once again, Margaux has convinced me to go on another date with Roman . . . though I'd be lying if I said I was disappointed about it this time.

Conflicted, yes.

Disheartened, not in the least.

This time feels different. There hasn't been a looming sense of dread hanging over me all day or the air of nervous anticipation coloring my thoughts. I feel no different now than if I were about to have dinner with a friend—but with a side of baby butterflies in my middle.

On top of everything else, with Margaux's pregnancy, it's more important than ever that she lands this promotion—though how she'll weave that into all this remains to be seen. Perhaps it would be an understandable excuse for her to cut things off with Roman when the time comes? Though that's for her to worry about, not me.

Until then, here we are.

"Thought I'd change it up a little," I add. The last two times we've hung out, I felt like I spent more time tugging and pulling my uncomfortable outfits into place than anything else.

"Hm." Margaux studies me with a critical eye.

Rather than raid my sister's closet, I opted for a few of my own pieces—black pants, a cream sleeveless blouse, and a pair of fuchsia-colored enamel earrings I purchased two years ago at the MoMA gift shop. Classic with a punch of pink for some feminine flair à la Margaux.

"No." Margaux rises from her bed and heads straight for her closet. A minute later, she retrieves a floral sundress and a pair of nude pumps. "It's a summer Friday in June, and he's taking you to Fiorucci's in Chelsea. You should dress like it."

I don't know what any of those things have to do with a floral dress, and I've never even heard of that restaurant, but she's the one calling the shots with this entire situation she's orchestrated, so I'll wear the damn outfit.

"You look like you're about to attend an art exhibit," she says like it's a bad thing.

Unbuttoning my blouse, I shrug it off my shoulders before draping it over the foot of her bed along with my pants. A minute later, I'm slipping her dress over my body and tugging it into place. It's a little snug in the waist and bust, but the forgiving A-line cut makes up for it. Our entire lives, I've always been a half of a dress size bigger than her. Sometimes a full size, depending on the brand. I've always chalked it up to the fact that Margaux doesn't sit still for two minutes most days, whereas I have the art of relaxation down to a science. My body shape is . . . softer . . . than hers, if only a smidge.

"Much better," she says with a proud sigh, clasping her hands together. "Will you let me curl your hair tonight?"

"No," I say.

"Then at least wear this." Grabbing an oversize headband from the top of her dresser, she places it on me, pulling pieces of hair out from behind my ears so they frame my face.

I turn to check my reflection in her mirror, and it takes everything I have not to burst into laughter at the sight of myself.

"This headband is *gigantic*," I say. "I feel like I'm wearing a crown or fascinator or something. I look like the Designer Imposter version of you. Designer Imposter Margaux."

"Don't be ridiculous." She plucks at and fusses with my hair some more, adjusting the headband just so. "It completes the ensemble. And you look stunning."

"I look like you."

"That's the whole point."

"Yeah, but . . ." I let my thoughts fade. She's right. I can't argue that fact. I'm not sure where I was going with that, but she pays it no mind.

"Isn't he going to be here any minute?"

I check my watch before sliding my feet into the skyscraper-height red-soled pumps she set out for me.

"If I break my ankle tonight, it's on you," I tell her.

"You act like you've never worn six-inch heels before . . ." Margaux rolls her eyes as she snickers. I'm glad she finds this amusing. "Just remember to walk *heel to toe and slow*. That's the secret. Mom taught us that, remember?"

I meet her reflection in the mirror.

"Speaking of Mom," I say. "You still haven't told her about the pregnancy . . ."

"I know, I know." Margaux waves her manicured hands. "I'm still figuring things out."

"You can't wait forever."

"Well aware," she says. "I'm reminded of it every time I try to put on a pair of pants. It's like everything's getting tighter by the hour. Nothing fits anymore, and I'm barely even showing . . . at this rate, I'll be the size of a house by the end of next month."

"That should be the least of your concerns right now."

Margaux starts to reply, until the ring of my phone cuts her off.

"It's Roman," I say after checking the screen. "He must be downstairs."

I take a deep breath.

She takes a deep breath.

"Remember," she says, placing her hands on my shoulders, "to be uninteresting."

"Yeah, yeah, yeah." I grab my clutch and phone and head outside, where Roman's leaning against his shiny black Escalade with a half-cocked smile on his face.

Like a moment out of a movie, my heart skips a beat, and everything feels electric and live wire—much like the way I felt when he asked me on this date a couple of days ago. While I wanted to scream "yes" from the top of my lungs, I had to give him an apprehensive maybe. I needed to consult with Margaux first. This is her project. This is all her doing.

Roman and *I* are not dating.

None of this is real.

"Look at you." He flashes a brilliant smile as he drinks me in, and then he reaches for my hand as he helps me into the back seat. The scent of new-car leather and his expensive cologne fills my lungs as I settle in, and the instant he takes the spot next to me, my stomach does a mini somersault.

I hate how real this feels . . . because it only means that one of us is going to get hurt in the end—which was never the goal here.

"How was work?" he asks. "Theodora's in Montauk for the weekend. I imagine the office was pretty calm today. When the cat's away, the mice will play, or however the saying goes. I try to stay out of the office on Fridays myself. It's my gift to my employees. I think it's good for morale."

It would've been nice for Margaux to share that little tidbit with me earlier about Theodora being gone . . .

"Fridays are usually pretty low key," I say. *Low key* is a phrase Margaux uses far too often, as well as *literally*. They're her favorites. She is literally always using the term *low key*. "I swear half the office was out anyway."

I remember Margaux mentioning that when she came home earlier . . . she was upset about a couple of people not finishing some report, and her assistant went home sick, though she's pretty sure she was just hungover. Margaux tends to complain about work more than most people, which has always been humorous to me because for someone who swears they love their job, she doesn't always act like it.

"Antonio, we're going to Fiorucci's," he says to the driver. I make a note of memorizing his chauffer's name this time. So many people in this city have drivers and housekeepers and assistants and treat them like they're nonplayer characters without names and feelings and entire lives outside of their jobs.

"Antonio, I'm . . . Margaux," I say, catching myself almost slip. "I don't think we've been properly introduced yet."

Our gazes connect in the rearview mirror, and he nods. "Lovely to see you again, Margaux."

The weight of Roman's gaze falls over me, though he doesn't say a word.

"How long have you been driving for Roman?" I ask Antonio as I lean forward to hear him better.

"Since he was barely old enough to tie his shoes." Antonio chuckles.

Roman feigns annoyance as he fights a smile. I'm sure he's relishing this on the inside.

"Started driving for his father about thirty years ago," Antonio adds as we coast to a gentle stop at a red light. "After Mr. Bellisario passed, Roman asked if I'd drive for him. Was hoping to be retired by now, but I like what I do and who I do it for, and so here I am."

"He's not allowed to retire," Roman says with a single lifted brow and a hint of amusement in his tone. "It's in his contract."

Antonio sniffs. "I'll be here until the cows come home. Or until the girls are off to college. Whichever comes first."

"We keep you busy, that's for sure," Roman says. "Work, school, day care, dance class, music lessons . . ."

"The thing about the Bellisarios, Margaux, is that they don't know how to sit still," Antonio interjects with a teasing tone. "It's in their DNA or something. Always busy. Always doing something. If there's a club or class, they're in it."

It's still difficult for me to picture Roman as a doting, hands-on father, but I can imagine staying busy keeps him from lingering in his grief for too long.

Busyness is an escape for many.

And an addiction for some.

A few minutes later, Antonio drops us off by the curb outside of a vibrant new restaurant in the Meatpacking District—a place rumored to have a monthslong wait list, according to my sister. How he got us in at eight o'clock on a Friday night is beyond me, but I'm excited to try the place.

There's a line outside stretching at least half a block, if not longer. Ornate brass letters against a chic black-and-white backdrop spell out *Fiorucci's*. Elaborate white flora in tall black pots flanks the entrance, which is accented with a plush red rug. The air outside is warm and soft and scented like perfume and Italian spices.

By the time we're settled in at our table for two a few minutes later, and our drinks have been ordered and delivered, a three-piece band in the corner begins to play old-world Italian music. The ambience is colorful, lively, charged with excitement.

Everyone seems happy to be here, and I get it. One step in here and you're magically transported to a place where all your troubles are left at the door.

Maybe it's the drinks.

Maybe it's the music.

Maybe it's the handsome man with the intense gaze pinning me into place . . .

I've reached the bottom of my first Aperol spritz when the room begins to spin like a merry-go-round. Maybe one of these days I'll accept the fact that I'm a lightweight. A cheap date. I meant to eat something beforehand so I wouldn't be drinking on an empty stomach again, but after Margaux vetoed my outfit, it completely slipped my mind.

"So your mother lives in France?" I ask. He'd briefly mentioned it earlier this evening before our server stopped to take our order, and the conversation veered to something else.

"With her new husband, yes," he says with a hint of subtle distaste in his tone.

"I take it you're not his biggest fan?" I arch a brow.

"Something like that."

I lift a single shoulder. "You love who you love."

"He's half her age, poor as a pauper, and she's funding his stalled-out music career, but yes, I suppose you love who you love." He takes a sip of whiskey, his eyes not leaving mine for a second.

"What kind of music does he make?" I ask.

Roman's upper lip curls, like he's attempting to stifle a laugh. "He, uh, he wants to be like a French version of Eminem—or something like that."

"Oh." I try to reserve my judgment, as everyone is allowed to have their dreams, but I imagine my reaction's written all over my face at the moment. I've never been good at wearing a poker face, and the cocktail coursing through my veins certainly doesn't help.

"Right," he says with a sniff. *"Oh."*

"Hopefully there's a prenup or something in the mix . . . you just never know with those kinds of relationships . . . the age difference and all of that . . . and creative types can be so fickle sometimes . . ."

"I don't even want to know if there's a prenup," he says with a hint of annoyance coloring his tone, which leads me to believe there likely isn't one.

"Does she see your girls often?"

"She comes back when she can." His tone is bordering on terse, leading me to believe it's a sore subject for him. I'm about to ask about his dad when I recall Antonio mentioning Mr. Bellisario had passed. "Do you have any brothers or sisters?"

"A brother," he says. "He's an entertainment lawyer in Los Angeles. We're not as close as we used to be these days. He's got his life, and I've got mine. We try to get together once a year."

"He didn't want to help you with the shipping business?" I ask.

"Different fathers," he says. "Though I don't think it'd have made a difference. He'd be miserable doing anything else but practicing law. It suits him. The man loves to prove a point any chance he can."

"It's so funny how some people are just born to do a certain job," I say. I'm about to wax on about Margaux and her social butterfly ways and how she found her calling—when I quickly remember that I *am* Margaux. "You could still teach art, you know. Maybe not now, but someday."

He takes another sip of his drink before shaking his head. "I try not to think that far ahead. I find focusing on the future tends to make me wish my life away."

"I don't know how to stop living in the future," I say. "It's all I think about . . . so many things I want to do, so much I'm looking forward to."

"I used to be that way," he says. "Before I became a father. The girls have forced me to slow down and be engaged in the moment. I'm not sure I even knew how to do that before they came along."

"What's your favorite thing about being a dad?" I prop my elbow on the table, leaning forward with my chin on the top of my hand as I await his answer. I've never been good at small talk. I like to dig deep, below the surface. I like the harder-hitting, soul-pressing conversations. Real and meaningful topics, no fluff.

Roman cocks his head ever so slightly, as if my question catches him off guard. And then he stares off to the side for a second, looking lost in contemplation.

"All of it," he finally answers. "The random *I love you*s. Getting to experience everything for the first time again through their eyes. Watching these little humans grow into their personalities. It's like nothing I've ever experienced before."

"It sounds magical when you put it that way."

"It's not always magical," he says. "But that's kind of the best thing about it. The highs always make up for the lows. I could be having the worst day in the world, but the second I walk through the door after work and they run up to me with smiles and throw their arms around me, everything else sort of . . . fades away."

"Okay, now you're making me want, like, ten kids," I tease.

"Are children on your radar at all?" he asks, though I can't tell if he's simply making conversation or vetting my stepmother potential.

"I think so?" I say. I've always loved the idea of having at least one kid. Maybe two. Nothing too big or overwhelming. Enough to experience motherhood in all its glory without sacrificing my career or passions. I'm not sure if it's possible to have it all, but I'd like to think I can give it the old college try. "Sometimes I don't know if I'd be a good parent, though. I don't know the first thing about kids. Never had any younger siblings or cousins. Never babysat."

"Used to feel the same way," he says with a pained smile. He looks down at the flickering candle centerpiece between us. "Everything changed after I met the right person. You figure it out as you go along. Together."

There's an ache in my chest that accompanies his words.

"Anyway." He tosses back the remainder of his whiskey. "Enough about me. You have any siblings? I know you're from Ohio."

We're back to small talk now . . . and a topic I was hoping to avoid.

"I have one sister," I say.

"Are the two of you close?"

"Too close." I chuff. "It wasn't enough that we were womb-mates . . . now we're roommates."

He squints, as if he doesn't get the joke.

"We're twins," I say. I release a slow exhale.

"Ah. I see. Identical?"

I nod. It feels good to be honest with him about something for a change. There's an unexpected lightness washing over me now, like I've peeled back a layer. The layer may be as thin as cellophane, but it's still a layer.

"My mother has sisters who are identical twins," he says. "They must be in their sixties now . . . never married, never had kids, still living together in a little town outside Milwaukee. I guess they never learned how to do life without each other."

"Sounds like your mother is more than making up for that . . . living in Paris and all."

Our server stops by. "Your food will be out shortly. Would you like another round of drinks in the meantime?"

Roman holds my gaze from across the table, waiting for me to answer first.

"I'd love another spritz," I say.

Roman lifts his glass and nods. "I'll take another Macallan."

The night is young, yet it feels like time is moving faster than it should.

"Tell me more about your mother," I say. "I'm intrigued. She sounds like someone who marches to her own beat."

He exhales a breathy semblance of a laugh. "That's putting it mildly."

"A divorcée who up and moves to France and marries a guy half her age has my vote. Not a lot of people could do something so bold."

"She's probably more reckless than bold," he says, "but I have no doubt she'd be flattered by your words."

"Tell me about her. Does she wear red lipstick and bateau-striped shirts? Does she chain-smoke and read Baudelaire and Verlaine? I'm imagining this fabulous, sophisticated woman. Paint me a picture."

His eyes glint with amusement as he studies me with his devilishly handsome dark gaze, one that drips over me slow like honey and heavy as steel at the same time.

Our server stops by with our drinks, but Roman's penetrating fixation never wavers. In fact, it's as if I'm the only thing in the entire room worthy of his attention. For the first time in forever, I feel seen. Truly seen.

Something is happening between us.

Something I can't describe because there are no words to accurately convey it.

For a moment, I'm frozen, all thoughts suddenly abandoning my mind and leaving nothing in their place. I don't know that I could form a sentence if I tried. It's all just . . . blank.

"Thank you," he tells her, breaking the intensity that fastened me into place a mere second ago. He waits for her to leave before directing his attention my way once more. "Her name is Claudia, and she's not much of a smoker. Not much of a reader either. She's adventurous. A young soul. After my father passed and I grew up and started a family of my own, I don't think she really knew what to do with herself, so she started fresh somewhere new. I always tease her and tell her she's in her second act."

"Is she happy?"

"Happier than I've ever seen her."

"Then that's all that matters," I say.

"I just hate to see anyone take advantage of her, that's all. She's a generous person, very personable, easy to like. She tends to attract a certain . . . type."

"She sounds nothing like my mom," I say. "Mine has never left Ohio. Still lives in the house I grew up in, and she'll never leave it. Her definition of adventure is staying in Cincinnati for a weekend at the Embassy Suites. She might hit up Columbus every great once in a while if she's feeling audacious. She's terrified of New York, though. She doesn't visit if she can avoid it."

"Terrified?" He laughs. "Of what?"

"She's a small-town girl. I think she gets overwhelmed by every-thing . . . the cars, the people, the buildings, the sounds, the smells. She hates feeling disoriented and out of her element," I say. "My sister and I flew her here for Christmas one year, thinking she'd love to see the Rockettes and how beautiful the city gets with the snow and the holiday decorations and everything."

"And how did that pan out?"

"She had a panic attack the second we left the airport. Ma—*my sister* fortunately had a bottle of Xanax in her purse that she keeps for emergencies," I say. A flash of heat burns my cheeks as I pray he didn't notice the slipup. "Needless to say, she needed a refill after that weekend."

"Do you go back to Ohio often?"

"A couple of times a year. Mother's Day usually. And either Thanksgiving or Christmas."

"You ever miss it?"

"I miss it when I'm not there. I get nostalgic for it. But every time I go home, all I can think about is wanting to be back in the city again. New York is my home now. I can't imagine ever living anywhere else. It starts to feel like a big little city after a while—if that makes sense."

A flash of amusement flickers in his dark irises before fading like it was never there to begin with. Per usual, it's impossible to know what he's thinking, though there's no question he's more engaged tonight than ever before.

I went into this entire thing with every intention of suffering through my time with him like some kind of martyr. Enjoying my time with Roman was the furthest thing from my mind. It wasn't even in the realm of possibilities. And now here we are. And here I am. Wishing I could stop time, if only for one evening.

"You're different, Margaux," he says out of nowhere.

"Different?"

"Not what I was expecting at all."

I reach for my drink, pausing to give him a sideways glance. "Is that a good thing? Or a bad thing?"

Two dimples appear at the centers of his cheeks as his lips tug up at the corners. This time his handsome smile doesn't disappear in an airtight instant. It remains. It lingers. It lights his eyes from the inside out.

"It's been a long time since I've dated anyone," he says, "but I seem to remember everyone feeling like they had to impress me all the time. They'd name-drop. Talk about their expensive vacations and their career achievements like they were interviewing for a job. But you . . . you're not like that at all. You're just . . ."

His voice tapers as he studies me.

And is he implying that we're dating?

A swarm of questions circles my head, none of which I can ask without making this all the more confusing.

I thought this was simply a dinner date redo?

"I'm terrible at small talk," I say with a shrug. Is he idealizing me, or is he truly impressed with me? Is my attempt at being boring and uninteresting having the opposite intended effect? "Plus, nobody likes a braggard."

He takes a slow sip of his whiskey. "It's been a long time since I had a real conversation with someone."

Before he can expand on that, our dinner arrives, officially kicking off the final segment of our evening. While nothing can ever come of this, it doesn't make me enjoy getting to know him any less. Plus, the way I catch him staring at me, like I'm some kind of beautiful art piece he's laying eyes on for the first time, gives me life. I don't even know if he knows he's doing it, but he hasn't stopped since he picked me up an hour ago.

What I wouldn't give to stop the clock, if only for tonight.

CHAPTER FOURTEEN

ROMAN

"I'm afraid you're going to have to roll me out of here if I take another bite." Margaux folds her napkin and places it beside her half-eaten tiramisu. "I'm tapping out."

"You went for the gold," I say. "No small feat."

"Guess I got silver then." She points to my polished-off cup of stracciatella gelato.

Before Emma, anytime I'd get dinner with a woman, she'd order a small salad or piece of grilled fish and a sparkling water or dry wine, pick at her meal like a rabbit foraging for food, and wave her hands vehemently when the dessert tray rolled up, insisting she was stuffed. Not only that, but oftentimes she'd sit so rigid, I'd have thought her spine was a steel rod.

I take it back. There was one girl a lifetime ago. A waiflike culinary dropout with eyes bigger than saucers. She impressively threw down three-fourths of a shared appetizer, a triple cheeseburger, her fries, and most of my fries, and washed it all down with a double chocolate milk shake. Our conversation that night consisted mostly of food-oriented topics. Recipes she wanted to try. Restaurants she loved. Her favorite grocery stores and cooking magazines. Anytime I changed the subject, she'd somehow find a way to circle the topic back to food. I'm not unconvinced that the poor thing had a tapeworm. And an unhealthy fixation.

But I digress.

Most of my previous dates rarely looked alive unless they were rattling off a laundry list of prestigious accolades or name-dropping some designer, renowned chef, up-and-coming artist, or pseudocelebrity from their inner circle. The conversations were always superficial and stilted, like a mind-numbing game of Ping-Pong.

But Margaux is different.

Who'd have thought dinner and a simple conversation could be so . . . simplistically satisfying? The first time we went out, I couldn't get home to my girls fast enough. Tonight, the thought hasn't crossed my mind once. And not because I don't miss my daughters but because I'm enjoying myself for the first time in forever.

It's easy to be around her.

It's even easier to talk to her.

She isn't trying to impress me, nor am I trying to impress her.

She isn't consumed with putting on some kind of performance that involves twisting her hair and batting her lashes and lame attempts at being flirty or witty.

She's purely . . . Margaux.

Sliding out my phone, I tell her I'm going to call Antonio and have him bring the car around.

"Actually, could we walk around the block a little bit first?" she asks. Her ocean-blue eyes are filled with hope. Or perhaps I'm imagining it. Occam's razor would suggest she merely wants to walk off this feast of a dinner we just put down.

"Of course." I put my phone away and take some cash from my wallet, placing it in the leather folder along with tonight's tab.

"Thank you for dinner," she says as we get up to leave.

I place my hand on the small of her back as we weave through tables upon tables of patrons and make our way to the exit.

A man in a gray suit steals a glimpse at her as we pass, his eyes lingering a little too long at her cleavage. Margaux doesn't seem to notice, but I shoot the classless bastard a dirty look anyway. His gaze darts away, returning to the poor, unaware woman sitting across from him.

Once outside, we're met with warm, sticky night air. I shrug my jacket off and throw it over my shoulder, hooking it on my finger.

"You okay?" I ask Margaux, who hasn't said a word since we left the table.

"Oh, yeah. I'm fine," she says. Her heels click against the pavement as we amble forward at an unhurried pace. She isn't in a rush, and neither am I. "I was just imagining a scenario where I literally burst out of the seams of this dress. Like what would I do, you know?"

I let out a laugh at her unexpected response.

Out of all the things she could've said, that was the last thing I expected.

"I'd give you my jacket," I say. "Obviously."

She exhales, gifting me a gorgeous smile as she peers up at me through a fringe of dark lashes.

"Now that we've solved that hypothetical conundrum, what are you thinking about now?" I ask. It always used to annoy me when Emma would ask what I was thinking about. At least at first. To me, my thoughts were private and personal, and if I wanted to share them with someone, I would have. But after a while, I learned it wasn't the worst thing to empty the contents of my busy brain onto someone who actually gave a damn.

Margaux cocks her head to the side. "I'm thinking that this headband has been giving me a headache all night, but if I take it off, I'll probably have a weird dent in my hair. Not that you'd judge me for that. At least, I don't think you would."

This woman's honesty is as refreshing as a drink of cold spring water after an arduous hike, and I'm here for it.

"Wouldn't dream of it," I say. "Take it off."

She slides the headband off and massages her fingers into her scalp, just behind each ear. Sure enough, her hair is "dented" in those areas, but it doesn't make her any less beautiful. If anything, it gives her an edge of imperfection—one of the things I look for most in the art pieces I collect.

"Okay, your turn," she says, beaming at me. "What's on your mind right now?"

If I'm being honest, I was thinking about how pretty she looked.

"I was admiring the dent in your hair," I say. Among other things . . .

Margaux bursts into laughter, giving my arm a playful punch followed by a gentle squeeze. My breath unexpectedly catches when she touches me, but only for a fraction of a second.

"Now, what are you *really* thinking about?" she asks.

"Nothing, really. I'm just enjoying the moment."

"Ah. I see. Maybe one of these days I'll learn how to do that."

"Are you not?" I ask.

"Not enjoying the moment?" She squints. Silence lingers in the space between our words. "Of course I am. But I'm never not thinking about something. So right now, you don't have a single thought in your mind outside of this walk we're on?"

"No," I say.

"You're not thinking about that load of laundry you forgot to put in the dryer this morning? Or that you need to pick up bread and milk from the store? Or that your student loan payment is due next week? You're not thinking about the dry cleaning you keep forgetting to pick up?"

I chuckle. "No."

"Must be nice." Her shoulder bumps against mine, though I don't think it was intentional.

When we left the restaurant a few minutes ago, there was at least a foot, maybe two feet, between us. That gap has since closed, and neither of us has made an effort to restore it.

"I used to have anger issues," I say. "As a kid, I mean. My parents put me in therapy for years, and while I don't remember much of what we talked about, I do remember this trick my doctor taught me. When you need to ground yourself and quiet the storm in your mind, stop what you're doing and engage with your five senses. It sort of . . . tricks your mind into being present."

"Hm."

"Right now," I say, "name one thing you can hear."

Margaux gathers a breath, stops in her tracks, and closes her eyes.

"Music," she says. "There's music coming from an apartment. Sounds like jazz. Old jazz, not new jazz. Like . . . Chet Baker, maybe?"

"Okay, good. Now, name one thing you can see."

Opening her eyes, she scans the cityscape around us. "A bus stop."

"What's one thing you can smell?" I ask next.

Dragging a deep breath into her lungs, she holds it for a moment before exhaling.

"Your cologne," she says. "It's peppery. And musky. Different but in a good way."

"What's something you can taste?" My attention lowers to her pillowy lips as she presses them together. It's been a long time since I've kissed anyone, but tonight I found myself flirting with the idea of what it would be like. Entertaining the notion, I suppose. Aunt Theodora would be beside herself with joy if she knew I was taking a mental step in that direction.

"My dessert from earlier. I can still taste the bittersweetness of the cocoa powder and espresso," she says after a moment of contemplation.

"All right. Last one. Name one thing you can touch."

Margaux faces me, squaring her shoulders with mine. Our eyes hold, and I lose my train of thought for just a second. With her lips cocked at one side, she lifts her hand slowly . . . cracking a full smile when she reaches her final destination.

Tucking her hair behind her left ear, she says, "The dent in my hair."

"Wow," I say, fighting a chuckle. "We've officially come full circle."

She places her hand on my arm, bracing herself as she laughs. But just as quickly as she reached for me, she lets me go, and we continue on our walk.

I step ahead, catching up with her, watching her dress sway with each stride.

"It quieted my mind," she says over her shoulder. "For the record. It worked."

"Of course it did."

We cross the street at the next corner and turn left onto Gansevoort.

"There's a little gallery up ahead," I say. "They have the best window displays in all of Manhattan."

"The Landry?" she asks without pause. "Hard disagree. Riverside Modern Collective has the best displays. It's not even a debate."

"Riverside?" I sniff, amused. "Are they new?"

"I *really* hope you're joking," she teases with a smile.

"You certainly know your art galleries," I tease back.

Hands clasped behind her back, she bites her lip. "I mean, I know *some* of them?"

"Are you a collector?" Surely it would've come up in conversation by now, but I have to ask. Only those in the know are familiar with these galleries. They're off the beaten path, smaller and more curated than some of their more established counterparts.

"I wouldn't call myself a collector, no," she says. "I have a few pieces. And the ones you gave me, of course. But I can't afford to play in the big leagues. I'm more of an appreciator of the arts than an accumulator."

"I should show you my collection sometime."

Margaux angles her head, turning her full attention my way. "I wouldn't say no to that."

"What's your schedule like next week during the day? Think Theodora can stand to lose you for a couple of hours?"

She doesn't answer immediately.

"I'll have to look and let you know . . ." There's a hint of reluctance in her voice, though I'm not sure why an "appreciator of the arts" wouldn't want to check out someone's private cache.

Maybe I'm coming on too strong, too fast. God knows I'm out of practice. I haven't felt excited about getting to know anyone in years, and when I'm into something, I tend to go all in. That and between running a multi-seven-figure company and raising two little girls, I'm seldom told no. In my everyday life, I snap my fingers, and everyone immediately does what I want without faltering.

Sliding my hands in my pockets, I put a little bit of distance between us.

If my mother were here, she'd tell me good things take time and are always worth the wait . . . which is exactly what she told me before she married Jacques "the French Slim Shady" DuBois. I was pointing out their insane age difference, and that was her response—that she waited sixty years to find the right person, and he was worth that wait.

But I digress.

"You know, I—" Margaux begins to say something only to be cut off when one of her high heels gets stuck in a sidewalk crack. She lurches forward, her arms outstretched in an attempt to break an inevitable fall. At the last second, I catch her, hooking my hand in the bend of her elbow and pulling her toward me.

"You okay?" I keep a hold on her as she steadies herself.

"I knew I shouldn't have worn these shoes tonight." Her cheeks are flushed, but she has no reason to feel embarrassed. This stretch of sidewalk has been in disrepair for years now. There must be throngs of people tripping and falling here on a regular basis. "But yes, I'm fine. Maybe you should call Antonio, though?"

We're easily more than two miles from her place, a jaunt I can't imagine would be comfortable in those sky-high stilettos.

I shoot Antonio a text, and he sends back a near-instant reply. Per usual, he was ready and waiting.

"He's ten minutes away," I tell her.

We find a bench nearby, sandwiched between a couple of newspaper racks. Margaux takes a seat, resting her purse on top of her crossed legs. I steal the spot next to her, draping my suit coat across my lap and soaking up what remains of our night together.

I thought it would feel different . . . the prospect of moving on.

I thought I'd hate it. I thought guilt would suck every last ounce of enjoyment out of the entire process.

Margaux, so far, has proved me wrong on all fronts.

"We could still make it to the Landry if we hurry," she says, nodding in that direction.

"Another time."

"You sure?" She glances up the street, then back to me.

"I was trying to impress you, but you made it clear that the Landry is less than extraordinary." I'm teasing, of course, but I keep a straight face.

"Really?" Margaux leans back, her chin tucked. "You know you don't have to do that . . . you don't have to impress me, Roman."

My name on her lips is like honey and glass, smooth and sweet and natural, and I realize this might be the first time she's ever actually said my name out loud in my presence.

A black SUV turns onto the emptied-out street that belonged only to us just a moment ago. The closer it gets, the clearer I see Antonio's silhouette behind the wheel. In an airtight instant, I find myself wishing he weren't so timely for once. If only he'd have caught a handful of red lights or hit a traffic jam on his way here.

"That's us," I say, rising before extending my hand to help her up.

Her fingers are soft and delicate against mine as she stands, and she doesn't let go until we get to the car.

The ride home is silent, mostly, save for the classical radio station Antonio is playing on low volume. I stifle a yawn. While it isn't exactly late, most nights I'm in bed by now. After I put the girls to sleep, I spend an hour or two tending to things around the house, getting clothes situated for our morning routine, running a load of dishes or laundry, and carving out a little time for myself in the form of a stiff drink and a book . . . or whatever strikes my mood that night.

Various street- and stoplights paint colorful shadows on the glass as we make our way through the city. When Margaux's not looking, I steal a couple of glances her way, studying her like I'd study a painting on exhibit at the MoMA. Riding beside me, her legs crossed at the knee and her hands resting on top of one another, she watches out her window with glistening eyes and a breathless sigh on her lips. She's a portrait of quiet elegance, approachability, and sophistication.

I've still yet to pick up on that chatterbox side of her Theodora insists is there; then again, some people need more time to warm up to people.

At the end of the day, this is merely our third time together.

We're hardly better than strangers.

Antonio arrives at Margaux's building, pulls into a spot, and climbs out before Margaux has so much as unbuckled her seat belt. He gets her door and helps her out. I step onto the pavement, straighten my shirt collar, adjust my tie, and meet her on her side of the car.

"You don't have to walk me up," she says. For a moment, there's a flash of something in her eyes. Hesitation? Reluctance? Rejection?

Her reaction stings more than I thought it would.

I'm not one to take things personally. The way people feel about me is almost always a reflection of themselves. But in this case, I thought we were connecting and enjoying one another's company? I'm not usually this off when it comes to reading people.

"I'm not expecting a nightcap and a good night kiss," I say, raking my palm along my jaw. I'd hate for her to think I was presuming that just because I took her out to dinner, I expected an invitation inside.

I have no problem being a man of decency in a world of modern men.

My father was fifty years old when he met my mother—twice her age at the time. As a result, most of the things I've learned about being a man . . . or rather, a gentleman . . . I learned from a man who came from a simpler generation. A man with old-fashioned notions of how a lady should be treated. It was one of the reasons my mother first fell for him, and his traditional charms were one of the many things she instilled in me as I grew up.

"Oh." Margaux holds her purse with both hands, resting it in front of her hips. "I wasn't . . . I didn't mean . . . I just . . . I didn't want to inconvenience you, is all. I'm sure you're anxious to get home to your girls."

My girls should've been in bed over an hour ago.

If they're still up, when I get home, Harper will have some explaining to do.

"Of course," I say.

"Thanks again for dinner." Her magnetic blue eyes rest on mine before she nods toward the front steps of her building. "I'll check my schedule for next week . . . I'd love to see your collection."

With that, she takes a step closer to the building, though her focus remains on me.

"Good night, Margaux," I say.

"Good night, Roman."

She says my name, sweet and smooth all over again. I wait until she disappears inside before returning to my SUV.

"I know you didn't ask," Antonio says when I'm inside. "But she seems nice." He shrugs as our eyes catch in the rearview. "I'm just glad you're getting back out into the world, kid," he adds before checking his side mirror and pulling out. "Long time coming."

CHAPTER FIFTEEN

SLOANE

The murmur of music playing from down the hall catches me off guard when I step inside my apartment. For a moment, I'd almost forgotten I wouldn't be coming home to an empty place.

I slide my killer heels off my aching feet, grab a bag of peas from the freezer for my sore ankle, and then head to my sister's room, where some catchy song by the 1975 plays.

"Knock, knock," I call when I open the door.

Margaux's sitting cross-legged on the floor, surrounded by mountains of clothing.

"What are you doing?" I ask, placing the shoes on the floor. I take a seat at her corner desk chair, cross my legs, and place my makeshift ice pack into position. Pointing at my swollen ankle, I add, "Almost broke this tonight, FYI."

"Nothing fits," she says with glassy eyes and an exasperated sigh. A flickering gardenia candle on her dresser fills the room with a thick floral haze. "I've got about five outfit options that have some stretch to them, other than that . . . everything else is going to have to go."

"You're donating that entire pile?" I point to the massive fabric mountain on her left.

"Some of it, yeah. The rest will go into storage." She eyes the little closet against the far wall, one that's packed all the way to the ceiling with designer pieces, bags, and shoeboxes. Margaux pauses her music on her phone, stopping to check the time. The sudden silence is jarring. "Why are you home so early?"

I shrug. "The date ended when it ended."

"What do you mean? Did something happen? Is he losing interest?"

"I thought you *wanted* him to lose interest?" I distinctly remember her telling me on several occasions to be boring—and losing interest would be a direct and expected outcome of that.

"Theodora's just so excited about the prospect of me being with her nephew . . . she brings it up almost as much as she brings up the new Tayla Haywood account I just landed. I told you about that, right? That YouTube-beauty-guru girl? She's doing a lipstick *and* skin-care line. Huge deal. Multiple-seven-figure contract. Anyway, I think we should maybe keep things status quo with Roman for a bit? Keep moving forward but don't rock the boat too hard either way."

"You realize he's a real person, right?" I ask. "I can't just string him along indefinitely. And what happens after you get the job? I dump him and break his heart?"

She folds a cashmere sweater into a neat square. "Obviously breaking his heart would be less than ideal—which is why I cannot stress enough that you need to be as dull yet likable as humanly possible."

"It's not that simple."

"Of course it is," she says. "I figure it's only a matter of time before I really start to show—and once I land my promotion, I can announce my pregnancy. Roman and Theodora should completely understand. Extenuating circumstances and all of that."

"Why don't you just announce the pregnancy now? And put an end to this ridiculous dating madness?"

I lift the bag of peas and check my ankle, where the skin has gone from its beige-crayon color to a wintry bright red. She still hasn't asked if I'm okay or apologized for forcing me to wear her heels—not that

Margaux would do either of those things, but it'd be nice to be appreciated every once in a while.

"I have a plan," she says, her tone matter of fact as she straightens her shoulders.

"I signed on for one date," I say.

"I know. I thought Theodora would have her mind made up by now. I'm sorry. I have no control over that."

I imagine it pains her to have no control over any of this—which is why she's obsessed with controlling every minute detail. This has always been Margaux's MO. Control Freak Sheridan. If I were the type to psychoanalyze, maybe I'd blame it on our parents' divorce, our mother's extreme anxiety, and Margaux's naturally perfectionistic ways. Her obsession with her body issues I could easily peg on her high school drill team days. It was a toxic group of women helmed by an even more toxic coach. All Margaux's foundational years were a perfect storm of dysfunction that crafted her into the type A person she is now. Sometimes, when I'm particularly frustrated with her, I remind myself that she didn't always have it easy.

Where I've always been able to roll with the punches, Margaux has struggled. Relinquishing control, in any amount, is pure torture to her. A death sentence to her ego. She would never. But it doesn't stop me from planting the thought in her head anyway.

"What would happen if you told Theodora about the pregnancy now instead of waiting?" I ask. "Just get it over with. Save yourself this balancing act. Besides, it's illegal to discriminate against pregnant people in the workplace."

"It's illegal, yes," she says. "But very difficult to prove."

"Maybe you should tell her that you don't want to date anyone right now?" I suggest. "Just be honest."

"And risk giving that position to *Franklin*?" Her jaw nearly hits the floor as she reaches for another sweater, this one a lavender cardigan with mother-of-pearl buttons. "Never. I've worked too hard for some fresh-off-the-intern-boat brownnoser to steal that out from under me."

Margaux rambles on, going on yet another tired tirade against Franklin. I'm not sure if it's ever occurred to her that some people work just as hard as she does.

"I don't want to hurt him," I cut her off. "Roman, I mean. He's a good man."

She chuffs. "Obviously no one wants to hurt anyone. That's not the goal here. But need I remind you, he had you fired? He's not exactly a saint."

"His wife died." I adjust the peas once more. "I think Halcyon was his wife."

"Halcyon?"

Of course she doesn't remember. She's never listening. She's never paying attention to anything that doesn't directly involve her these days.

"That artist I told you about a while back," I remind my sister. It's been years, though, now that I think about it. She can barely remember what she had for breakfast most days. "Anyway, when he had me fired, it was because I sold a painting out from under him . . . but not on purpose. There was a mix-up at the gallery between me and another salesperson. I think he was trying to buy his wife's painting back, and it went to someone else who refused to let it go."

"Still not a valid reason to have someone fired."

"I'm guessing he wasn't his best self at that time . . . he'd just lost the love of his life . . . and he was raising their two little girls alone . . ." I think back to that day, when I walked into my boss's office to find him on the phone with a man all but screaming into his ear. I couldn't make out the entirety of what he was saying, only bits and pieces.

. . . unprofessional . . .

. . . joke of a gallery . . .

. . . never doing business with you people again . . .

My boss—who was typically lacking a spine even on his best days—told me I had to fix it or I was done. I called my buyer and did my best groveling to get her to change her mind and cancel the sale of the painting, but she refused, hanging up on me before I could explain the situation or that my job was on the line (not that she'd have cared).

"I don't want to keep leading him on," I say.

"Then don't." She blinks once, like it's that easy. "Just be neutral. We've talked about this a hundred times."

"It's not that simple . . . I like being around him . . . and he wants to see me again . . ." I'm not sure where I'm going with this. "If things were different, if this were real, I think we'd have a connection."

"Oh, come on." She laughs, eyes rolling hard. "You've met him, what, all of three times? Sure, he's rich and attractive and maybe he plays the poor-widower-single-dad card pretty well, but don't act like you've suddenly met your soulmate after three mediocre dates. Let's be real."

Two dates.

Technically.

One of which was mediocre.

The other of which was . . . promising.

Rising from her chair, I slide the zipper down the side seam of this skintight dress, shrug out of it, and carefully lay it across the foot of her bed. I don't recognize the designer label, but knowing Margaux, I'm sure it wasn't cheap.

"You can go on the next date," I say, knowing full well that she won't. It'd be too risky at this point. He could easily bring up something we talked about on a previous date, and if she looked like a deer in headlights or said the wrong thing, this whole charade would come crashing down. Not to mention the fact that she's pregnant and starting to show. She could dress carefully, but there's always a chance the fabric might pull the wrong way, or he might catch a glimpse of a round belly that wasn't there the last time he saw me.

"Sloane," she calls after me as I head to my room.

I change into pajamas before making a beeline to the bathroom to wash this makeup—and effectively this night—off my face.

"Sloane." She knocks on the door, her voice muffled by the wood that separates us.

I take her earrings out and place them next to the toothbrush before turning the faucet to warm and grabbing my face wash. The bottle feels lighter than usual, a sign that Margaux has likely been helping herself.

You'd think after twenty-seven years, I'd be used to her self-centeredness by now, but lately it's growing more out of control by the second . . . much like her ever-expanding baby bump.

"I'm sorry." Her voice is lower than before, with no hint of a tease in her tone. While there's no way to know if she's truly sorry or if she's simply apologizing so we won't spend the rest of the weekend avoiding one another is beyond me. "Open the door, please."

I finish washing up first, taking my time as I dry my face on a fresh hand towel. It wouldn't kill her to be inconvenienced instead of being the inconvenience-r for a change.

When I'm done applying my nighttime moisturizer and serum, my damp reflection stares back at me in the mirror with heavy eyes, like a live portrait of a woman straddling two lines she never wanted to straddle in the first place.

She's as dewy as she is conflicted.

"Sloane-*nuh*," she says again, this time dragging my name out into two syllables.

"Yes?" I open the door and fold my arms.

"I think it's sweet that you care about him," she says. "And I know I'm asking a lot from you."

She gathers a deep breath as she braces her arm against the doorframe.

"I just . . . I really, really want that promotion." Her left hand slides over her small belly. "Correction: I *need* that promotion. Now more than ever."

Living in one of the most expensive cities in the world, I don't even want to imagine the cost of childcare—or anything else that comes with raising kids.

Alone, to boot.

But while Margaux has my sympathies, so does Roman.

I can't imagine how hard it must be for him to put himself out there after suffering the worst kind of loss imaginable . . . only to get his heart broken all over again.

Maybe I shouldn't flatter myself.

Maybe he's simply biding his time with me, wetting his whistle, getting his bearings back after being out of the game for so long.

But maybe not.

Because while I've tamped down my excitement to nearly undetectable levels in his presence, I can't help but notice the glint in his eyes or the way he steals a look at me when he thinks I'm not paying attention.

I also can't help but notice the electric charge passing through me anytime we touch.

Or the way my stomach somersaults whenever he cracks a rare and elusive dimpled smile.

There was a moment earlier tonight when we were discussing art galleries that my mind flashed to a brief what-if scenario, picturing the two of us together.

Roman and *Sloane*—not Roman and Designer Imposter Margaux.

My flash-in-the-pan reverie fades in a millisecond when I remind myself that it'll never be an option for us. I can't go on pretending I'm my sister indefinitely. And if he ever finds out the truth, he'll feel betrayed.

This isn't the kind of thing a person could laugh off.

It isn't cute. We're not in some real-life rom-com.

And while Roman would be angry, maybe slightly humiliated for being played for a fool, he'd eventually move on, quick to forget any of this ever happened.

But me, on the other hand?

I imagine I'd think about what might've been for the rest of my life.

CHAPTER SIXTEEN

ROMAN

"The girls mentioned Harper was over last night," Theodora says Saturday morning after we finish breakfast. The girls are at the kitchen sink washing the syrup off their hands, playing with soap bubbles and none the wiser about the conversation we're about to have at the island. "I take it you went out?"

"I did," I say before changing the subject. "How were the Hamptons?"

She arches a thin brow. "Margaux again? I presume?"

Per usual, I can't get anything past her, and she's not going to let this go.

"Yes." I don't want to say too much. This is all so new, and it would serve no purpose getting ahead of myself or filling my aunt's head with false hope. No one ever knows how things are going to go after a handful of dates. Hell, no one ever knows how things are going to go once you tie the knot, either, but that's neither here nor there.

"And?" She leans closer, tapping her long red nails against the marble countertop. "Aren't you going to fill me in? Or wait, a gentleman never kisses and tells."

"I believe it's a lady never kisses and tells," I correct her. "But in this case, there's nothing to *tell* anyway."

She straightens her spine, examining me. "You're just like your father, taking things at a snail's pace. It used to drive your mother insane with anticipation. I see exactly what you're doing. Classic Bellisario move."

"I'm not . . . doing . . . anything. Just letting things progress naturally."

"Sometimes there's no harm in giving nature a little push in the right direction." She traces her fingertips along her razor-sharp jawline, a feature courtesy of a lower face-lift she had a few years back. "No shame either."

"Aunt Theodora, can I show you my new Squishmallow?" Adeline asks, tugging on my aunt's arm.

"What on God's green earth is a Squishmallow?" Theodora chuckles. "I've never heard of such a thing in my life."

"Come to my room and I'll show you." Adeline gives her another tug.

"Well, all right," she says, disappearing down the hall.

I head to the sink to help Marabel finish washing her hands.

"Look at this, Daddy." She scoops out a mountain of tiny dish-soap-scented bubbles and blows it into the air. It soars high for a brief second or two before floating to the countertop like a heavy little cloud. She giggles and does it all over again, this time with an even bigger handful. "Can we go to the park and blow bubbles today?"

Grabbing a nearby dish towel, I dry off her hands and the foamy mess on the counter before helping her down from the step stool.

"I think that sounds like a great idea," I say. "Maybe Aunt Theodora can take you to the bodega on the way home to pick some up?"

"Okay." Marabel flashes a mile-wide grin reminiscent of the very one her mother used to wear, only Marabel's is accented with dimples courtesy of her Bellisario DNA. "Daddy, why did Harper babysit us again last night? Where do you keep going at night?"

While it's only been twice now that Harper has watched them on a Friday night, I imagine to a four-year-old, it feels more substantial, given it's such a rare occurrence.

"I had dinner with a friend," I say.

"You have friends?" She wrinkles her nose.

I snicker. She has a point. I've let almost all my old friendships dwindle into disconnect over the years. Friendships aren't unlike houseplants. They need water and sunlight to thrive. If you leave them in the dark, eventually they shrivel up and die.

After losing Emma, I shut out a lot of people I used to care about.

Eventually the phone calls and text messages became fewer and farther between, and the Christmas card pile got smaller each year. I never blamed any of them, though. I was an insufferable, miserable person to be around, especially that first year. I'd have quit me too.

But I don't want to be that guy anymore.

The one feeling sorry for himself.

The one who's too busy being angry at God to take a second to stop and breathe and *live*.

"What's your friend's name?" Marabel asks. "Wait, I want to guess it." She presses her index finger against her lips, which are twisted at one side. "Is it Cora?"

"Nope."

"Is it Sawyer?" she asks.

"Guess again."

"Is it . . . Mrs. Templeton?"

I snort a laugh. "No, it's not your preschool teacher."

"Oh, I know." She does a little bounce. "It's Crew, no, it's Jax B. No, Jax W."

"Way off. And just so we're clear, I did not have dinner with any of your friends from school," I say, "or any of your teachers."

"Then who was it?" she asks, blinking up at me.

I begin to answer, only to stop myself. I don't want to so much as breathe Margaux's name in front of my daughters unless it's for good reason. There's no way of knowing how it'll affect them or how they'll interpret it.

"Come along, Marabel." Aunt Theodora returns to the kitchen with Adeline in tow. "Apparently we're off to get some more Squishmallows."

"Can we get bubbles too?" Marabel asks. "Daddy said we could blow bubbles later."

"Of course we can." Theodora cups her little chin before bopping her on the nose. "Now go get your shoes on and wait for me by the front door."

"The last thing they need are more Squishmallows," I say. "Did you not see the massive collection in the corner of their room?"

"Apparently there's some limited edition neon-rainbow version that Adeline insists she must have." Theodora places her palm across her heart, her expression growing grave. "And who am I to get in the way of a collector of the stuffed animal arts?"

"You spoil them," I say.

"As I should." She winks from behind her shiny red glasses before turning on her heel to leave. Stopping after a few steps, she turns back to me. "You should call Margaux while we're out today. Maybe invite her to get lunch or coffee or something."

"I just saw her last night."

Sliding her glasses off her nose, she chews on the tip. "Actually . . . one of her best clients just opened a new bakery downtown. If I recall, she's supposed to be there for the grand opening today."

"Yeah, no." I stifle a chuckle. "I'm not just going to show up like that at one of her work events. I'm not a stalker."

"All right, fine." She places her glasses back with a single, swift move. "Now that I said that out loud, it does sound creepy. It was sweeter in my head. Anyway, we're off."

With that, Theodora and the girls leave to hunt for Squishmallows.

And while I have no intentions of showing up at Margaux's client's bakery, I pull up my phone and cue up her number. Thumb hovering over the green button, I contemplate my move. It's barely been half a day since our date, and I certainly don't want to seem desperate—lord knows I'm not.

Playing games has never been my thing.

I'm a straight-to-the-point type.

Which is why I'm going to call her up and nail down a date and time for the private collection tour I offered.

That, and I want to know when I'm going to see her again.

The sooner, the better.

CHAPTER SEVENTEEN

SLOANE

"Wish me luck." Margaux shimmies her feet into a pair of strappy nude sandals and stops by the mirror in our entry to fluff her hair. Once she's satisfied with the way the curls frame her face, she fusses with her skirt, which appears to be digging into her waistline. "The last thing I need is to be surrounded by delicious baked goods, but I've spent a year working with this client on his merch, so it'd be wrong for me to miss the grand opening."

"Isn't this the kind of stuff you live for? Seeing the products you helped develop on real shelves? In the hands of real people?"

"Yeah." She presses her lips together, blending her lip gloss.

"You don't sound excited . . ."

"I'm not." She checks her purse next, rifling through it until she finds her phone. "I'm supposed to meet with Ethan right after . . ."

"Oh—he finally got back to you?" Last I knew she'd sent him a couple of texts but hadn't heard back. Margaux eventually sent him a picture of the ultrasounds. I wasn't aware that he'd responded to that yet. "So what are you wanting out of—"

"—I don't know. Can we just talk about this later?" She returns her phone to her bag. It's hard to tell if she's snippy because of hormones or because she's anxious about talking to Ethan or if she's just Margaux being Margaux. More than likely it's a combination of all three.

"Of course."

My sister leaves in a frazzled huff—though no one but me would be able to tell. She still looks as poised and put together as ever.

She isn't gone but two minutes when Roman calls me. I'm midway through a bite of buttered toast when the first ring comes through. I wash it down with a gulp of orange juice before answering.

"Hi," I answer after the third ring, in my most neutral voice.

Checking the time, I calculate that I need to be ready and out the door in forty-five minutes. My former colleague Julissa invited me to check out the new Pietro Palomar exhibit at Hartsfield Galleria. It's a soft opening—industry insiders and select collectors only. Pietro isn't my personal favorite, as his style is more along the lines of glamorous gore, but I have a handful of clients who are huge fans of his work, and keeping in the know is part of my job.

"Good morning." His voice is velvet against my ear, stirring something in my middle. "Was just looking at my schedule for the week. You still interested in seeing my collection?"

I've never been more interested in seeing anything in my life.

But I can't tell him that.

"Sure. What day did you have in mind?" I play it cool, nervously brushing toast crumbs off my counter and into the sink. Half of them stick to my palm.

"I could leave the office early on Thursday—three o'clock. Would that work?"

I have no idea if it would work for Margaux, but it's going to have to. If she protests, I'll tell her I'll take this in lieu of her firstborn child like she promised years ago.

"I'll make it work," I say.

"Great. Pick you up then." He hangs up without an awkward or even subtle goodbye—without any kind of goodbye, actually.

I'm sensing a pattern here.

The man hates to say goodbye.

Which only makes the reality of this situation all the more crushing.

CHAPTER EIGHTEEN

ROMAN

"Circle around for a bit," I say to Antonio when he drops me off outside the Hartsfield Galleria. "I won't be long."

I'd almost forgotten about the invite-only exhibit until a reminder popped up on my phone this morning. Pietro Palomar's work is notorious for being the stuff nightmares are made of. I'd never hang one of his pieces in my personal home, but I've always been fascinated by the way his creative mind works. He thinks in a way most people don't.

That and I have good reason to believe he microdoses hallucinogens when he paints.

I took a hit of acid in college once. While it was my first, last, and only time dabbling in such things, I'll never forget the colors I saw—colors that don't exist in nature as we know it. Colors I couldn't even begin to describe because there are no words accurate enough to convey their otherworldly beauty.

Sometimes when I close my eyes, I can imagine them, but they're often gone within seconds.

I feel the same way about Emma sometimes. Our time together was so brief yet intense. And when I close my eyes and think of her, it's like trying to remember a distant dream. I know it was real. I know what I saw. But it's not the same. It's surreal. And I hate that.

"Good morning, Mr. Bellisario," the gallery owner greets me the instant I step inside with a smile as phony as his toupee. "How are you on this fine Saturday morning?"

Rick Hartsfield is a schmoozer. A hustler. A face-lifted, veneer-wearing Muggle of a man desperate to look half his age. But the man knows his stuff, and his connections are second to none.

"The Palomar exhibit is straight back." Rick points behind him before plastering another fake grin on his face to greet the couple who comes in behind me.

Heading back, I stop to admire a series of Hortensia Hayward ink sketches—a raisin, a pear, and a carrot that look so hyperreal you could almost grab them off their cardstock paper. A descriptive placard below mentions they were all drawn with Pilot gel pens. Seems like the trend lately is to create art with unconventional materials. Many artists are growing bored with tradition, desperate to set themselves apart from their competition or challenge themselves in new ways. The price tag below each sketch lists them at $1,000 apiece. I imagine some new-moneyed soul will walk away with these at some point in time, but they're far from the investment-quality works I prefer.

I follow the sound of voices, soft chatter and idle conversation, until I get to the Palomar exhibit in the back of the gallery. It's the usual crowd—a trendy couple from Brooklyn, a middle-aged man in head-to-toe Patagonia, a woman in a vibrant, asymmetrical red dress that looks like an FIT student sewed it together for a final-exam project, two lanky runway models with matching high cheekbones, a group of ageless women lost in conversation. In the corner are two more women—one with hair as dark as midnight, and the other with the same honey-blonde locks as Margaux.

My heart catches in my throat.

It can't be her—she's at a bakery opening . . .

Still, it wouldn't be the first time I've sworn I spotted her in the proverbial wild. Lately I'm seeing her everywhere I look.

"Roman, hi." An old classmate of mine, Stacey Bronstein, saunters up to me with a smile so wide it stretches from ear to ear. A lifetime ago, we lived on the same floor and were in the same study group (which later evolved into a party group). "I haven't seen you in forever. How have you been?"

Before I get a chance to answer, she places her hand on my arm and leans close.

"I heard about Emma." She bites the inside of her lip, and her eyes are half-squinted as if she's attempting to convey emotional pain, but her Botox-paralyzed facial muscles won't allow her such an expression. "So tragic. I'm so sorry. I can't even imagine . . ."

Her voice trails when she spots a young man in a three-piece suit wielding a tray of mimosas around the room. She waves him over, taking two champagne flutes and handing one to me.

"Champs always makes these Saturday exhibits a bit more tolerable," she says with a wink and a smile, as if she'd completely forgotten we were talking about my dead wife a mere moment ago. "So what all have you been up to?"

She lifts her flute to her pillow-size lips, and in the process, a glimmering diamond on her left ring finger catches the light. The rock must be at least the size of a postage stamp. There's no missing it—and I imagine that's the whole point.

Stacey was always sidling up to the rich kids at college. When I rebuffed her, she moved on to the son of an oil magnate. When he tossed her aside, she set her sights on a guy whose mother was the heir to a media conglomerate. After that didn't pan out, she cozied up to the troubled son of a Hollywood A-list couple.

I'd love to know who she suckered into giving her that gem so I can thank him for taking one for the team.

I scan the room again, searching for the Margaux doppelgänger.

"Are you still living in the city?" Stacey asks, taking a small sip of her drink and blinking her mile-long lashes. Tracing her fingertip along her exposed collarbone, she angles her body as if she's positioning herself in front of a camera.

I could never be with someone who feels the need to shapeshift themselves into oblivion.

Confidence whispers; insecurity screams.

"I am," I say, still looking for the Margaux lookalike. I finally spot her in front of the largest Palomar piece—a phantasmagoric wet dream of a painting of naked women riding winged horses through a blood-colored river.

"These paintings are so Pietro," Stacey says, flicking her wrist. "So wild. My husband is obsessed. Have to say, I don't really understand the appeal. I think they're a little corny." Placing her palm against my chest, she tucks herself in. "I hope I'm not offending you. Clearly you're here for a reason."

"Nah, you're good." I don't meet her laser-pointed gaze. I focus on the other people in the room, desperate for someone to come save me from this woman lest I'm here all day.

"So you're a fan?" she asks.

"What?" I ask before digesting her question. "Oh, yeah, no."

"Then why are you even here?" She arches a brow, drinking me in.

I'm debating on whether to tell her the boring truth—that I'm killing a little bit of time while my daughters are out—before thinking better of it. She's not entitled to an explanation. She could barely contain her excitement a few minutes ago at the fact that I'm a widower.

"Oh, let me introduce you to my husband." Rising on her toes, Stacey flags down a silver-haired man easily twice her age. "Roger, this is an old friend of mine . . . Roman Bellisario."

Roger's face is shaped into a permanent scowl, but he extends his liver-spotted hand my way.

"Good to meet you, Ronan," he says.

I don't correct him, and neither does Stacey. I'm not entirely convinced she even noticed. She's been too laser focused on me to pay much attention to anything else.

"Roger owns a hedge fund firm downtown," she says.

Of course he does.

"Maybe you've heard of it?" she asks. "Willingham, Conway, and Draper."

"Sounds familiar," I lie out of politeness. There are a million financial firms in this city, and all of them sound the same.

"If you ever want a consult, I'm sure Roger could fit you in?" Stacey shrugs before giving her husband a nudge. "He's not accepting clients anymore, but I know he'd do me a favor. Isn't that right, babe?"

Calling a man old enough to be a grandfather "babe" sends a flash of burning bile up the back of my throat, but I swallow it down and refrain from any further judgment. It's not my circus and definitely not my monkeys.

The honey-blonde woman moves away from the bloody river painting, disappearing behind a white partition. Everything from the way she walks to the way she tucks her hair behind her ear screams Margaux, but she's yet to turn around so I can see her actual face.

"I'm sorry, will you excuse me for a moment?" I ask.

The light leaves Stacey's emerald eyes, but she nods. "Don't leave without giving me your number, though. Roger and I would love to have you over for dinner sometime. So much catching up to do!"

Roger glares at me from behind his squinty, hooded eyes, but I don't take it personally.

In fact, I have no doubt this is a common occurrence.

A tiger is incapable of changing its stripes.

I'm halfway to the partition when my phone rings with a call from Theodora. It hasn't even been an hour since she left with the girls.

"Hey," I answer.

"Oh, thank goodness you answered." She's breathless. "Everything's fine, but Marabel took a spill on the sidewalk and hit her head on a newspaper rack. The cut is pretty deep, and it's bleeding pretty good, so we're heading to the ER to see if we can get her stitched up. Can you send me a photo of your insurance card?"

"Which hospital are you going to?" I ask, already turning on my heel and heading for the front exit.

"Thank you so much for stopping in, Mr. Bellisario," Rick Hartsfield says as he sends me off with a wave and his signature fake smile. "Please come back soon."

"Lenox Hill," Theodora answers.

"I'm on my way."

"Oh, it's not necessary, Roman. Really. No need to overreact. She's fine. I just wanted you to know—"

"—I'll call you when I get there." I end the call and head up the block in search of Antonio, who just so happens to be rounding the corner.

I flag him down, climb in, and tell him to hightail it to Lenox Hill.

We're passing the gallery when the door swings open, and out steps the honey blonde. Her head is down as she looks at her phone, and a breeze blows her hair in front of her face, but it's *her*.

It's Margaux.

This time, I'm certain.

CHAPTER NINETEEN

SLOANE

"He almost saw me today," I say the second Margaux gets home Saturday night.

"Who?" She shrugs her purse strap from her shoulder and places her bag on the entry table.

"Roman," I say, as if I could possibly be talking about anyone else.

Margaux shakes her head. "Oh, right. Wow. Okay, what happened?"

"I went to an art gallery exhibit," I say. "He showed up while I was there. As soon as I noticed him, I went in the back and hid in the ladies' room. When I came out a few minutes later, he was gone."

Margaux frowns. "I don't understand how that's a big deal. If he would've run into you, he would've just assumed you were me."

"I was with Julissa," I say. "My old colleague? You've met her before. Anyway, if he would've called me Margaux in front of her, or if she would've called me Sloane in front of him . . ."

My sister takes a seat at the end of the sofa, collapsing as if she's had the longest day of her life.

"You seem out of it," I say. "What's going on? How was dinner with Ethan?"

Staring ahead, her gaze unfocused, she says, "It was . . . unexpected."

"Unexpected good or unexpected bad?"

"Good." Her voice is monotone, and there's no light in her eyes. "I'm just trying to wrap my head around everything."

"Care to elaborate? I'm not getting any younger here."

"So, his mother was there," she begins. "I'd never met her before today, but she was there with him and she's . . . strangely excited about this whole thing. I guess she's been after Ethan to settle down and start a family for years. He's never going to settle down because he's, well, Ethan, but he promised to support me—us—as much as he can. His mom doubled down on that and offered me this three-bedroom rent-controlled apartment on the Lower East Side that's been in their family for decades."

"Holy shit."

She turns to me, her eyes suddenly expressive. "I know, right? It all seems too good to be true. I was expecting to go there tonight and have him plead with me to . . . I don't know . . . not have the babies or to give them away. I was expecting to have to come home and make a decision, but now it's like things are magically falling into place."

"This is great." I inch toward her and place my hand on her knee. "Why aren't you jumping for joy right now? A rent-controlled three bedroom? Support from Ethan? An excited grandmother? This is incredible."

"His mom offered to hire a nanny for us, too, so I wouldn't have to worry about day care," she adds. "And on top of that, she's really nice. She's sweet and loving and warm and friendly and completely over the moon about the babies."

"Wow."

"Ethan's pushing forty," she continues, "and he's her only child. She said being a grandmother is the only thing she wants in this world, and she wants to make sure I'm healthy and happy and have everything I need to give her grandchildren the childhood they deserve."

"I know she's not technically your mother-in-law, but I don't think it gets any better than that."

"It's weird, right? Like, I don't deserve any of this. It's like I won the lottery, but I can't figure out why I'm not happier about it." She rests her chin against her hand, focusing on the lifeless TV on the other side of the room. It's the first time I've ever seen my sister in this deflated state. There's no confidence oozing from her porcelain skin or emanating off her in electrostatic shock waves. "It's not like it's a promotion or something that I've worked for, you know?"

Suddenly everything about my sister makes perfect sense.

It's always about control for her.

She can control how hard she works. She can control what positions she applies for and how well she interviews for promotions.

She can't control failed birth control. She can't control that it's two babies instead of one. She can't control that the next eighteen years of her life have suddenly been written for her, without her having any say in the matter.

"It's not about deserving this or that," I say. "You're allowed to be happy about all of this. Maybe it's not what you had planned, but all you can do is adjust your sails and go from there. One day at a time, one thing at a time."

She pulls in a ragged breath before moving her hand to her lower belly.

"It's weird, right? All of this?" she asks. "I keep trying to picture myself as a mother, and then I think about all the houseplants I've killed over the years. I'm not sure I'm capable of taking care of two human beings when I can't even keep a plant alive for more than a month at a time."

"The plants died because you forgot to water them," I say. "Let's not compare apples and oranges. Also, when are you going to tell Mom?"

Margaux massages her temple. "Soon, I guess. Now?"

Our mother has a tendency to worry herself sick—quite literally. It's uncanny. Whenever she's stressed or upset or worried about something, her body breaks out into a fever, and she can hardly keep food down. Other times, she'll have debilitating migraines for days. She's a sensitive soul, and she'd have definitely fretted herself into a frenzy over Margaux's situation a week or two ago. Now that Ethan's mother is coming in clutch, this whole thing will be much easier for our mom to stomach.

Rising from the sofa, I grab her phone from her bag in the entry and carry it back.

"Here." I take a seat beside her. "We'll do this together."

She's dialing our mom's number when my phone begins to ring.

My breath catches when Roman's name appears on my screen. I press the option to autorespond to his call with "I can't talk, can I call you later?"

We have plans to get together this coming Thursday, so I'm not sure what he could possibly be calling for right now. All I know is my stomach somersaults when I think about hearing his voice, and maybe I shouldn't . . . but I'm already counting down the minutes until I can return his call.

CHAPTER TWENTY

ROMAN

"You realize you're living my dream, don't you?" Margaux steps inside my front entrance Thursday afternoon. "A limestone prewar town house with a mansard roof on a gorgeous, tree-lined street in a historic neighborhood. A lifetime ago, you would've been neighbors with Jackie O."

"My father knew her, actually," I say. "This home has been in my family for generations."

"Did you grow up here?" She points down.

"I did."

"And now your daughters get to grow up here?" She rests a hand over her heart, her pretty face tilted to one side. "I love that so much."

Turning around, she peeks out the sidelights that flank my front door.

"What are you doing?" I ask.

"I'm thinking about all the people who have probably walked this sidewalk before," she says with a wistful sigh. "Truman Capote, maybe. Jean Shrimpton. Edith Wharton. Margaret Sanger. Andy Warhol."

"Al Pacino lives around the corner. I see him walking his dog sometimes," I say. "My mother was good friends with Beverly D'Angelo. I think Oprah has a place the next street over. I'm sure there are more, but I don't really pay attention to that sort of thing."

Turning back to me, she says, "It doesn't matter how many years I've lived here, sometimes I still feel like a tourist . . . just a starstruck small-town girl from Ohio taking everything in with stars in my eyes."

"Hold on to that with everything you've got," I say. "Don't ever let the city take your sense of wonderment away."

One of my favorite art professors fed us that line back in the day, though he was speaking in the context of art. It's solid advice either way. I've seen far too many people move to the city and become hardened, jaded, and cynical. New York will do that to a person, though. It's a kaleidoscope of everything that's right and wrong in this world, all the ugly and beautiful things.

Margaux steps out of her black heels and places them neatly off to the side of the rug.

"Everything is on the sixth floor," I tell her as she follows me to the elevator. We step inside, and I press the button. "I like to think of it as my own private art gallery."

The elevator slows to a stop when we reach the top floor, and I tap in my code. Years ago, I had the elevator replaced with a more security-oriented option. No one can access my art gallery without a code, and no one can access the floor my daughters sleep on without a code as well. On top of that, I've taken great measures to fireproof both priceless spaces.

The doors part, and I motion for Margaux to step off first. In her skintight dark denim, white blouse, and colorful PUCCI scarf tied around her neck, she is a vision of poise and style. Her hips sway ever so slightly as she heads to the first wall, reminding me of the day I spotted her at the Hartsfield Galleria.

I'd called her later that night, and sure enough, she confirmed it was her and apologized for missing me. I would've asked her about the bakery grand opening, but Theodora was the one who told me about that—not Margaux.

We spent the rest of that night talking on the phone, breaking only once when I had to put my daughters to bed. It wasn't until two in the morning that our conversation had more yawns than words and we decided to call it a night.

"More Halcyon," she says, pointing to two side-by-side paintings meant to have a mirror effect. "You're obsessed."

"Hoping to pass these down to my daughters one of these days," I say. "This particular set reminds me so much of them, how they complement one another while maintaining their own individuality. As alike as they are different."

"Sounds like my sister and me . . ." She moves on toward the next painting, a Chagall the size of a postcard.

"Is this a real Chagall?" Margaux claps her hand over her mouth. "It is, isn't it?"

I chuckle, slipping my hands in my pockets as I live vicariously through her. I've seen this one enough that it's lost its luster a bit, but it's a top-notch investment piece. Still, I miss the days when I would walk into this room and feel like I was seeing it all for the first time again.

"If you like this, you'll love my Duchamp over there." I nod to the far corner, where an earth-toned cubist painting hangs against a stark-white wall. "Got into a bidding war with this one. Earned myself an enemy by the name of Rolf Fischer. It's been several years, but every time I see the man around town, he still shoots me dirty looks."

"Rolf Fischer . . . as in the billionaire German software engineer?" she asks. "The one married to that Serbian supermodel that's in all those Givenchy perfume ads?"

"That's the one. How do you know him?"

Her lips part for a second, but she doesn't answer right away.

"People talk," she says with a casual shrug before moving on to the next work. "Oh, my god. You own *Orpheum at the Hillside*?"

She moves closer to the landscape oil painting, one that set me back a cool seven million two years ago. The artist was a favorite of Emma's, and I purchased it on what would have been her thirty-second birthday.

"How does it feel to know you have superior taste to ninety-nine percent of art collectors worldwide?" she asks before gifting me a teasing smile. "Seriously, though. You have made some impeccable choices here."

"So you're impressed?" I tease back.

"No. I'm spellbound." She saunters to the next item, a pottery piece from an eighteenth-century Prussian artist whose name I'd likely butcher if I attempted to pronounce it in front of her. All I knew when I purchased it was that it was rare and valuable, and I was looking to diversify my collection at the time. "Good luck getting me to leave . . ."

I don't know that most women would be impressed by an art collection.

But Margaux's not like most women.

Not even close.

"Don't tell me you have a Picasso. Are you kidding me?" She lets out a squeal as she leans in to examine the unfinished work. The man painted until the very end, sometimes two pieces a day. "This was supposedly his very last painting," I say. "Painted shortly before he died, hence the reason it's unfinished."

"This has to be worth hundreds of millions . . ."

"You'd think." It's just a blank canvas with a few navy-blue brush-strokes and some hair-thin pencil outlines on the other side. "It's priceless to me. Maybe someday someone else will feel the same."

I stand back as Margaux makes her way around the rest of the room, fangirling in awe, much like she did at the Halcyon studio. Her zest and enthusiasm are contagious, and I find myself grinning like a schoolboy as she fills the room with her giddiness.

This is true, unfiltered, genuine happiness. The elusive kind. The kind you have to capture in a bottle because it's so mysterious and wonderful and you never know when it's going to strike again.

No one can tell me otherwise.

Checking my watch, I ask, "You want to grab a coffee? I've got a couple of hours until the girls get home from school, and there's a place around the corner. I can't guarantee you'll see Al Pacino there, but I also can't promise you won't. Word on the street is the man loves his three o'clock pick-me-ups."

"I could go for a decaf iced latte right about now," she says with a curious glint in her eye. "And then you can tell me how you managed to snag that Jacinto Lombardo painting . . . I thought they were all destroyed?"

Years ago, 95 percent of Lombardo's lifework perished when a museum hosting a traveling exhibit caught fire. As a personal fan of Lombardo's work, I reached out to the owner of the collection and asked if I could buy any remaining fragments and have them restored to their former glory—if that was even possible.

After I wired him a pretty penny, the owner overnighted me an eight-by-ten scrap from a larger painting that had been badly burned. It smelled of soot and ash and had some frayed and burnt edges, but I found a local professor who was willing to take the project on as a favor. In fact, she was so excited she said *she* should be paying *me* for the honor.

"I'll tell you all about it," I say as we head to the elevator.

A few minutes later, we're strolling the sidewalk at a leisurely pace, the summer sun warming the tops of our heads as a gentle breeze rustles the leafy trees. For the first time in years, there's a tranquil mood in the atmosphere, like everything's going to be all right.

Like the best is yet to come, perhaps.

A guy could get used to this.

CHAPTER TWENTY-ONE

SLOANE

"What do you think their story is?" I lean in as I nod toward the couple two tables over. They're young. Early twenties, I'm guessing. And they haven't stopped snapping selfies since they sat down. "Do you think they're into each other, or are they just taking pictures for the Gram?"

I expect Roman to peel his heavy gaze off me and steal a peek at the lovebirds, but I remain his sole focus.

"I don't know," he says, "and honestly, I don't care."

"Do you think it's possible for people to be that in love, though?" I ask as the two of them nuzzle against each other and interlace their fingers. It's like they're the only ones in their own little world. The rest of us are nonplayer characters. Background noise. Extras. "Okay, she just climbed into his lap. Maybe they *want* the attention?"

"Then why give it to them?" He sips his Americano like a man without a care in the world.

"It's not about that. I just find them interesting. People, I mean, not necessarily them. It's like when you look at a piece of art and you study the details and intricacies and the nuances. People can be just as complex and layered as a painting."

"Maybe their love language is physical touch," he muses.

I steer my attention back to him.

"The fact that you know what love language is, is almost as impressive as you owning a Lombardo." I rest my chin on top of my hands. "What's your love language then?"

"Quality time," he says without hesitation. "Without question. Time is my biggest asset. It's a luxury. If I'm sharing mine with you, that means more than any kiss or sweet nothings or gift ever could."

"Interesting."

"What about you?" he asks.

"Same. I'm picky about who I spend my downtime with."

"So you're saying I should be flattered that you're spending your Thursday afternoon with me?"

"To be fair, you lured me with art. It's like offering candy to a kid."

"Way to knock a guy down a few pegs," he says with a playful glint in his chocolate irises.

The more time I spend with him, the more he lightens up. While it's only been a handful of weeks, the Roman sitting across from me right now is a completely different person compared to the one who sat across from me on our first date.

Er, *Margaux's* first date.

I keep forgetting this isn't real.

Roman checks his watch.

"Everything okay?" I ask.

"My nanny just picked the girls up from school. They'll be home soon," he says, almost as if he's apologizing—but then it hits me . . . he doesn't want his girls to see him with me.

At least, that's what I'm picking up on here.

"I'll have Antonio drive you home," he adds as he taps a text into his phone. "He should be here in about five minutes, after he drops the girls off."

His generous offer is only a confirmation of my assumption. He's having Antonio pick me up here so the girls don't see me—and I understand. It's a thoughtful and considerate move and demonstrates how deeply he cares for their emotional well-being.

"Thank you so much for the tour today," I say as I gather my things. "It's an experience I'll never forget as long as I live. I know I sound cliché, but I'm still reeling. I'm going to be reeling for a while . . ."

"What are you doing tomorrow night?" He ignores my gushing. "I want to see you again."

"You don't mess around, do you?"

"I don't have time to mess around. And even if I did, I still wouldn't."

"Can I just say how refreshing that is?" I rise from the table and slip my purse over my shoulder. "In a world full of men who play mind games like it's a professional sport, you're truly a breath of fresh air." Covering my face, I blush. "I'm just full of clichés today, aren't I?"

Roman walks me to the door, his hand on my lower back. Once outside, we move to a vacant section of sidewalk. My apartment is in the opposite direction of his, so there'll be no walking me home or even to the end of the block.

"You still haven't answered my question," he says, his dark brows furrowing as he concentrates on me. He's all but pinning me into place, though it's not like I'm in a hurry to leave. Our time together is fast becoming one of my favorite things. "What are you doing tomorrow night?"

I don't want to give him a solid answer without talking to Margaux first, but I also don't want to send him home with his tail between his legs, because I want to see him again too.

"What did you have in mind?" I ask.

"I have two tickets for the New York Philharmonic," he says.

In the six years I've lived in the city, that's one of the things I've yet to experience. It's always been on my bucket list, but I've never taken the time to make it happen.

"I'd love to," I say, "but can I let you know?"

His expression stays calm, collected. There's no disappointment. No hope. At least none he's willing to let slip past his stony facade.

"Sure," he says, taking a step backward. This is his version of goodbye—a non-goodbye. "Antonio should be here shortly."

"Thank you," I wave as he walks away. "And thanks again for today . . ."

I'm sure I've thanked him more today than I've ever thanked any one person in my lifetime, but I want him to know how truly grateful I am that he shared his private art collection with me. Many of my clients, most of whom I've worked with for years, have yet to do the same.

I plant myself at a wrought-iron bench outside the coffee shop and scan the passersby in search of Al Pacino—or any other famous faces—as I wait for Antonio to arrive.

Three minutes later, a shiny black Escalade pulls up to the curb. The passenger window rolls down, and Antonio gives me a wave before starting to climb out.

"You don't have to do that," I say as I trot to the car, climb inside, and buckle in.

"How's your day going?" he asks as he merges into traffic.

"Great," I say. "Roman showed me his art collection, so no complaints. Yourself?"

"Really." His hazel eyes flick up into the rearview mirror, intersecting with mine. "He took you up there, did he?"

I nod.

"Huh." He flicks on his turn signal when we come to a red light.

"What's that supposed to mean?"

"He doesn't take anyone up there." We pull onto another street and come to a crawl behind a stretch limo attempting to parallel park outside a historic hotel. "At one point, he was talking about putting everything into an archive or something."

"I'm glad he didn't," I say. "He's got some pretty extraordinary pieces . . . it'd be a shame not to share them with people who truly appreciate them."

Antonio dials down the radio, which I hadn't even noticed was playing until now. The display on the front shows it was tuned to the Kidz Bop station.

"You know, the number of times that man has smiled—*genuinely* smiled—in the past three years, I could probably count on one hand, maybe two. Excluding when he's around his girls. They're the only thing that makes him happy these days," he says a few minutes later, when we arrive at my street. "But then you came along, and now I'm seeing glimpses of the old Roman again." Inching up to the curb, he finds a place to park and flicks on his hazard lights. Angling his shoulders, he turns to look at me. "With all due respect, young lady, whatever happens with you two, just don't break his heart."

CHAPTER TWENTY-TWO

ROMAN

"Why do you keep leaving us?" Marabel is perched on my bathroom counter as I shave my face. Her eyes are glassy, tearful almost, and her little lips are shaped into a pitiful pout. It's almost enough to make me think twice about this whole moving-on thing.

Just because I'm finally ready to take that step, it doesn't mean they are.

The girls were one and two when Emma passed. I'm all they know. I'm their entire world. To have to share me with someone new could be devastating for them.

"Daddy has a new friend," I say. "And we're having fun. That's all."

"But why can't we go with you?" she asks.

I rinse my razor in the sink before going in for another section.

"Because it would be boring for you," I say.

"But you just said you're having fun. How could it be boring if you're having fun?"

For a four-year-old, her logic is unparalleled. Her lawyer uncle would be impressed.

"It's grown-up fun, not kid fun," I say. "We're not blowing bubbles or going to the park."

"Then what are you doing?"

"What are you and Harper going to do tonight?" I redirect the conversation. "I told her you could have dessert if you eat all your vegetables, and I made sure your favorite orange sherbet is in the freezer. Friday-night desserts have become a Bellisario tradition lately."

She sticks out her tongue. "I hate orange sherbet."

"I thought you loved it? I thought it was your favorite?"

"That was before, Daddy." She crosses her arms as if I should have known. And maybe I should have known . . . I've been spending more time away from them than ever lately. Not physically, per se, but mentally. Even when I'm home with them, my mind drifts to other places—namely Margaux.

"How about I bring you something back?" I offer.

Her pout fades. "Like chocolate cake?"

"Sure." I'm not sure if the Peruvian restaurant we're going to tonight serves chocolate cake—and then there's the whole issue of lugging it around at the symphony, but I'll see what I can do.

"With marshmallow frosting," she adds. "And rainbow sprinkles."

"That's a very specific request."

"But it's my favorite," she says.

"Noted." I finish shaving, rinse my face, and reach for my aftershave.

"Adeline, Daddy's bringing us home chocolate cake with marshmallow frosting and rainbow sprinkles," Marabel says when Adeline ambles into the room.

She, too, looks a little more somber than usual.

"Why the long face, kiddo?" I ask her.

"What's a long face?" Marabel asks.

"It means she looks sad," I say.

"My boyfriend broke up with me," Adeline says, taking a seat on the cold marble floor. She rests her chin in her hands.

"First of all, you're in kindergarten," I say, "so you're not even allowed to have a boyfriend. Second of all, you're too good for him. Plain and simple."

She looks up at me as if nothing is registering, like I'm speaking a foreign language.

The doorbell chimes before she has a chance to question anything.

"That's Harper," I say. "Should we let her in?"

Adeline jumps up, her somber expression wiped away and replaced with a smile that takes up her entire face. Marabel climbs off the countertop and races her sister to the front door.

"Wait, girls," I say, following after them. "You know the rule. You don't answer the door without a grown-up with you."

A minute later, the girls are completely preoccupied with Harper and the "bag of fun" she always brings—mostly snacks and dollar-store items. When they're not looking, I use the opportunity to sneak out.

Guilt eats away at me with every step I take to my waiting SUV, but once inside, it's quickly replaced with the thrill of anticipation that floods my core when I think about seeing Margaux again.

On the way to pick her up, I remind myself that I wouldn't be ditching my girls to be with this woman if I weren't absolutely sure about how I feel about her.

While I never expected to like the woman my aunt chose for me— let alone fall for her—here I am . . . falling . . . harder and faster than I ever expected.

And there's not a damn thing I can do to stop it.

CHAPTER TWENTY-THREE

SLOANE

"Why don't we just make something from scratch?" I ask Roman. It's nearly 11:00 p.m., and the last three bakeries we stopped at were out of chocolate cake for the day. The first two places we went to were closed, despite Google saying they were open. The second one was permanently closed and, by the looks of it, had been for a while. There's a bakeshop in Brooklyn that has chocolate cupcakes with rainbow sprinkles but no marshmallow frosting—so far that's our best bet. "Would be a lot easier than driving all over town."

He rakes his hand along his jaw. "I don't even know if I own a cake pan. Even if I did, I don't know the first thing about baking."

"Let's just grab a few things at the Westside Market up the street, take them back to my place, and I'll teach you . . ." It's risky taking him to my apartment, and it's reckless extending this date beyond dinner and a concert, but I'd hate to send him home empty handed after he made a promise to his daughters. When he spoke about them at dinner earlier, I could sense the guilt in his tone despite him trying to play it off like a cute little conversation they had.

He drags in a long breath of humid summer air. "You sure you want to do that? It's already getting late."

"I don't have anywhere else to be . . ."

Roman studies me, like he's been doing all night.

Like he always does.

"Come on." I take a few steps in the direction of the grocery store and wave for him to follow me. I haven't baked a cake in forever. When you live in a city with some of the best bakeries in the entire world, it doesn't make sense to whip up a box of Betty Crocker devil's food. But that's exactly the plan tonight. "Betty's going to save the day."

"Betty?"

"Crocker."

He cracks a smile, one that showcases his deep dimples and makes me think of what Antonio said yesterday about not hurting him.

As our dinner progressed tonight, we found ourselves connecting over films we love and trips we hope to take. The conversation flowed nonstop until we arrived at Lincoln Center, but as the orchestra played some of the most beautiful music I've ever heard, all I could think about was what if . . .

What if this worked out?

What if I came clean and he didn't storm off in a cloud of hatred, never to be heard from again?

What if he understood the situation and found humor in it, and we could move forward with a clean slate?

What if this is the kind of thing we could laugh about someday?

We're wandering the near-empty Westside Market a few minutes later under a sky of fluorescent lighting and a soundtrack of elevator music when Roman slips his hand over mine. The touch alone sends a start to my chest, painful almost, but a good kind of pain—like when you stretch a muscle that hasn't been used in ages.

Who'd have thought such a simple move could be so titillating?

If my body reacts this way to a simple holding of my hand, I can only imagine how it'll respond when he kisses me—something I'm certain is in the cards for us. More times than I can count tonight, I've caught him looking at my lips.

Roman's palm is soft against mine, and he steers me close to him. The warmth of his intoxicating cologne invades my lungs, sending a dizzying sensation to my head. If I could bottle this feeling and drink it, I'd be a goner.

"This aisle," I say, pointing with my free hand toward a sign that says **BAKING MIXES, OILS, AND FROSTING**. We head toward the section of colorful boxes with coordinating frostings. Grabbing a chocolate cake mix, a jar of marshmallow frosting, and a shaker of rainbow sprinkles, I place them in our basket. "Easy enough."

He gives my hand a squeeze.

I squeeze it back.

I don't know what it means, but whatever he's feeling, I'm feeling it too.

We could wax on for hours about all the art and music and film in the world, but at the end of the day, talk is cheap. Words mean nothing without the emotions and intention behind them. The connection I'm feeling with Roman is happening beneath the surface, on a deeper plane. It's taking place between the words and the stolen glances and the dimpled smiles.

My heart hammers in my chest with each step we take—hand in hand—toward the checkout. I keep expecting him to let me go at some point . . . for logistic reasons . . . but he manages to place our basket on the conveyor with his free hand before retrieving his wallet from his pocket.

Fifteen dollars later, we're on our way to my place in the back of his Escalade. Darkening my phone screen, I quickly tap out a text to my sister, telling her about the cake situation along with instructions to stay in her room for the night and don't come out until I give her the all-clear.

The message shows as delivered but not read.

Last I knew, Ethan was going to show her that three-bedroom apartment tonight, but I haven't heard from her in hours. Lately she's been complaining about fatigue, even going so far as to steal catnaps in her office in the afternoons. There's a good chance she's already asleep for the night.

Antonio drops us off at my building, and we head upstairs.

My apartment is dark. No music. No candles. No TV droning in the background. I flick on a light and place our grocery bag on the counter by the stove before preheating the oven to 350.

Roman shrugs out of his sports jacket, places it on the back of a kitchen chair, and rolls up his sleeves while I grab the baking pan, eggs, oil, a measuring cup, a hand mixer, and nonstick spray.

I'm not sure why it didn't occur to me earlier, but the cake will need to cool completely before we can frost it. We can stick it in the fridge, of course, but this is going to be—at minimum—a two-hour ordeal.

"Okay, how good are you at cracking eggs?" I hold up two eggs.

"What kind of question is that?" He gives me a teasing eye roll before taking them from my hand. Our fingers brush in the process, and I think back to the supermarket.

I dump the chocolate cake mix into a bowl and measure out the oil and water.

"Crack the eggs into the mix," I say before dumping the liquids in.

Two perfect cracks later, and we're ready to mix.

"You want to do the honors?" I hand him the mixer. "Start on low and in the middle. We're mixing until it's well combined. We want it to be the same color and consistency all over."

He turns the mixer on, following my instructions to the letter. While he's doing that, I check my phone. My text to Margaux is still showing as unread. I'm almost positive she's passed out. If all the kitchen commotion wakes her from her slumber, I only pray she checks her phone before rolling out of bed.

Next, I hand Roman a spatula from the drawer.

"We're going to spread the mix into this baking pan," I say. "And just so you know, it's totally okay if you leave a little bit behind. Pro tip: licking the leftover batter is the best part about baking a cake."

I place my hand over his as we pour the batter into the dish. Maybe it wasn't necessary, but I wanted an excuse to touch him again. Now that those floodgates have opened, I don't know that I can go back to keeping my hands to myself, so to speak.

They say if you have to question whether a man likes you, then he doesn't like you.

I think it's safe to say Roman has made himself crystal clear on where I stand with him.

The oven beeps when it reaches 350, and I slide the dish onto the center rack before setting the timer.

"Thirty-five minutes?" he asks. "That's all it takes?"

Confused, I squint. "How long did you think it took to bake a cake?"

With a glint in his dark eyes, he says, "I was kind of hoping it took longer than that . . ."

"Oh?" I say before reading between the lines. He was hoping he was going to have more time with me. "*Oh* . . . um, well, after it bakes, it's going to have to cool for a while. An hour at least. Maybe longer? Two if we want to be extra safe. I imagine marshmallow frosting melts pretty easily . . ."

Reaching, he grabs my hips and pulls me close, until my body is pressed against his and I can hear his heart beating fast in my ears.

Or maybe it's mine.

Everything's happening too fast to process.

A slow smile spreads across my face as every inch of me comes alive at his touch. The war that's been going on between my head and my heart all this time turns cold. For the first time in forever, my thoughts grow quiet, and my body does all the talking.

Placing his finger beneath my jaw, he tips my chin up until our mouths are perfectly aligned. His lips part, as if there's something he wants to say, but whatever it is, he keeps it to himself.

"I've been living in the dark for so long," he says, "and for the first time in years, I feel like someone has come along with a candle to show me the way out."

My heart breaks at the thought of him wandering around in his own darkness, not able to find his way out until I came along.

"I've never met anyone like you." He brushes a wisp of hair from my forehead. "I'm feeling things I never thought I'd feel again, finding pieces of myself I thought were gone forever."

I search his face before surrendering to his powerful gaze, soaking in his every word.

How can something so wrong feel so perfect, so meant to be at the same time?

I don't have time to make sense of it because his hands tighten around my hips. He pulls me against him once more, as if I wasn't nearly close enough before. Then without another word, his mouth crashes down on mine, sweet like sugar, hot like cinnamon. His tongue slips between my lips, meeting mine. My body turns liquid hot, melting in his arms. Complete surrender.

Within an instant, his hands are in my hair, and I'm kissing him so hard I'm forgetting to breathe. Every fiber of my body wants every atom of his.

The heat of his kiss ignites a frenzied rush in my soul, one that dances down my spine before spiraling all the way to my fingertips. I'm flooded with a lightness unlike anything I've ever felt before—one that makes me feel like I'm standing on a cloud yet anchored into place at the same time.

His kiss breathes life into my soul.

His touch grounds me.

I exist wholly in this moment, in the sweet intoxicating now.

Roman's hands abandon my hair, sliding down my sides before cupping my ass. With a single lift, he carries me to the living room. We end up on the sofa, me straddling him, his mouth pressing hot kisses against my neck as he hikes my skirt up to my waist. Tracing his fingertips along my exposed outer thighs, he gifts me with a biting kiss that ends with my lip between his teeth.

"The things I want to do to you," he says, his voice low and breathless against my ear. "The things I *could* do to you . . ."

"Show me." I grind against him, working the buttons of his dress shirt and inhaling the pepper-and-musk cologne that wafts from his uncovered skin. His cock pulses beneath me, unapologetically straining against the layers of fabric that separate us. "Or I could show you . . ."

Rising from his lap, I take his hand and lead him down the dark hallway and into my room, locking the door behind us. He kisses me hard as we stumble toward the bed. I give him a gentle push until he falls back against the soft mattress.

Sliding to my knees, I unfasten his belt, unsnap his navy suit pants, and tug his zipper down until he's fully exposed. Taking his generous cock in my hand, I pump its length before circling the tip with my tongue.

Roman releases a quiet moan and grabs a handful of my hair as I take him in my mouth, and each stifled, pleasured groan that follows only serves as encouragement to keep going.

"My god . . . ," he says between sighs.

I glance up at his face, watching it contort as he tries to fight off the inevitable release.

"You like to watch?" he asks with a half-cocked smile when he notices me watching him. "So do I."

Guiding me to my back, he positions himself between my thighs. Peeling my panties off, he tosses them aside and returns his attention to my pulsing sex. Sliding a finger between the seam, he circles my clit before giving it a gentle suck.

A shiver rides through my body, causing my hips to buck and my back to arch.

This man and his Midas touch . . .

He drags his tongue along my slit before sliding two fingers inside me, curling them against my G-spot as he devours me.

With my hand clamped over my mouth, I stifle the moans that threaten to escape. Margaux pounding on the door right now would steal all the wind from these sails in an airtight instant.

Glancing down, I find him watching me, delighting in my ecstasy as much as if it were his own.

"I'm so close," I whisper, tensing every muscle in my body in an attempt to stave off the inescapable end.

"Don't come yet." He removes his fingers from my wetness and kisses a trail along my inner thigh.

I take a deep breath. I'm not sure how long we've been going at this now. It could be five minutes; it could be fifty. All I know is time always seems to play tricks on me whenever I'm with him.

"Take it slow," he says, kissing the inside of my other thigh. "I want to enjoy this. I want to enjoy *you*. But more importantly, I want you to enjoy me too."

The level of eagerness in my body is akin to a virgin about to lose her v-card on prom night . . . the nervousness, the excitement, the wanting to *do it already* but also wanting the night to go on forever. All I know is, I've never wanted someone inside of me so desperately that I can't think straight.

My guard is down, my body is fair game, and tonight I'm all his.

Without a word, Roman climbs off the bed. "I need to text my babysitter and tell her it's going to be a while."

Sliding his phone from his pocket, the screen lights his face in the dark, highlighting our delayed gratification.

Biting my lip, I inhale another sharp breath and close my eyes. A cocktail of anticipation floods through me like someone injected it straight into my veins. The metallic tinkle of his belt hitting the rug beneath my bed sounds next, and I brace myself for him to come back.

A moment later, he returns to my side. His weight against the mattress is followed by his fingers working to free me of my skirt, blouse, and bra.

Slivers of light from the streetlamps outside peek through my blinds, painting our naked bodies like we're one and the same.

Roman brushes my messy hair from my face, taking a moment. A sly smile curls across his lips. The mouth that once got me fired is now the very same one exploring me without abandon.

His legs tangle with mine as he kisses me, his hand cupping my jaw.

Half of me wants to lie here with him all night, traveling and sampling one another's bodies until the sun comes up. The other part of me wants to feel him in the deepest parts of me. That part wants him to fill me to the hilt, to not stop until we're deliriously spent.

Reaching toward my nightstand, I pull out a condom. I'm no stranger to occasional hookups, and I always keep a box on hand in case. It also prevents guys from using the excuse that they don't have one on them—not that Roman would be that type.

Without protest, he takes the gold packet from my hand, rips the foil between his teeth, and slides it down his shaft.

My sex pulses in response.

Positioning himself between my thighs, he teases the tip of his cock against my entrance before sliding it all the way in, one throbbing, generous inch at a time. Once he's all the way in, he exhales, crushes my mouth with a punishing kiss, and sinks into me again and again.

My hips meet his thrust for thrust as I dig my nails into the hot flesh of his muscled lower back. I guide him deeper, deeper still, and it's still not deep enough.

"Harder," I whisper into his ear before giving it a playful nibble.

He rams his shaft into me, this time with more vigor.

"*Harder*," I whisper again. "*Deeper.*"

Roman slides his cock out of me without warning, quickly motioning for me to get on all fours.

"You want me to go deeper?" He caresses my ass cheek before giving it a soft smack. A moment later, his cock presses against my sex from behind, slipping back into my warm wetness.

I let out a soft moan before biting my tongue.

Burying my face into my pillow, I release a soft gasp as he thrusts into the deepest parts of me, faster and faster still.

"I can't fight it anymore," I say, gasping against the tangled mess of sheets in my clenched fist.

"Then don't," he says, driving into me. "Let go . . ."

With his words, I do exactly that. I let go. I come harder and longer than I've ever come in my life. He groans with his final thrusts, emptying himself of every last drop.

I collapse on my stomach, facedown, questioning whether I left my body a moment ago because I've never had an orgasm so intense.

"You okay?" I roll over, brushing the hair from my sweaty forehead and taking a closer look at Roman. A brisk chill sweeps over my naked body—a body that very much expected to be lying in his arms as the last little orgasmic earthquakes work their way from between my thighs.

Instead, he's perched at the foot of the bed, silent but still very much naked.

My stomach sinks.

Is he regretting this?

Did we take it too far?

"Yeah," he says, a second later. When he turns back to me, I spot his phone in his hand. "I was just making sure Harper got my text earlier about being late. And I just told Antonio he's off the clock for the night."

A cold sweep of panic zips through me.

He can't stay the night—I can't keep Margaux locked away in her room for that long.

Speaking of Margaux, the house is still oddly quiet . . .

"Just going to Uber home," he adds, almost as if he sensed my panic, though I can't imagine how.

Gathering my sheets, I pull them around me. He was literally inside of me less than thirty seconds ago, and now he's talking about the logistics of how he's getting home? What happened to basking in the afterglow?

I'm not one who needs cuddles after sex, but I've never had a man switch gears *this* fast.

"You sure you're okay?" I ask again.

He shoots me a look, as if *I'm* the one not making sense here.

"I think I hear the oven timer." Climbing out of bed, I dig a T-shirt and a pair of shorts from my dresser drawer, pull them on, and head to the kitchen.

Between the hand mixer, the sex, and the oven going off, it's a miracle my sister hasn't come out to investigate even once. She's always been a light sleeper, something she would constantly advertise at childhood sleepovers so no one would mess with her if she passed out first.

I take the cake out and place it on a trivet, letting it cool. After that, I head to the bathroom to clean up. On my way out, I stop at Margaux's door, twisting the knob as softly as I can and peeking in.

Only Margaux isn't there . . .

. . . which means she hasn't been home this entire time . . .

. . . which also means she could come home at any minute.

"Margaux?" Roman's voice startles me. I turn around to find his head sticking out of my bedroom door. "Everything okay?"

"Yeah." I wave it off. "Cake is cooling. I was just checking on my sister."

His eyes scan past my shoulder.

"Turns out she's not even home," I say.

Guess we could've been as loud as we wanted . . .

Roman steps into the hallway, his pants already zipped up and his belt secured just beneath his rippled abs, which taper to a chiseled V. We'd been going at it so intensely, I hadn't taken the time to stop and appreciate Roman's Adonis-like physique. Shrugging into his white dress shirt, he works the buttons one by one without peeling his gaze off me.

"If you need to get going, I can always drop the cake off in the morning," I say.

Roman frowns, stepping toward me and meeting me in the hallway. "What? No." He cups my cheek before leaning in to steal a kiss.

"It just seems like you want to go." I fold my arms, not because I'm mad, but I feel like I could use an extra barrier between us for some strange reason. Never mind that Roman was inside me just minutes ago.

"I don't."

"You don't *what*?" With everything suddenly being clear as mud, I'm going to need him to be more specific.

"I don't want to go." He runs his hand through his messy hair, the very hair I was tugging and pulling and running my fingers through mere minutes ago. "Not yet. Not unless you want me to."

"I feel like something happened in there . . . afterward, I mean . . . it was like you flipped a switch . . . you shut down."

There's a dark flash of pain in his eyes, though I'm not sure that pain is directed at me, at his late wife, or at his girls. Maybe perhaps all four of us.

"We were having a good time, right?" I ask. "The whole night? From beginning to end? I wasn't just imagining it, was I?"

"You weren't imagining any of it." His tone is confident and reassuring as he pulls me against him, but I keep my arms crossed tight. "I wasn't planning on coming home with you tonight. I wasn't planning on sleeping with you. I wasn't planning on any of this."

"I'm sorry—"

"—please let me finish," he says. "Everything that happened tonight—I wanted it. All of it. But as soon as it was over, I don't know . . . like you said, I shut down. I started thinking about things outside of this apartment. The people who work for me, the people who were still on the clock, waiting for me, for starters."

"You couldn't, I don't know, wait a few minutes before com-partmentalizing?" I ask with a slight chuckle to hopefully hide my bruised ego. I feel silly for assuming the worst, but the whole thing still stings.

Roman untangles my arms, drapes them over his shoulder, and pulls me close.

"I could have," he says. "And I should have."

He kisses my forehead before breathing me in. The scent of his faded cologne on his dress shirt fills my nostrils, a fleeting souvenir of the night we shared that was *almost* perfect.

I don't know what it's like to lose a spouse or the parent of my children in such a devastating and tragic way. I don't know what it's like to try to make sense of that or to give yourself permission to live again, to feel *pleasure* again.

"Next time, don't leave so soon, okay?" I ask. "Stay a while."

"I haven't left yet, have I?"

"Emotionally," I say. "Stay with me emotionally."

"Right." His lips press flat, and while he looks like he has the weight of the world on his mind, he keeps his thoughts to himself.

"I'm going to stick the cake in the fridge to cool . . ." I untangle myself from his embrace and trek to the kitchen, placing a dish towel under the pan and sliding it onto an empty shelf in our little white Frigidaire—halfway between Margaux's organic french vanilla greek yogurt and a cup of pomegranate arils.

When I turn around, I'm suddenly face to face with Roman. I release a startled gasp. I hadn't heard him follow me.

"Sorry." He runs his hand down the side of my arm before inter-linking his fingers with mine. "Just came to see if you needed any help."

"Should be ready for frosting and sprinkles in a half hour or so." I gesture to the living room. "We can watch something while we wait?"

Though I'm half tempted to hide him in my room in case Margaux comes home.

"I just need to check on my sister." I grab my phone and check my texts. My last one to her now shows as read, but she's yet to respond. I fire off a series of question marks.

About to head home soon, she finally writes back, following up with, Wasn't aware I was out past my curfew?

Take your time. I'm going to need at least forty-five minutes, I send. Margaux shoots back an annoyed emoji followed by a sleeping emoji. I get it. She's tired.

Need I remind you I'm doing this for you? I type out because it bears reminding. I add a smiley face to keep things from escalating in the wrong direction.

No one told you to take him back to our freaking apartment! she writes back almost instantly.

I compose another message to her. Going to his place wasn't exactly an option.

"All good over there?" Roman calls from the living room.

"Yeah, just texting my sister. Be there in a sec. The remote should be on the coffee table."

I shoot her one last text before joining Roman. Forty-five minutes and not a second before. He places his arm around me the second I sit down, and I rest my head on his shoulder.

In the half hour that follows, he watches some random show before gently nodding off, and I debate when to tell him the truth. A hundred variations of the same conversation play out. Some of them funny. Some of them horrific. Many of them emotional and heartfelt.

But the fact is, until the conversation is had, there's no point in theorizing how it's going to go. There's only one way to find out, and the longer I wait, the greater the odds are that this conversation isn't going to go the way I hope it will.

I cover him with a throw blanket and leave him asleep on the sofa while slipping away to the kitchen to frost and sprinkle his daughters' cake. When I'm done, I quietly locate the cake pan lid from a drawer and pop it on.

Regardless of what happens next, no matter which way this shakes out, I just hope he knows I truly care about him.

I like him.

A lot . . .

More than I ever thought possible.

"Roman." I wake him with a whisper and my palm on his shoulder. "The cake is ready."

He stirs, drawing in a sharp inhalation. His eyelids are heavy, and a disoriented expression washes over his handsome face. For a moment, I imagine what he looks like first thing in the morning, waking from a deep night's sleep. The heavy pit in my stomach tells me I'll probably never experience that with him. The fullness in my chest tells me not to give up hope, that anything is possible.

"You fell asleep," I tell him, "so I finished it."

I decided halfway between frosting the cake and covering it with a million sprinkles and then some that I need to come clean to him this week.

It can't wait.

It shouldn't wait.

Not a day longer.

As much as it pains me to jeopardize Margaux's promotion, and as much as I worry he'll never speak to me again, it's the right thing to do. If I have to help Margaux financially with the babies, so be it.

At the end of the day, Roman Bellisario is a good man who doesn't deserve to be a pawn in someone else's game.

CHAPTER TWENTY-FOUR

ROMAN

"Kristie," I say when my assistant answers my call Monday morning. "It's Roman. I'm taking the day."

Antonio glances up in the rearview, his gray brows knitting together.

"If you could reschedule my appointments," I add, "I'd appreciate it."

"Of course, Mr. Bellisario," she says against a background of idle office chatter and rustling papers. "Is everything okay? It's not one of the girls, is it?"

"No," I say. "I mean, yes, everything is fine. And no, it's not the girls. Just taking a personal day. I'll be in tomorrow."

After sharing an intense and unexpected Saturday night with Margaux, I've been feeling . . . different. Nothing bad. A little lighter, perhaps. Colors are slightly brighter. Music is more appealing to my ear. It's almost as if I've stepped out of a black-and-white movie and into a world of high-definition Technicolor.

"Got it," she says. "I'll work on moving everything as soon as possible."

"Perfect. And Kristie?"

"Yes?" she asks.

"Take the afternoon when you're done." I'd have to be blind not to notice how the poor thing sits around bored to tears half the time. Once or twice I've caught her with a single white AirPod in her ear, listening to some audiobook or podcast from her phone. The problem isn't that she's lazy or unmotivated—quite the opposite. She's too efficient. She finishes her work by ten o'clock each day, ten thirty at the latest. I could easily cut her down to part time if I wanted to, but I'd never do that to her. She lives with her disabled grandmother in Brooklyn, and Kristie's salary pays their rent.

"Are . . . are you sure about that?" she asks.

"You're welcome to stay the entire day if you'd like?" A teasing smirk covers my face. Sometimes I wish Kristie wouldn't be so serious, so eager to please. Sometimes I wish she'd give me guff every once in a while.

"Oh, um, I just . . ." She stumbles over her words. "This isn't like you. Are you sure everything's okay?"

"You'll be the first to know if it isn't. Now get to work. The sooner you finish, the sooner you can go home for the day."

"Y-yes. Okay. Thank you," she says.

I end the call and meet Antonio's gaze in the rearview again.

"You going to tell me what's going on, kid?" he asks when we stop at a red light.

"I feel like painting today." I utter words I haven't spoken in years. Three years to be exact. "Take me to the studio."

His grip loosens on the steering wheel. "Now that's what I'm talkin' about."

With rush hour traffic, it'll be a while before we get downtown. But if I close my eyes, I can almost feel the wooden handle of a paintbrush in my palm and the resistance of bristles against a freshly primed canvas. I can see the painting materializing in my mind's eye—an image so vivid it woke me from a dead sleep at five o'clock this morning, and I haven't been able to get it out of my head since.

After my wife died, I never thought I'd paint again.

Hell, I never *wanted* to paint again.

My biggest fan, my muse . . . was gone forever, never to return.

I don't know much about death or dying, and I try not to think about the afterlife in any sort of detail because it tends to give me an existential crisis. I've never been one to give much credence to signs or "messages from beyond," but if I did . . . I'd have half a mind to wonder if Emma had a hand at putting Margaux in my path.

She always had a knack for knowing what I needed, even when I was too bullheaded to realize I needed it in the first place.

Never in a million years would I have thought that sleeping with a new woman would breathe life into my inner artist again.

Not only was the moment intense—and beyond satisfying after a three-year hiatus—it was truly life changing. It was a closing of one chapter and the start of a new one. Same book, of course. Same story line.

If life is an unreliable narrator, Margaux Sheridan is my plot twist.

The key chain, the apartment, the reigniting spark of artistic creation . . . it's too specific, too perfect to be coincidental.

It's Emma.

It has to be.

Emma did this for me.

An hour later, Radiohead's *OK Computer* album is blasting from the Bluetooth speaker in the corner of my studio, I've stripped down and slipped into my paint-stained coveralls, and the newest Halcyon piece is coming to life in real time.

I won't lie—it feels pretty damn good to be back.

CHAPTER TWENTY-FIVE

SLOANE

"So, uh . . . care to tell me what *this* is?" Margaux hands me a small envelope the second she gets home from work Monday evening. "Roman sent flowers. *To my office.* The arrangement was so enormous I couldn't even carry it home, so now I have to look at that floral monstrosity every day until those petals wilt. I mean, it's gorgeous. But still."

"Did you take a picture?" I ask as I slide the card from the envelope. Roman has impeccable taste. I highly doubt the flowers were a hideous monstrosity.

The inscription reads, **I CAN'T STOP THINKING ABOUT SATURDAY NIGHT. I FEEL LIKE A DO-OVER IS IN ORDER . . . ROMAN**

"What the hell does he mean, a do-over?" Margaux's brows are angled and angry. These days it's hard to tell if it's pregnancy hormones or just Margaux being Margaux. Either way, she's none too pleased about this. Kicking off her shoes and placing her bag and keys on the foyer table, she asks, "Did you *sleep* with him?"

I don't answer out loud. I don't need to. The look on my face tells her everything.

"Oh my god." She lets her hands fall loose against her sides before gripping fistfuls of air. "I thought you guys just baked a cake? You didn't tell me you went all the way . . . Why? Why would you do that? And when were you going to tell me?"

I planned to tell her the first chance I got, but after Roman left, I was too spent to wait for Margaux to get home. I went to bed, and by the time I woke up in the morning, she'd already come and gone. Far be it from her to miss her standing brunch reservation with seven of her closest friends. Sometime around noon, she texted me saying Ethan's mom was taking her on an impromptu baby-shopping spree at Bergdorf's. By the time she got home that night, I woke just enough to hear her stumble to her room and collapse on her bed in a heap of exhaustion. This morning, she was already out the door for work by the time I got out of the shower.

"This is the first time I've had a chance to talk to you since Saturday night," I say. "So, now I guess."

Margaux crosses her arms, which only makes her growing bump that much more prominent. Or maybe it's the nonmaternity dress she's squeezed herself into. I'm convinced she's in denial, that she thinks she's going to wake up one morning and it'll all have been a dream and things can go back to normal. I'm not sure why else she'd be so against maternity clothes or why she's trying to fight the inevitable. It won't be long before she'll look as if she swallowed a basketball, and last I checked, Gucci and Chanel don't exactly design for that type of silhouette.

If she plans to continue to hide her growing midsection so as not to risk her promotion, she's going to have to embrace it, to work with it instead of in spite of it. There are things she can do—the way light and dark colors play with the eye and create illusions. I see it all the time at work on canvases. I'd suggest she utilize these techniques with her wardrobe if she were in a more receptive mindset.

Another time, perhaps.

While Margaux stands here shooting daggers my way, I look at this situation from an alternate angle: Margaux has been in the driver's seat of her life from day one. She's always had her pick of friends, schools, jobs, boyfriends, and designer wardrobes. She's always had the luxury of calling all the shots when it came to every life decision.

Deep down, beneath her tear-filled eyes and shaky voice and accusatory tone, is a woman terrified of living a life commandeered by fate.

To a control freak like her, it's one of the worst things that could happen.

I only pray motherhood softens her a bit.

If it doesn't . . . lord help us all—and those two sweet babies.

"I like him," I say. Lightness blankets my chest with those words. The sensation feels so good I say it again. *"I really like him."*

It feels even better the second time around, like breathing forbidden words into existence makes them all the more real.

"I heard you the first time," she says.

"And he likes me."

"You don't say . . ." Margaux does nothing to hide her annoyance.

"I have to tell him the truth," I say, "about everything."

"You can't." She juts her chin out, asserting what little control she has left into this situation. "You'd destroy any chance I have at ever getting a promotion at Lucerne. Theodora would kill me for lying to her. No—she'd fire me in a heartbeat and have me blacklisted from the industry before I finish packing my office."

"He's a person," I say. "A human. With real feelings. This isn't some game to him. This is his life. I can't keep stringing him along and then drop him as soon as you land your new job. I'm sorry, Margaux, but I'm going to tell him this week—the next time I see him."

My sister blinks, staring up at the ceiling as thick, soggy tears slide down her pink cheeks.

"I wish you wouldn't." Her words are terse, pointed, and broken, as if she's staving off a wave of sobs desperate to escape the back of her throat. "Maybe . . . maybe you can just wait a little longer? Hold off until I get my new position? Then I can come clean about the pregnancy, and we can let him down easy. This way everyone wins."

"Except Roman. He's still just a pawn in someone else's game," I say.

"No one told you to get attached." She folds her arms before adding, "I hate that he's falling for you. Not because I'm jealous or because you two aren't a good match. But because it was never supposed to happen. It wasn't part of the plan."

Ah, yes. Margaux's master plan.

"I'm sorry, but I'm telling him. It's the right thing to do." I take a step closer, reaching out to place my hand on her shoulder. Despite the fact that we've reached an impasse, she's still my sister, and I'm still inclined to comfort her.

She jerks away.

Message received loud and clear.

"Look," I say, placing some distance between us again. "No one could've seen this coming. Roman and I both went into that first date on the same page . . . that we weren't looking for a relationship. This wasn't supposed to happen. But it did. And now here we are."

Margaux swipes at a tear, keeping her gaze trained anywhere but on me.

"You realize you're choosing a guy—some guy you barely even know—over your own flesh and blood, right?" She tightens her arms across her chest. "And how the hell am I going to afford raising two babies in Manhattan on my current salary?"

"I'm not choosing him over you—I'm choosing my conscience. There's a difference," I say. "And we'll figure out the financial stuff. I'll help if you need me to."

"Funny how you didn't have a conscience a few weeks ago," she says, ignoring my offer to help her financially. That's another thing about my sister—she's as independent as she is stubborn. Asking for help is a sign of weakness. Taking help is an act of desperation.

I'm hopeful that with Ethan's mom being so generous and willing to step in, she might loosen her reins a bit. Only time will tell.

"You're right," I say. "I didn't have one then. I was only thinking of you in that moment and no one else. I deeply regret that . . . which is why I'm coming clean to him."

"And how, exactly, do you foresee this little conversation going?" Her eyes are wild, full of a cocktail of unrestrained emotions.

"No idea. But I'd rather be honest and risk losing him than break his heart so that you can get a promotion."

Turning, I head down the hall toward my room. After a long day at the gallery, the last thing I want to do is stand here and bang my head against the brick wall that is my sister. I know from experience that she can argue with the best of them, rarely backing down until she gets what she wants.

But my mind is made up.

I'm halfway to my room when Margaux shoves past me, her shoulder brushing so hard against mine she nearly knocks me off balance. She doesn't apologize; she simply disappears behind her bedroom door, slamming it closed. A moment later, music blasts from inside her room, her way of literally tuning me out.

Either way, I don't let it get to me.

I know I'm making the right choice.

And the thing about Margaux is she'll eventually get over this. It might not be tomorrow or next week or even a year from now. But she won't hate me forever.

I only wish I could say the same for Roman.

There's no telling how he's going to take this news.

CHAPTER
TWENTY-SIX

ROMAN

I pull up my old Halcyon email account while I wait for Antonio to arrive at the studio. There must be hundreds, maybe even thousands, of unread messages. I delete them all before composing a single message to a select handful of local galleries, informing them that "Halcyon" would like to have a small exhibit in the coming weeks.

It feels ridiculous, even now, writing in the third person, pretending this entire charade isn't as comical as it is insane. When Emma and I first dreamed up this little side gig, it was nothing more than a passion project. She saw how unfulfilled I was working for the family business and suggested I find a creative outlet doing something that brought me pure pleasure. Something to feed my joy-starved soul. Something for me and only for me.

Under the influence of sweet wine and edibles, we dreamed up my Halcyon alter ego, carefully planning all the ways it could be mysterious and anonymous. But what began as a joke quickly took on a life of its own, growing into something more than either of us bargained for. I was never looking for fame, money, or recognition. And with the freedom anonymity could provide, I could continue painting for the fun of it. There was never any reason to stop . . . until there was.

I press send on the email, slide my phone into my pocket, and lock up my studio—but not before stealing one last glimpse at the piece I finished an hour ago: one solely inspired by Margaux.

If it never leaves this building, if it never hangs on someone's wall, then at least it exists.

That's all that matters.

In my early Halcyon days, Emma and I would hole up here every weekend. I'd hold marathon painting sessions while she curated playlists and ran out for coffee and bagels in the mornings and pizza at night. That was always our thing—it was sacred, and I'd never re-create that with Margaux. But one of these days, when the time is right, I'll tell her the truth about Halcyon and how everything came to be.

If she's anything like I think she is, she'll understand why I didn't tell her. The value of my work almost completely hinges on the fact that I'm anonymous. It gives the art more of an edge, an air of mysteriousness that only adds to its value and demand. If all of that were to go away, hundreds of people would lose millions of dollars.

I can't, in good faith, screw the very collectors who padded my pocketbook all those years ago. The idea that these multimillion-dollar paintings might suddenly be worth hardly more than the canvas they're painted on makes me sick to my stomach.

"How was it, kid?" Antonio asks when I climb into my back seat a few minutes later. "How'd it feel to get back at it, eh?"

"It's good to be back." I dial Margaux as we head uptown.

"Hey," she answers on the second ring.

"Hi."

The line is silent, and for a moment, I check to make sure we're still connected. I guess I was expecting more of a greeting than a neutral little *hey* . . .

"Did you get the flowers I sent?" I break the silence.

"I did," she says after a short pause. "Thank you."

"And the note?"

"That too," she says, though there's no hint of playfulness in her voice that leads me to think she's excited about the do-over I proposed.

After Ubering home with the chocolate cake in tow, Saturday night I caught what little sleep I could get before spending Sunday with the girls. While I know it's in good taste to touch base after sleeping together, I was hoping the flowers would hold her over until we could talk again—or at the very least, let her know I was thinking about her.

"When can I see you?" she asks.

That's more like it . . .

"The girls have piano lessons tonight," I say. "Tuesday night, I have an after-hours conference call with our Australian office. Wednesday night the girls have dance. We could do Thursday? I could see if Harper's free to babysit?"

"I can't do Thursday." Her voice is laced with disappointment. "Friday?"

"Friday works." I'd already mentally set my Friday aside for her anyway.

"You want to come to my place? We could just stay in? Do something low key?"

"Actually, there's a hotel two blocks from me. Sweeping views of Central Park. A Michelin-starred restaurant on the premises. A rooftop bar that serves the best old-fashioneds in all of Manhattan. Twenty-four-hour room service . . ."

I haven't stayed a single night away from the girls in three years, so knowing that I'd be a mere two blocks away would give me tremendous peace of mind and allow me to fully enjoy all the things I plan to do with this woman . . .

"Not that that doesn't sound incredible," she says, "but you don't have to do all of that for me."

"I know I don't have to—I want to." I feel awful for compartmentalizing the other night, for shifting my attention to anything but her when I should have been holding her in my arms. In retrospect, it was a sick move, and she deserves better than that.

I intend to make it right.

"Honestly, the hotel thing sounds amazing, but I'd prefer if you just came here Friday night," she says.

The half-cocked smile that framed my lips a second ago flattens.

Something is . . . off . . . here.

"Of course," I say. "Everything okay?"

"It's just been a . . . stressful day," she says, with an apologetic breath.

"Let me know if I need to pull Theodora off you. She tends to work her—"

"—no, no. It's not her," Margaux says. "We'll talk Friday, okay? I have to go . . . I've got another call coming in."

With that, Margaux ends our conversation, and I ride home in silence, ruminating on all the things she didn't say, wondering if I'll have the patience to wait four more days before she can finally say them.

I don't know that I can.

Perhaps I'll pay her a visit at the office this week.

It's easier to gauge someone's reaction face to face, rather than over the phone. If she's excited to see me, I'll know right away. And if she isn't . . .

I don't want to think about that just yet.

Not if I don't have to.

The idea of going back to what I was before I met her—a melancholic, uninspired shell of a man—holds zero appeal.

I want Margaux.

I need Margaux.

In the short time I've known her, she's breathed more life into my weary soul than I ever thought possible. At this point, she's as essential as oxygen.

"Everything okay?" Antonio asks. "Awful quiet back there . . ."

I change the subject. "Yeah. The girls good for you at pickup today?"

"Do you even have to ask that?" He rolls his eyes, chuckling. "You know how I feel about stupid questions."

I repeat my father's tired old mantra from a lifetime ago. "No such thing as stupid questions, only stupid answers."

He snaps his fingers. "Was just going to say that."

We head uptown to a soundtrack of stop-and-go traffic, yacht-rock radio, and small talk.

But in the back of my mind, I can't stop thinking of Margaux.

CHAPTER
TWENTY-SEVEN

SLOANE

"Did you hear?" My boss, Brenna Tiernan, rushes up to me the second I arrive at the gallery Tuesday morning. Her red hair is particularly wild today, but behind her emerald-green frames, her baby doll eyes are even wilder.

"No . . . what?" I place my purse into my locker in the employee break room before taking a sip from my coffee cup.

"Halcyon . . . is painting again." A mile-wide smile takes up the entire lower half of her face. She does a little happy dance, the heels of her signature black Louboutins clicking daintily on our marble floors.

In haste, I swallow my sip of coffee . . . only it goes down the wrong pipe, leaving me in an embarrassingly difficult-to-contain coughing spell.

Without missing a beat, Brenna grabs me a bottle of Evian from the communal fridge, uncaps it, and shoves it into my hand.

"You okay?" She lightly pats my back as I sip the ice-cold water. There's not a comforting bone in Brenna's body, but God love her for trying.

"How . . . how did you hear about this?" I ask when I'm finally able to use my voice again.

"Halcyon's representative sent an email to a bunch of galleries last night. I already wrote back and told them that whatever their best offer is, I'll top it by fifteen percent."

Holy shit.

"I might lose money on this in the short run, but can you imagine the foot traffic it'll drive? It'll put our little gallery on the map. Well, not that it isn't already, but you know. You can't buy this kind of PR."

"When?" I ask. "When are they wanting to have this exhibit?"

"The email said sometime in the next couple of weeks. It'd be a small collection—ten pieces or so. But in this case, I wouldn't even bother pricing anything. There'll be multiple offers on every last painting, I just know it. We'll have bidding wars upon bidding wars."

Brenna flits around the break room, starry eyed and talking a mile a minute, manic almost.

"People will be talking about this comeback for years to come," she continues, though I suspect she's mostly talking out loud rather than talking to me. A bell chimes, letting us know we have a customer out front. "Hon, would you mind taking that? I need to start lining up a caterer, a press release, the whole nine yards."

I don't tell her that there's a chance Halcyon might not choose our gallery, that it's likely not about money. But I don't know those things for sure, and I'm not about to rain on her parade. In the three years I've worked here, I've never seen Brenna so manically giddy, so tunnel visioned with excitement. She's like a child about to visit Disney's Magic Kingdom at Christmastime.

Heading out front to assist a walk-in, I think back to the Halcyon studio tour Roman gave me and all those unfinished paintings. While Roman didn't confirm or deny that Halcyon was the pseudonym of his late wife, the writing was clearly on the wall. Knowing that losing *You or Someone like You* mattered to him so much he was willing to have a stranger fired over it, I'm worried he's not thinking clearly right now. Perhaps sleeping together last weekend sparked something in him. Maybe this is his way of ushering in a new era.

A bittersweet closure to his past.

While placing those priceless works into the hands of people who will love and appreciate their splendid beauty is a great idea in theory, once they're gone, there'll be no getting them back. Not for a long time. And not without spending a small fortune. In all the years I've dealt art, Halcyon resales are as rare and fabled as unicorns.

I just want to make sure he's doing the right thing.

When those paintings are gone, they'll be gone forever—like his beloved Emma.

Two hours later, I finally get a reprieve from our morning customer, and I sneak to the back to make a quick call to Roman, only to get his voice mail.

"Call me when you get this, okay?" I say after the tone. "I have a quick question for you . . . it's important."

As the rest of the afternoon ticks by in virtual slow motion, I check my phone every chance I get. But he's yet to call back. I'd just hate for him to make a mistake—to let go of the last of his late wife's priceless art—all because he thinks he has a future with me.

CHAPTER
TWENTY-EIGHT
ROMAN

I end my conference call with our Melbourne office and peek my head into the family room. The girls are watching *Sesame Street*. Harper wasn't available tonight, so I had to rely on Elmo and Big Bird to keep the girls occupied for the past two hours.

"All right, girls." I grab the TV remote. "Tell your puppet friends good night. Time to get ready for bed."

Over the hour that follows, I draw the girls' baths, dress them in pajamas, and read them a stack of bedtime stories, all the while reminding myself I still need to call Margaux back. She left me a message earlier today, but I spent all day catching up on yesterday's work and wanted to talk to her when I wasn't so rushed.

"Good night, Daddy," Marabel says when I kiss her forehead after we finish the final book.

"Good night, Marabel," I whisper. Adeline is already asleep, and once she wakes up, it's almost impossible to get her back to sleep without repeating our entire bedtime routine from top to bottom. "Sleep tight."

"Don't let the bedbugs bite," she whispers back with a giggle.

"No, *you* don't let the bedbugs bite," I tease.

"No, *youuuuu* don't let the bedbugs bite." She giggles, clamping her hand over her mouth.

I switch on their dresser lamp—a ceramic rainbow butterfly Emma found at some flea market when we were six months along with Adeline a lifetime ago. I dial the dimness down until their bedroom is washed in a dreamy haze of light, and then I pull the door softly shut behind me.

Ten minutes later, I sink into my favorite wingback chair with a freshly poured scotch in one hand and my phone in the other, and I call Margaux.

"Hey," she answers—her tone still as neutral as it was when we spoke yesterday.

"Meant to call you sooner," I say. "Just got the girls off to bed. What's going on?"

"Did you know Halcyon is making a comeback?" she asks.

Of course I know . . . but the more important question is . . . How does Margaux know?

After showing her the studio a while back, I thought she might start piecing things together or at the very least, ask pointed questions. But for some reason or another, she didn't ask a single one.

It hasn't occurred to me until now that perhaps Margaux assumes my late wife was Halcyon. Perhaps her lack of inquiring was only a way for her to be sensitive to my loss and to avoid inflicting more pain than necessary by bringing it up.

"Even if I did, I'm not at liberty to say." I hate that I have to be vague with her, but this is the kind of conversation we should have face to face this Friday. Clearly she has connections in the art world if she heard about Halcyon's return. One slip of the tongue and my true identity could easily land in the wrong hands. "How did you hear about it, if you don't mind my asking?"

Margaux doesn't answer me—not right away.

I know there are certain art-collector circles where everything is hush-hush and sources are never revealed, and I would never want her to breach someone's trust, but I have to ask.

"I'm not at liberty to say." She feeds my words back to me, though she isn't being facetious about it.

Fair enough.

Three more days . . .

Three more days until I can tell her everything.

CHAPTER TWENTY-NINE

SLOANE

"Sloane, so sorry to interrupt. I know you're with someone right now." My colleague Derrick taps my shoulder and leans close to my ear. "But you have a call on line two. It's your sister. She says it's urgent."

My stomach plummets to the floor faster than the smile fades from my lips.

Margaux has never called me at work.

Ever.

"Would you mind going over our Ronceau collection with Mrs. Seidlin while I take that?" I ask him, doing my best not to showcase the fact that my insides are swarming with adrenaline-hot panic.

"I'd be happy to," he says with a gracious smile.

I hurry back to the break room, lift the receiver on the wall, and press the button for line two.

"Margaux," I say. "What's going on? Why are you calling me at work?"

"Oh my god . . . oh my god . . ."

"What? What?" My heart must be beating at least two hundred miles per hour. The room begins to spin, so I reach for a chair from a nearby table and take a seat.

"I called your cell like fifty times and sent you a bunch of messages," she says.

"What's going on? Is it Mom?"

"No." She exhales, though she's still very much breathless. "Roman just showed up. He's here, Sloane. He's at my office."

Oh, no.

No, no, no.

"He's with Theodora right now," she says, keeping her voice low. I imagine her peeking through the blinds that cover her office window. "He's been in there for about fifteen minutes. Why is he in there? He's never come to the office before. Ever. What's he doing? What does he want?"

"I don't know . . . Maybe he wanted to surprise you—*me*?"

"What do I do? What the hell do I do?"

"Get out of there," I say. "Grab your purse and say you're taking an early lunch, just . . . leave."

Ironically this is the most the two of us have spoken all week. Ever since our little blowup Monday night, she's looked through me like a ghost anytime we've been in the same room. Now look at us—coming together for a common cause, though our motivations are quite different.

She doesn't want to get fired, naturally.

I don't want him to find out the truth from her of all people.

"What happened to you telling him the truth?" Margaux snips, despite this being the worst possible time for her to start WWIII all over again.

"He told me he's busy all week . . . we're supposed to get together Friday. Are you leaving or are you hiding?"

"Neither," she says, her voice somber and heavy. "He just saw me."

"Smile," I say because I can't hear a hint of it in her tone. I picture her face—pale and shell shocked. It's as if a catastrophic train wreck is about to happen and there's not a damn thing I can do to stop it. "Smile and wave."

"I am," she says through what sound like clenched teeth. "Oh my god, Sloane, he's walking over here right now with Theodora. I have to go."

The line goes dead.

And I make a move for the nearest garbage can because I'm almost certain I'm going to throw up.

CHAPTER THIRTY

ROMAN

"So lovely of you to stop by today," Theodora says as she ushers me out of her office. "Little things like this make for the best surprises. How I wish you'd come by more often . . ." Brushing her hand against my arm, she chuckles. "Though I won't flatter myself. You and I both know the real reason you're here."

She points across the room, toward a door with a sign that clearly reads **MARGAUX SHERIDAN, CLIENT RELATIONS DIRECTOR**.

Twenty feet away, past a double set of shiny black reception desks and a small waiting area adorned with various plants and framed accolades, Margaux stands on the other side of a glass window, her silhouette partly obscured by miniblinds as she stares at me with a half-gaped mouth.

I had a break in my schedule today, so I thought I'd swing by and take her out to lunch as a surprise. I even called her assistant earlier to confirm her calendar was open, and I made her promise to keep this a surprise.

Margaux doesn't smile when she sees me—at least not at first.

Lifting her hand, albeit in slow motion, she offers a gentle finger wave as her full lips pull into a confused arch.

"Hi," I say when I reach her door.

"H-hi," she says, eyes squinting. There's something different about her, though I can't put my finger on it. Her hair is curled—but it's not that. "Come on in."

She reaches behind me, closing the door. Taking a deep breath, she drags her palms along her sides, as if they're damp and she's trying to hide any evidence of nervousness. Maybe I shouldn't have surprised her at work like this, but I figured Theodora wouldn't mind if I stole her away for a couple of hours. All of this is her doing anyway.

"What . . . what are you doing here?" she asks, though her tone is almost accusatory.

I lift a brow. "You seemed a little tense the last couple of times we talked . . . thought maybe I could take you out to lunch, cheer you up a bit?"

Chewing on the inside of her lip, she nods. "I see."

"The girls loved the cake, by the way . . . I forgot to tell you that. Marabel said it's the best chocolate cake she's ever had in her entire life—you can quote her on that." I'm attempting to lighten the mood, but Margaux's shifty gaze indicates I'm doing a piss-poor job at it.

She swallows, saying nothing, as she stares down at the industrial gray carpet.

This isn't at all how I pictured this. I thought there'd be a smile. A hug. Some stolen kisses behind her closed door. Not . . . *this*. Not a depressing, awkward exchange.

"You shouldn't be here," she says, though her voice is so low I'm not sure I heard her clearly.

"Yeah." I drag my hand through my hair. "I should have called you first . . . I called your assistant . . . she said your schedule was open, I just thought . . ."

Margaux worries her bottom lip, pacing the space in front of her window before coming to a stop.

"If something's wrong, if something's bothering you, just say it," I tell her. "If you changed your mind, if you don't want to do this anymore . . ."

I don't want to finish my sentence.

I don't want this to be the end.

I don't want to give her an out, but right now it looks like that's exactly what she needs.

Nothing about her implies she's happy to see me.

"This is really . . . um . . . I don't even know how to say it." Margaux crosses her arms just below her chest, causing the fabric of her dress to strain tight against her body and shift. It's then that I can't help but notice a slight yet undeniable roundness to her belly—a belly that was flat mere days ago.

"What the fuck is going on?" I ask.

Margaux's eyes turn glassy, and her lower lip trembles, but she blinks away any sign of tears and forces a smile that is more jarring than anything else.

It's like I'm standing next to a complete stranger. Nothing about this woman—aside from her facial features—resembles the Margaux I've come to know. This woman is shifty, agitated, emotional, and very fucking pregnant.

"I'm Margaux," she says with a breathy chuckle as she extends her hand to me. "The *real* Margaux."

My jaw tenses.

I don't meet her hand with mine.

I don't move.

I'm not even sure I'm breathing.

All I see is red.

"Sloane was going to tell you everything . . . ," she adds.

"Who the hell is Sloane?" I ask before recalling the piece of mail I saw at her apartment that day.

"My sister," she says before adding, "my identical twin sister."

Pinching the bridge of my nose, I close my eyes and draw in a sharp breath.

"Please don't be mad," she says.

Opening my eyes, I shoot her an incredulous glare. "Don't . . . be . . . *mad?*"

I'm a lot of things right now.

Mad doesn't begin to touch any of them.

She releases a nervous giggle. Gone are those crocodile tears she was about to shed a mere moment ago.

"It's actually a funny story," she says.

"I highly doubt that." I check my watch. I'd blocked off the next two hours of my schedule to spend them with her—uninterrupted. Now it appears as though I'll be spending them in a blinding rage instead.

My blood boils beneath the surface of my skin, and the collar of my dress shirt digs into my throat.

"She was supposed to be boring," Margaux says, waving her hand. "You were never supposed to fall for her. It's all kind of hilarious, if you think about it."

"This entire time, I've been seeing your sister? Thinking I was seeing you?" My jaw refuses to unclench, causing me to speak through my teeth. "Forgive me for not finding the humor in being made to look like a goddamned idiot."

"I told her not to get carried away," Margaux says, throwing her hands in the air. "I tried to warn her. I told her she was playing with fire."

I move for the door, refusing to tolerate this shit show a moment longer.

"Wait," she says, reaching toward me but standing firmly in place.

"I'd rather not." My hand is on the doorknob and my mind is already a million miles from here. I show myself out without giving her a chance to protest again.

Besides, I don't want to hear another word from *this* Margaux.

I want to talk to . . . Sloane.

By the time I get back to my SUV, I have no recollection of walking from the office to the elevator to the sidewalk. Everything is a blacked-out blur.

"Take me to Margaux's apartment," I say, sparing him the truth for now.

"Ah, she wasn't there?" Antonio asks.

"No," I say. "She wasn't there."

Ten minutes later, he pulls up in front of the familiar brown building with the black iron steps. I climb out before he so much as shifts into park, and I sprint up the stairs. Slamming my fist on the buzzer to her apartment, I ring her multiple times . . . and wait.

There's no answer.

She's not home. Either she's out on the town or she's at work—which serves as nothing more than a reminder that I don't know where that would even be because I don't know a damn real thing about this woman.

I buzz one more time—in vain.

And then I return to my Cadillac.

"Take me home," I tell Antonio as I slam the rear passenger door shut. I'm in no condition to be at the office right now.

"Sure thing, kid." He doesn't ask. He knows better.

By the time we arrive, I've worked myself into a tension headache that'll likely last for days. Hitting the sidewalk, I decide to walk off some of this steam. I need to cool off before my daughters get home from school in a few hours.

Pulling out my phone, I hover my thumb over her contact information, tempted to call her and demand an explanation.

Was this all a joke to her?

Was any of it real?

Shoving my phone away, I change my mind.

In my current state of mind, I'll no doubt say something I might come to regret.

I can't talk to her now.

Or maybe ever again.

CHAPTER
THIRTY-ONE

SLOANE

"He just left," Margaux says over the phone.

"That didn't take long . . . What did you say?" I'm squeezing the phone so hard my hand throbs.

"I told him that I'm the real Margaux, and that you're my twin sister, Sloane," she says.

"And how did he take that?"

She's quiet. "Um, he looked like he wanted to punch something really hard?"

I sink my back against the wall, exhaling.

I hate that he found out like this. It should have been my voice he was hearing, my eyes he was looking into, and my lips speaking this awful truth. No one else's.

"What did he say when he left?" I ask.

"Nothing. I tried to stop him, but he stormed off," Margaux says. "I don't think he's talked to Theodora yet, but I'm pretty sure I'm about to lose my job so . . ."

I roll my eyes despite the fact that she can't see them.

A man just had his heart shattered into a million pieces, and per usual she's making this about her.

My sister can get another job. Maybe not her dream job. Maybe not tomorrow. Maybe not at the snap of her fingers. Maybe not an enviable position with a handsome salary and a laundry list of fringe benefits. But she'll get back on her feet at some point. She always does.

Roman, on the other hand, has only one heart.

"I should call him," I say.

"What's the point?" Margaux asks with a huff. The sound of miscellaneous office supplies rattling around in drawers fills the background.

"The point? The point is I was going to tell him myself on Friday. The point is he had to hear it from you and not me—the woman he's been falling for this entire time."

"No, the point is he's rich and handsome, and he can swipe an app on his phone and have a replacement woman Ubered to his door in thirty minutes or less. Trust me, the man's going to be fine," Margaux says. "Me, on the other hand . . ."

"Damn it, Margaux! Not everything is about you." I raise my voice at my sister before clamping my hand over my mouth. I'm not a yeller. I rarely get angry. And the last place I want to do either of those things is at the gallery, where my boss is holed up in her office across the hall and our main floor is filled with colleagues and collectors alike. Lowering my voice, I add, "When you're done packing up your office, maybe you can pack up your bedroom too. How soon can Ethan's mom get you into that apartment?"

My question is met with dead silence.

It's rare for the proverbial cat to have Margaux's tongue.

I can only hope she's thinking about this from someone else's perspective for a change.

Brenna steps into the break room, her face twisted behind her emerald-green frames.

"Everything okay?" she mouths when she sees I'm on the phone.

Without saying goodbye, I hang up on Margaux.

"I heard shouting . . ." Brenna winces.

"I'm sorry. I've got a bit of a personal situation going on. I should probably take the day. I'm not sure I'd be all that helpful if I stuck around . . ."

She lifts a thin scarlet-colored brow. "Again? Didn't you have a personal emergency the other week?"

"I did," I say, vividly recalling the day I took Margaux to her ultrasound and IUD removal.

Not once did she thank me for that . . .

And now that I think about it, two years ago, I asked her to take me to my LASIK surgery appointment, and she claimed she couldn't get the time off. I had to inconvenience a friend instead. Over the years, she's used countless bottles of my face creams and lotions and oils, and not once has she offered to replace a single one. On top of that, she'll crumple my laundry in a wrinkled heap on top of the dryer when she needs to use it—instead of placing it in a basket like a sane person. She refuses to use AirPods to listen to her music when I'm trying to sleep or relax, claiming they "feel weird" in her ears. Margaux has no qualms about using the last of the coffee creamer or borrowing my favorite boots or umbrella when she forgets to plan ahead for inclement weather. She erases my shows from our DVR to make room for hers without so much as an apology.

I realize now that I could write a novel on all the ways my sister is the most selfish human being on the planet. How I didn't see this before is beyond me. Perhaps I didn't want to see it? Just like Margaux is happily in denial about her growing belly, maybe I, too, was turning a blind eye to all the ways my sister has always put herself first.

Our entire life, I've made excuses for her. She was always so anxious, so emotional, so high strung. My parents sidestepped around her mood swings and bent over backward to keep her smiling while I faded into the background, content to be the "easy" daughter.

While it's simple to point fingers at Margaux and stew in this soup of outrage, the person I'm the most upset with right now . . . is myself.

I've always been the docile twin.

The quiet twin.

The affable, amiable, self-sacrificing, peacekeeping twin.

I've allowed her to take advantage of me more times than I can count over our lifetime, and in doing such, I've created a monster.

I've enabled *all* of this.

"My goodness." Brenna places a hand on my shoulder, though she's touching me so lightly I can hardly feel it. "I can tell you're extremely upset right now. Whatever it is, go home and deal with it. We'll see you tomorrow."

Grabbing my things from my locker, I exit out the back and hit the sidewalk, opting to walk home to help clear my head and flood my body with much-needed oxygen.

Halfway there, I call Roman.

He doesn't answer—not that I expected him to.

I don't leave a message.

CHAPTER THIRTY-TWO

ROMAN

I silence Sloane's call and let it go to voice mail.

I don't have anything to say to her—not right now.

I watch my phone, waiting for a chime to indicate she left a message, but it never comes. Perhaps she knows there's nothing she can say to make any of this better. There isn't a single word that can undo what they've done. There isn't a broad enough brush she could use to paint this in a better light.

What's done is done.

She lied.

She lied again.

And then she continued to lie.

I slam my phone facedown on my coffee table, rest my elbows on my knees, and bury my head in my hand, breathing through my fingertips.

For the life of me, I can't surmise why the two of them did this. If the real Margaux had no interest in dating me, why would she send her sister in her place? And why would her sister continue to date me week after week? Why would she sleep with me? Did she not think everything would come to light eventually?

My phone dings with a text alert.

Lifting my head, I steeple my fingers and stare at the back of my phone, deciding whether I want to read the damn message—if it's even from Sloane.

After a minute of contemplation, I flip it over, tap the screen to life, and check my texts.

Sure enough, it's Sloane—though my phone identifies her as Margaux.

Please call me, she writes.

Lifting my phone, I call Harper instead—to see if she's available to take the girls to dance tonight. They shouldn't have to see me like this. No one should.

It's in everyone's best interest if I keep to myself for the next several hours.

After Harper confirms she's available, I pour myself two fingers of scotch, change into sweats and sneakers, and locate my MetroCard in the junk drawer. It's been ages since I've had to take public transportation, but I need to get to the studio without inviting a line of concerned questions from Antonio.

Being just another nameless, faceless New Yorker riding on a subway car and staring blankly ahead sounds good right now.

I need to get out of my element.

I need to be someone else for a change, if only for a hot minute.

An hour later, I'm holed up in my studio loft, music blaring as I paint the canvas in front of me the vilest shade of red I can find. And when I'm finished, I trash the fucking thing—the same way Margaux, or Sloane, or whoever the hell she is, destroyed my dignity, shattered my trust, and used my heart like a pawn in some twisted little game.

I hope she's happy.

Actually, no.

I hope she's miserable.

I hope she's sorry.

I hope she feels emptier than the gaping hole in the middle of my chest right now.

By the time I'm done, the canvas is lying in a broken, splintered, ripped heap on the floor, and my hands and forearms are covered in half-dried red paint.

I wouldn't say I feel better—but the intensity of what I spent the entire afternoon feeling has ratcheted down a notch.

After cleaning up and catching my breath, I grab my phone and type out a single text message: I hope it was worth it. My thumb hovers over the send button for a solid eight seconds before I delete it.

My silence is the only response she needs.

CHAPTER
THIRTY-THREE

SLOANE

My feet throb, hot and aching in my cross-trainers. I must have walked a dozen miles today. Or at least it feels that way. After leaving the gallery, I ran home, changed into something more comfortable, laced up my sneakers, and spent hours wandering our sun-scorched city—partly because I didn't want to run into my sister in case she got canned today and came home early. But mostly I couldn't sit at home.

I sent Roman a text earlier, asking him to call me.

He hasn't, though I can't blame him.

I keep asking myself if it would've gone differently had I been the one to break the news to him. If he heard it from my lips, would the words have been easier to swallow? I'd like to think they would have been. I'd like to think there's some alternate universe where today didn't happen, where we're still on for Friday, and where we have a heart-to-heart that involves more laughter than anguish.

But what's done is done.

Up ahead, I spot an empty bench and decide to take a break from my aimless, melancholic journey around the city. My belly rumbles, reminding me I haven't eaten since breakfast. I don't know that I could stomach anything right now anyway, but I should probably think about grabbing a bottle of water. Sweat collects across my brow, and I drag the back of my hand across it. Scanning the street, I search for a bodega or a Duane Reade—only to spot something else entirely: Halcyon's loft.

I was so awestruck when Roman took me here that I didn't think to jot down an address or even a street, but I remember the scaffolding outside the warehouse-like structure and the flower market on the corner, the one sandwiched between a Verizon store and a sushi bar.

Counting the windows, I focus on the row that lines up with the seventh floor—Halcyon's loft.

The shades are all pulled down, but the lights are on.

My heart hammers, and my breath quickens.

The outline of a dark, masculine figure moves behind the window.

Transfixed, I watch a little longer, letting my mind trek down curious alleys and avenues. What if Halcyon was never Roman's wife? What if Halcyon was Roman the whole time? It would make sense . . . he has unrestricted access to the studio and knows the names of all the paintings. Not to mention he gave me three of them without so much as asking for permission.

Oh my god.

It was so obvious.

It was right in front of me the entire time.

How could I not see it?

I was so focused on the fact that his wife's death coincided with Halcyon's abrupt departure from the art world that I wasn't thinking clearly.

Settling in on the park bench, I wait.

. . . and wait.

. . . and wait some more.

I wait until the sun goes down, turning the city into a neon nightscape.

I'm not sure how many hours have passed before the light inside the loft finally goes black. Rubbing my strained eyes, I blink and squint and refocus my attention on the building's entrance. Halcyon—whether it's Roman or someone else entirely—should be walking out any minute now.

The door swings open, and my stomach flips.

But it isn't him. It's an older woman with white-blonde dreads and so much beaded jewelry she jangles with each step.

A second later, the door opens again, only this time it's a couple of guys with long, shaggy hair. One has a skateboard. The other lights a cigarette. Both of them are far too thin to match the silhouette I saw in the window tonight. They say their goodbyes and head off in opposite directions.

I take my gaze off them for a moment, just to check the time on my phone. I've got a dozen missed calls and text messages—all of which are from Margaux. The messages are composed mostly of question marks and demands for me to call her.

I ignore them all.

"What are you doing here?" A familiar voice pulls me out of my daze and sends a start to my heart. Glancing up, I find Roman's imposing physique standing before me.

"It's not what it looks like," I say, before realizing it's absolutely what it looks like. Maybe I didn't come here on purpose, but I 100 percent stayed, watched, and waited like some crazy person. "I was in the area."

He clucks his tongue, glancing away.

"I walked around the city all afternoon . . . and when I realized where I was, I sat down to take a break . . . and then I saw the lights were on in your loft," I attempt to explain, but his expressions imply he's not buying any of it.

If I were him, I wouldn't either.

My word is shit.

"You're Halcyon." I change the subject. His steely gaze holds firm on mine. "You were him the whole time."

I don't suppose he ever owed me the truth. And he never technically lied. But in a way, I wasn't the only one keeping secrets.

"If you're trying to compare what you did with what I did, save your breath," he says.

Lifting my hand over my heart, I shake my head. "They're not even close. I would never. I just . . . there's a lot we don't know about each other."

He rolls his eyes. "To put it mildly."

"What all did Margaux tell you?" I ask, softening my question with a wince.

The space above his jawline divots. "I'm not having this conversation right now."

His attention scans past my shoulder, toward the street. I follow his gaze, expecting to find Antonio rolling up in his shiny onyx Escalade. Only it's a brunette in a Chevy Malibu. She gives him a wave. He gives her a nod. My stomach sinks. While he was never mine—and never supposed to be mine—my sister was right . . . he can order up another girl anytime he likes. Men like him don't stay heartbroken for long—or by choice.

"I'm sorry," I tell him as he walks to her car. "I know my words mean nothing right now, but please know that I'm sorry. I'm sorry I didn't tell you sooner. I'm sorry you found out the way you did. I'm sorry I agreed to help my sister. I wish I could take it all back. I wish we could've met like normal people meet."

I roll my eyes at myself. I sound like some pathetic sap rambling on at the end of some cheesy nineties romance movie, but this might be the only chance I get to have his ear. I'm sure the second he's gone, I'll think of a hundred other things I want to say to him. Meanwhile, he'll be deleting my number, I'm sure. Ready to move onward and upward and forget the entire last month of his life ever happened.

"I was going to tell you Friday," I add before he's gone forever. "That's why I didn't want to do the hotel thing . . ."

His eyes soften—or maybe it's wishful thinking on my end.

"Remember Monday? I asked when I could see you next," I remind him. "We decided on Friday. And when you called me and you kept asking if everything was okay . . . I knew you knew something was off. But I didn't want to say it over the phone. I wanted to tell you in person."

His lips flatten as he studies me.

"For what it's worth, Roman," I add, "it was real. It was real to me. Every second of it."

"Everything except your identity."

We linger in silence, and he glances toward the woman waiting in the car, who shoots him a quizzical look. She's parked in a no-parking zone with her hazards on. Another car careens past, blaring its horn.

Rising from the bench, I take the opportunity to share one more thing before he leaves.

"For the record, I loved getting to know you, loved spending time with you," I say. "And the last thing I ever wanted was for you to get hurt. I'll spend the rest of my life regretting that, wishing things could've been different for us."

He doesn't flinch, doesn't react, doesn't speak as his thousand-yard stare burns into me like hot coal.

"If you ever change your mind," I say, "or if you ever feel like talking, if you ever find it in you to look past the insanity of the situation and see if maybe we could try again . . ."

I let my words dwindle into nothing.

"Wow, um." My cheeks burn hot, and it isn't from the heat of the day this time. "Now that I'm saying that out loud, I realize how insane I sound."

He continues to glare, gifting me with a single slow blink.

"I'm sorry—I don't want to keep her waiting." I point to the girl in the Malibu. "She seems like she's anxious to get going."

"Right. She's my Uber driver." He breaks his quiet streak with a detail that gives me a raindrop-size speck of hope despite the fact that it shouldn't. I have no right to feel relieved at the fact that he's not running off with some mystery woman to spite me. "And your apology—at least I think that's what this is—is wasting that poor woman's valuable time." Clearing his throat, he rakes his hand along his jaw. "Not unlike all the ways you've wasted mine."

I deserve that.

"Right. I just . . . I wasn't expecting to see you tonight and . . ." I bite my tongue to stop from rambling. I could say a million other things to him right now, but the fact is, none of them would change a damn thing. There isn't a single sentence I could utter that would make him magically look at me the way he used to—like I meant something to him.

Those days, those tender, sweet moments, are officially gone.

Roman pinches the bridge of his nose, his shoulders falling as he exhales.

"Are you done?" He waves his hand in a circular motion. "With all of this? Did you get it all off your chest? Do you feel better now? Can I go?"

I cock my head as his words sting, though it's not like I don't deserve them. I guess deep down I hoped if we could talk face to face, he'd see how truly sorry I am and offer a microscopic sliver of grace.

I step backward, away from the direction of Roman and his waiting ride, and I offer a tight-lipped nod—a silent apology or white flag.

Turning on my heel, I walk home with a tightness in my chest, thankful for the dark blanket of sky to help disguise my tears and the unfazed New Yorkers who pay me no mind because they've seen crazier things than some random woman crying on the sidewalk.

CHAPTER THIRTY-FOUR

ROMAN

"Did you know about this?" I ask Theodora over the phone later that night. The girls are tucked into their beds, fast asleep, and I should be doing the same, but my mind is far too loud to let me so much as think about relaxing. While I'd love nothing more than to shut the book on this shit show of a day, I'm not quite there yet. "Did you know Margaux sent her twin sister on that date? Did you know I'd been seeing Sloane the entire time?"

"Roman, of course not." The horror in Theodora's voice tells me she's not lying. "I'm just as disgusted by this entire thing as you are. Not to mention, beyond disappointed in Margaux. She was one of my shining stars. I took her under my wing and sang her praises, and she turned around and lied to my face. There goes her promotion. I should have known there was something off about her. I always thought she was charming and social, maybe a tad bit on the narcissistic side. Usually I can see through that sort of thing but—"

"—wait, wait, wait. Back up. What did you say?"

"I said usually I can see through that sort of thing."

"No," I say. "Before that. You said something about a promotion."

"Right. She and Franklin are up for a new executive position we're adding." Theodora chuffs. "Needless to say, Franklin's a shoo-in now. And it's a shame. Margaux would've been a perfect vice president of Client Relations. She was looking at a huge raise, extra time off, a corner office . . . was just about to have HR write up the offer too. Such a shame."

"How long has Margaux known about this promotion?"

"We announced the position back in May, but we're not filling it until August. What are you getting at?"

"Margaux wanted that promotion . . . you wanted to set her up with your nephew . . ." Everything's piecing together in real time. "Sloane kept going on dates with me so I'd think things were going well with Margaux . . . so Margaux could stay in your good graces . . ."

Theodora sniffs. "That's almost diabolical. Who would do such a thing? I'm just . . . I can't wrap my head around any of it. I mean, I believe it. Clearly. I'm just having a hard time reconciling that Margaux would go to such lengths."

Theodora rambles on, dropping names of people I've never heard and waxing on about all the high-profile clients and seven-figure contracts Margaux has landed over the years.

"I'm calling her into my office first thing tomorrow and letting her go. This sort of thing is not rewarded, nor is it tolerated," Theodora says. "I'll have to make sure she receives a copy of the noncompete contract she signed when she first started working for me. She's prohibited from working for any of our direct competitors for the next five years. I hope this was all worth it. Anyway, I've got to go, darling. I'm going to take an Ambien and attempt to get a solid night's rest. Tomorrow's going to be one of *those* days."

"You can't fire Margaux," I say.

"And why not?" Theodora releases a sharp exhalation.

"I'm pretty sure she's pregnant."

Theodora is silent on the other end.

"I mean, I did think she was looking a little curvier these days . . . I suppose I . . . well . . . huh," she says before she stops mumbling altogether. "I never want to assume something like that about a woman. I certainly would never ask her about it. Do you know for sure?"

"No. But there was definitely something there . . ." I think of that day in her office, the way her lower belly was soft and round beneath her dress. I know from experience exactly what a pregnant woman looks like.

"Well, isn't this just lovely," she says with a sigh.

"How much were you pressuring Margaux to date me?" I ask. I would never dream of asking any of my employees to date someone I knew, let alone a close relative, but Theodora is a different breed.

"I probably emphasized it more than I should have . . ."

"Probably?"

"You know how I get about things. Once I get an idea in my head, I hold on to it for dear life."

"That you do."

"You know, I always looked at Margaux like she was the daughter I never had. I guess my intentions of fixing her up with someone were coming from a noble place. I thought she'd be the right person to bring you out of your shell, and I thought you'd be a stable person in her life. She was always talking about these disastrous dates and pseudorelationships . . . What did she call them? Oh, yes. Situationships. Anyway, my intentions were pure. I hope you know that."

"I do."

With a final exasperated sigh, Theodora adds, "Looks like I've got a bit of a mess to clean up now. Wish me luck."

We end our call, and I sink back into my chair, staring at the lifeless fireplace on the other side of the room as my mind replays the events of the day for the dozenth time. Earlier, when the real Margaux dropped that earth-shattering bombshell—not once did she show an ounce of accountability, humility, or apology. In fact, she made it a point to mention—on several occasions—that *Sloane* was supposed to be boring, that *Sloane* got carried away, that she warned *Sloane* not to play with fire . . .

But when I spoke to Sloane earlier tonight, she apologized profusely for hurting me, never once throwing Margaux under the bus when it's crystal clear to me now that Margaux is the one who put her up to switching roles in the first place.

Margaux masterminded the entire thing.

Margaux was the one who stood to benefit from the charade, not Sloane.

And Theodora's pressure certainly didn't help things.

There was a comment Margaux made . . . something about how she told Sloane to be "boring." Thinking back to our initial date, Sloane was definitely holding back. At the time, I chalked it up to first-date nerves. Now I know she was simply following orders.

And I was so convinced the key chain and apartments were signs that I was the one who pushed for a redo.

I was the one who took her to the loft.

I was the one who brought her to the symphony.

I kissed her first.

I'm the one who advanced this entire thing every step of the way, and while Sloane never once protested, I'm beginning to think she never had a choice in the matter because the promotion was still up in the air.

Margaux needed Sloane to carry on—but Sloane *wanted* to carry on.

Like Sloane said earlier tonight, all of it was real to her.

As much as I want to hate her, as much as I try to scrape every thought of her from my mind and scrub every moment we shared from my memory . . . I can't.

It was real to me too.

Still is.

CHAPTER THIRTY-FIVE

SLOANE

Opening the box of my freshly delivered pizza Friday night, I'm met with a mess of melted cheese, stringy and chunky and sticking to the top of the cardboard. The delivery guy must have dropped this at some point.

Sighing, I grab a fork from the drawer because I'm too hungry to wait another forty-five minutes for a replacement pizza. I salvage what toppings I can, scraping them off the underside of the lid and back onto the naked crust, and then I situate myself at the empty kitchen table.

With a topped-off glass of pinot as my only company and the ticking clock on the wall promising this day—no, this week—will be over in a few hours' time, I finish my literal hot mess of a dinner and manage to not check my phone a single time. Considering it's all I've done these past two days, it's an impressive feat.

Ever since things exploded in all of our faces Wednesday, I can't seem to shake myself out of this. And it isn't that I'm heartbroken and feeling sorry for myself—I mean, I am. I was falling for this man. Never mind that we'd only been in each other's lives for a month. We were connecting. We were on the same page. We were an accidentally perfect match.

But my thoughts are more of the guilt-ladened variety.

I hate that he's hurting, that he's embarrassed, that he feels like a fool.

He may or may not forgive and forget me, but I'll never forget my part in this. Hopefully maybe one day I'll manage to forgive myself too.

Taking my plate and glass to the sink, I shuffle to my room, slip an AirPod into my ear, and zone out with a lo-fi playlist. Lying at the foot of my bed, I fix my gaze on the three Halcyon paintings above my headboard and replay the last few weeks in my head like a movie. Although now it all feels like a dream where some details grow fuzzy and tainted with conflicting emotions.

I'd give anything to close my eyes and relive it just once more.

And I'd have come clean earlier. I'd have stood up to Margaux and saved Roman's heartbreak. At least, I like to think it would've happened that way.

If this week had gone according to plan, Roman would be here right now, and we'd be in the midst of the conversation we were meant to have, the way we were meant to have it.

Margaux sightings have been few and far between since our falling-out. While she hasn't mentioned it, I assume she was fired. When I got home from work Thursday, she was gone, but there was a cardboard box sitting on her bed filled with plants, picture frames, and random office miscellany.

She didn't come home last night, and when I texted her to make sure she was still alive today, she replied with a single word: Ethan.

I'm glad that they're spending so much time together, given the fact that they're about to become parents in the coming months.

Or she's simply trying to spend time away from me.

Knowing my sister, she likely blames me for everything. She's incapable of feeling guilt or admitting to being flawed in any way. While she mourns the loss of the promotion she so desperately felt she deserved, it'll only be a matter of time before she lands another job and sets her sights on conquering another corporate playing field.

Everything is a game to her.

And all is fair in love, war, and workplace politics—as long as she wins.

My music fades away as a text message chime plays. Scrambling for my phone, I pull up my messages—only it isn't Roman like I'd secretly hoped.

It's a group text from my boss to all the gallery employees.

BIG NEWS, she writes in all caps. I'm beyond thrilled to share with you all that Halcyon has selected OUR gallery for their exhibit! The event will be invitation-only, so I'd like for you each to contact your respective clients next week and personally extend an invitation so we can put together our guest list. The showcase will be next Friday, August 4th at seven PM. All are required to work that night. NO exceptions! It's going to be a mad dash to the finish line and a lot of long hours in the week ahead, but if anyone can pull this off, it's us.

A handful of coworkers write back with enthusiastic, ass-kissing replies, and while I should probably do the same, I'm too stunned to form a comprehendible sentence at the moment.

Out of all the galleries in the city, he chose *mine*?

Was it intentional?

Did he google me and find out where I work?

Or is it nothing more than a strange coincidence?

I'd ask him myself, but I'm quite certain I'm still the last person he wants to hear from.

While my mind fills with hopeful little reveries about some kind of movie-scene moment where the guy realizes he loves the girl after all and they run into each other's arms, I'm quickly reminded that "Halcyon" never attends their exhibits.

I don't imagine he'd start now.

CHAPTER
THIRTY-SIX

ROMAN

"So." Margaux—the real Margaux—is seated across from me, her blonde hair pressed into curls so shiny they rival the untouched silverware on the table. We're not here to eat, drink, or be merry. "So? What did you want to discuss?"

I reached out to Margaux yesterday, asking if she'd be available to meet Saturday morning, as I had some pressing questions I wanted to put to bed. Imagine my shock when she replied within seconds. I suppose she has nothing but time on her hands now. While Theodora decided not to promote Margaux on account of her dishonesty, she opted not to fire her either (on account of her suspected pregnancy). Regardless, Margaux resigned immediately.

I imagine her pride got the best of her.

Some people can't handle when those who once held them on a pedestal no longer sing their praises.

The more I thought about the dynamics between Margaux and Sloane, what each one had to gain (and lose), and the night-and-day differences between their apologies (or lack thereof, in Margaux's case), the more I wanted to confirm my suspicions.

A person can assume all they want, until they're blue in the face or the cows come home, but all of it's a self-serving waste of time without the full story.

Margaux bats her lashes and offers a disarming smile. I imagine this is what she does when she's particularly uncomfortable. She dials up her charms and graces in hopes of distracting people from her shortcomings.

Fortunately, I see through it.

She isn't the first narcissist I've encountered in my life, and I'm sure she won't be the last.

"I have to know . . . What made you send Sloane in your place that night?" I ask. "To the blind date?"

She swallows, looking sheepish for a flicker of a second before tilting her head and rolling her eyes.

"I was sick." Margaux straightens her shoulders. "I, um, thought I had food poisoning. Turns out I was just, um, pregnant. With twins."

Just as I suspected . . .

I refrain from reacting.

"And it was morning sickness—which, as it turns out, isn't restricted just to mornings," she continues. "Anyway, Theodora was so eager for us to finally meet and she was so excited and I didn't want to cancel. Sloane offered to go for me instead."

She chuckles, as if she's telling a humorous little story. And maybe to some it would even be considered cute, but I'm not here to be entertained.

"Sloane offered?" I ask. "As in it was her idea?"

"No," Margaux says. "I asked and she offered."

Big difference.

"I see," I say. "And you said you told her to be *boring*?"

"Exactly. I didn't want you to fall for her or anything. I told her not to be off putting but to be dull enough that you wouldn't be asking for a second date." Margaux toys with a shiny blonde curl before brushing it over her shoulder. "If she'd have listened to me . . . none of this would've happened."

She couldn't be more wrong.

Had *she* not sent Sloane in the first place, none of this would have happened. Subsequently, I wouldn't have semiwalked Sloane home. I wouldn't have seen her apartment building. Or that Halcyon key chain.

If it had been Margaux that evening, I would've walked away relieved that the night was over.

"So this is all Sloane's fault?" I ask, seeking clarity. "Is that what you're getting at?"

"I mean, yeah. Basically." Margaux checks her phone. "I'm sorry. Ever since I left Lucerne, my phone won't stop ringing. Everyone wants to know what happened. Not with work, but with you and everything. You know how people talk . . . one of my friends actually wants to write an article about it for *Cosmo*." She splays a manicured hand, tucking her pointed chin. "Don't worry, though, she won't use any real names."

The audacity of this woman to humblebrag about her friend using our situation as entertainment fodder is enough to send me packing, but I keep my feet planted on the floor and finish what I came here to do.

"Is it true you were up for a promotion?" I ask next.

She considers her answer for a second. "Yes."

"Did you think that by dating me, you'd improve your odds of getting it?"

She wrinkles her nose. "You know how Theodora is."

"I know exactly how she is," I say. "Her family is everything to her. I'm the closest thing she has to a son. You thought that if you disappointed her, you'd jeopardize that position."

Theodora spent nearly an hour on the phone with me the day Margaux resigned. After my aunt realized the scope of what she'd done—pressuring her employee to date me while leaving the new position unfilled—she was horrified at herself. She must have uttered her apologies at least a dozen times if not more. She felt awful for pushing

Margaux to date me, and she felt even worse that I was used like a game piece for Margaux's corporate strategy.

"I didn't think going on one date with you was going to hurt anything." Margaux gives a casual shrug. "And Theodora was so sure we were going to hit it off, that we were quote-unquote perfect for each other . . . so naturally, I was curious. Who knows. Maybe we would have been? Clearly you have a type."

I resist the urge to insult her with the truth.

I do have a type—and she's light-years away from remotely being in the same orbit as it.

"Did you ask Sloane to keep spending time with me?" I change the subject, keeping this on track so as to keep this entire exchange as short as humanly possible. I don't want to be around this woman a second longer than necessary.

"Do you even have to ask that? I think you pretty much solved the crime, Inspector Gadget." She laughs at her lame joke.

I don't.

"Oh, come on. Are you always this uptight?" She waves her hand across the table at me.

"Are you always this insufferable?" I ask.

Her enchanted smile vanishes, replaced with some semblance of a frown. "Excuse me?"

"You said you warned Sloane not to play with fire." I ignore her question because I said what I said and she heard me crystal clear, even if she pretends otherwise. "What did you mean by that?"

For the last few days, I've been trying to make sense of that . . . If Sloane was dating me at Margaux's insistence, why would Margaux warn her about anything?

"Because she was falling for you," she says. "She felt bad about the whole thing. And obviously you guys couldn't keep your hands in your pants because she slept with you." Margaux rolls her eyes, and I don't appreciate her insinuating it was her sister's fault that we slept together, as if she lured me in with her siren song and seduced me.

I slept with her because I wanted to.

And because she wanted to.

Because every minute I spent with her only made me want more of her, *all* of her.

Looking back, maybe the distance in Sloane's voice over the phone earlier in the week wasn't because I compartmentalized after sex . . . maybe it was because she realized *this* was becoming real, and she needed to tell me the truth before we took it even further.

That's why she asked when she could see me again.

That's why she wanted me to come to her house for a quiet night in—she even said so Wednesday night outside the loft.

"Oh my god." I run my hand along my jaw. "This all makes sense now."

"Oh, okay, good for you?" she says, phrasing it like a question. "Did you have any further questions, Counselor, or am I free to leave the witness stand?"

She's already gathering her keys and phone and the enormous Jackie O.-style sunglasses she plunked on the table the second she sat down a few minutes ago.

I wave my hand, silent permission for her to leave.

Slipping her designer-logo-encrusted bag over her shoulder, she turns back to me.

"You should consider yourself lucky," Margaux says.

"And why is that?"

"You were never supposed to like her. It was never supposed to be more than one date," she says. "If there's anything I know, if you screw with destiny, destiny screws right back."

Placing a hand over her small baby bump, she raps her long fingernails.

I'm not sure if what she just said is profound or poignant or neither at all, but I don't think she's completely wrong.

"As soon as you took her to that painting place, that studio or whatever it was," she says, "that's where you went wrong. That sort of thing wouldn't have impressed me one bit. In fact, it probably would've been boring. But my sister's a sucker for art. She came home all starry eyed, talking about these pictures you gave her and how they were literally priceless and how it was the nicest thing anyone had ever done for her." Margaux sighs. "Anyway, art is her thing, you know? She's an art dealer, director, something. I don't know her exact title, I only know that when she's talking about work, sometimes it sounds like she's speaking another language."

"Wait, what? Where does she work?"

"Oh, right. She probably never told you what she did for a living since you thought she was me. Yeah, she's the director of the Westfeldt Gallery."

"Westfeldt? In SoHo?" I ask.

"I believe that's the one."

Westfeldt Gallery is hosting the Halcyon exhibit this Friday . . .

I chose them because the gallery owner, Brenna, made me an offer I couldn't refuse—that and that gallery was always Emma's favorite. After she passed, I couldn't set foot in there, so I had my associate handle any and all purchases brokered from there.

"If she didn't tell you where she really worked, then she probably didn't tell you that you almost got her fired once." Margaux points a long pink nail my way.

"What?"

"Yeah. Something about a painting that you wanted to buy, but she'd already sold it and you demanded she get fired or something . . ."

Holy shit.

You or Someone like You.

It was the only painting Emma had done under the Halcyon name. She was always into printmaking—that was her preferred medium. That was her wheelhouse. She'd tried her hand at painting over the years— oil, watercolor, and acrylic, but things never turned out the way she wanted them to. They always looked better in her head, she'd say. So one day I told her to close her eyes. I placed a paintbrush in her hand and moved the easel in front of her.

"Paint with your eyes closed," I told her.

And she did.

The piece definitely stood out in its own special way. The shapes and colors played with your mind if you stared at it a little too long. Nothing about it made sense, and yet it was perfect at the same time.

When I asked her what the name meant, she told me she wasn't sure—it just felt right.

We included it in the next Halcyon exhibit, not expecting it to go for much given that it was a little "off brand" compared to the rest of my body of work. Only we couldn't have been more wrong. People were so thrilled by this "experimental" piece that it became the talk of the proverbial town. When a bidding war ensued, Emma was floored to find out someone offered $1.2 million to buy it. But it wasn't the money she cared about—it was the fact that people loved her painting.

The week after she died, the sale fell through, so I had my art buyer arrange to purchase it for the same price. It was a matter of principle and respect for Emma's memory. Only when the day came to finalize the sale, we were told it had already been sold to someone else. They claimed after the initial sale fell through, one of their brokers offered it to the second-highest bidder without talking to anyone first. The contract had been signed. The money had been wired. The painting was already in transit.

I wasn't my best self at the time, and while I don't remember exactly what I said, I imagine it wasn't pretty. And I have no doubt that I tried to have someone fired.

"Anyway, I should get going. Sloane told me to pack my things and move the other day," she says. "And I can't wait to see the look on her face when I call her bluff."

Slipping her giant glasses over her nose, she bounces on the ball of her foot like she's waiting for a formal send-off.

Sloane told *Margaux* to move out?

She already lost me—now she's willing to lose her sister too?

"It was kind of her," I say, rising until I'm almost towering over her. "Doing what she did for you. Did you ever stop to think about that?" I don't let her answer. "All you've done today, all you did on Wednesday, was throw her under the bus. You blamed her for *everything*. You washed your hands of all responsibility when you were the one driving *all* of this every mile of the way."

She swallows, peering up at me with big blue eyes and comically thick lashes that serve to make her look more like a Park Avenue blow-up doll than the Upper West Side socialite air she's going for.

"Your sister," I say, "apologized to me so much I lost count. And not once did she place an ounce of blame on you—though I can't, for the life of me, figure out why. After talking to you this morning, I think I've found my answer."

Margaux sniffs. "What?"

"She's not an asshole."

With that, I leave Margaux in the middle of the café, hit the sidewalk, and never look back.

I've got a big week ahead of me, and I want this Halcyon exhibit to be the best one yet—and the first one I've ever actually attended.

CHAPTER THIRTY-SEVEN

SLOANE

"Have you seen the paintings? My goodness, I could just die and go straight to heaven." Brenna clasps her hands in front of her chest before gathering a long breath. "Now if only my Xanax could kick in."

Brenna, in all her attention-loving glory, ironically loathes public speaking. Anytime she has to do her two-minute welcome speech at the start of each exhibit, she turns beet red and breathless by the end of it. Lately it hasn't been as bad—now I know why.

"Did you see Prince al-Moussa flew in?" she asks.

"I heard he was coming, yes."

"He isn't just coming, he's here." She smooths her blown-out scarlet locks behind her ears and checks her reflection in a nearby wall mirror. "Anyway, I'm going to go out and mingle a bit before everything starts. Please make sure you've seen each piece and familiarize yourself with titles and everything. We haven't priced anything, but we're not taking less than seven figures on anything tonight."

Brenna strides out of the break room, her red-bottomed heels clicking with each step, and I steal a glimpse in the mirror myself. Smoothing a flyaway, I make sure my hair is in place, and then I tap the pad of my ring finger along my lips, blurring any uneven lipstick into place.

It doesn't matter how many times I assure myself Roman isn't coming tonight; I can't ignore the atomic-particle-size voice that assures me he is.

If only I could tell the difference between a gut feeling and wishful thinking . . .

Drawing back my shoulders, I lift my chin and hit the floor to check out the Halcyon pieces. While all my cohorts were fawning over them earlier today, I avoided them like the plague. I'd already seen them anyway, and I didn't want to stir up any emotions in front of anyone.

But I can't avoid them forever, and our exhibition starts in ten minutes.

The buzz of droning conversation fills the space as people arrive. I scan the room, holding my breath in case I spot those familiar, heavy coffee-colored eyes that used to pin me into place with a single glance.

But he isn't here.

A young man in a caterer's uniform passes by with a tray of champagne. He stops to offer me one, likely assuming I'm a guest and not an employee. Reaching for a flute, I toss the bubbly liquid back in one swallow and place the empty glass back on the tray.

He blinks, lingering as if to question what he just saw, and then he goes on his way.

Taking a deep breath, I run my hands along my thighs and head to the first row of paintings, all of which are hauntingly familiar. Eying the neon stoplight painted on newspaper, I lean in to read the title.

Lost after Midnight

My chest is tight—heavy with sadness, yet filled with delight at the same time.

That's the name *I* gave that picture.

He kept it.

Surely if he hated me, he would've replaced it with something else?

"Oh, look at this one," one of our patrons says, pointing to *Sour Apple*. "It makes me feel . . . a certain way. Dirty, gritty, alive. I want this in my bathroom, like, yesterday."

"Good luck. You and I both know you can't afford anything in here. You could hardly afford your half of the Uber ride tonight," his counterpart says under his breath.

"A man can dream," the first guy says before they move on to the next piece.

"Screw dreaming. I just want to know who Halcyon is," the friend says. "I'm here to do some scouting. Last I heard, it's some Greek heiress. Though some people think Halcyon's the pseudonym of this Dutch glassblower who was tripping on acid one night and accidentally realized he could paint."

I chuckle. I'm not sure how they got on the guest list for tonight, but I admire that kind of dedication to a beloved artist. If Roman were here, I imagine he'd get a kick out of these stories.

Either way, his secret is safe with me.

I'd take it to the grave if I had to.

"Sloane, there you are." Brenna sneaks up from behind me. "I'm about to make my welcome speech, and I need you all to line up beside me so everyone knows who you are."

I meet her back at the podium as someone places a mic pack on her. This is the only part of our exhibits I dread—being lined up and named off like the Von Trapp children. I know Brenna thinks it makes it easier for our guests to find and identify help throughout the evening, but I find it a little . . . campy.

Unnecessary.

Cringeworthy, even.

Besides, we're wearing shiny gold name tags that all but give off Bat-Signals under all this bright light.

Five minutes later, Brenna's welcome speech is done, and we've been instructed to "disperse and converse."

I scan the room once more, secretly searching for a man who definitely isn't here.

My heart sinks a little lower than it was before.

"Rupert," I say when I recognize the petite silver-haired fox in the kelly-green blazer. "So glad you could make it."

"Sloane, love." He leans in, kissing the air beside both of my cheeks. "Did you hear the bad news?"

"What bad news?"

My stomach drops.

The disappointed look on Rupert's face morphs into a contagious grin as he wags his hand. "I'm on a budget tonight. My accountant told me this week that my art spending is getting a little . . . overzealous."

I exhale, relieved there wasn't any actual, relevant bad news related to tonight's event.

"That's the most tragic thing I've heard all day," I say, feigning compassion. Winking, I add, "You should check out *Sour Apple*. It'd look divine in your Midtown office. I can picture it over your desk. All that natural light would really make it pop."

"Would it, now?" He arches a brow, sips his champagne, and adds, "Just point me in the right direction . . ."

I wave him off to the southwest corner of the gallery and prepare to "disperse and converse" once again, only something catches my eye.

In the center of the room, all by itself, and bigger than any other piece in this room, is a Halcyon painting I've never seen before. Standing at least eight feet tall and six feet wide, it appears to be a simple candle against a black background at first glance. But upon closer inspection, the body of the candle is made of some kind of folded paper covered in typed words. Squinting, I attempt to read the writing. It takes a minute or so for me to deduce that he used some sort of cut-up and folded menus for the base of the candle.

But not just any menus.

The restaurant menu from our first date.

One from the coffee shop we went to that lazy afternoon.

Another is from the cocktail bar at the symphony.

There are receipts, too, mixed in for variation. Receipts from all these places.

Searching for the placard, I stifle a gasp when I read the name of the piece: **YOU OR NO ONE LIKE YOU**. In a smaller italicized font are the words *Display only, not for sale.*

I gasp, lifting my hand to my mouth.

Thick tears threaten my vision, but I blink them away.

Now is not the time.

And I have no business assuming any of this means anything. Artists are strange beasts. They have their methods and their madness, and it's not our job to understand it, only to appreciate it.

Besides, context—much like beauty—is in the eye of the beholder.

This could be the most personal painting I've ever seen, but it doesn't mean Roman feels the same way. Maybe he's simply capitalizing on his heartbreak.

He'd have every right.

"Something about this one." A man's voice sends a shock to my heart. Turning, I'm met with a tall, broad-shouldered Adonis with a navy suit and a devil-may-care smirk on his handsome face. "I don't know what it is, but I like it. Makes me feel . . . I don't know. A certain kind of way."

Roman.

My heart beats so fast I feel light headed for a moment, but I quickly reclaim my composure.

"Me too." I play along. "It's inspiring. I'd like to imagine the candle in the dark is symbolic of the hope the artist must have been feeling when he painted this."

"What do you think that means?" Roman points at the title placard. "*You or No One like You.*"

"I'm sure whatever it means, it's deeply personal to the artist and the person he had in mind when he painted this," I say.

"Roman Bellisario." He extends his hand.

Cocking my head, I shoot him a sideways glance before sliding my palm against his.

"Sloane Sheridan." A thrill runs down my spine before settling in the base of my stomach.

Safe to say he still has that Midas touch.

"It's lovely to meet you, Sloane." He keeps my hand in his for a moment longer than expected. "You know, I'm pretty sure I've met your sister. Margaux, is it?"

"Yes." I continue to play along, not sure where he's going with this. "That would be her."

"Have to say, I'm a bit worried for her."

Brows knitting, I ask, "Why?"

My sister and I are still not on speaking terms, and just a few days ago, she packed up her room and informed me she'd be out by the end of the week. Her things were still there by the time I left for work today, but tonight I'm fully anticipating coming home to a truly empty home for the first time in my life.

"She seems to think the world revolves around her," he says. "I worry if no one ever tells her, she'll go the rest of her life believing that's true."

Our gazes hold, and there's a softness to his that wasn't there last time.

A knowingness.

"You're a good sister," he says. "And an even better person. You didn't deserve what she put you through."

"Neither did you."

"I'd like to take you out sometime, Sloane Sheridan." He says my full name with a playful half smile on his lips.

"I'd like that. Roman, was it? I'm sorry, I'm terrible with names . . ."

"Roman, yes." His eyes glint with amusement.

"Sloane?" Brenna's voice cuts like a knife through the soft music and dull timbre of conversation. We lock eyes from across the room, and she waves me over. "Sloane, I need you over here, please."

"I have to go," I tell him.

He says nothing, simply pins me into place with that heavy gaze of his. Reaching into his pocket, he retrieves a small paper folder, no bigger than a credit card. Opening the folder, I'm met with a hotel logo and a room key.

"Room 1217," he says. "See you tonight."

With that, he swipes a champagne flute from a nearby catering tray and disappears into a crowd of his biggest fans.

I don't see him the rest of the evening, though I don't stop searching for him until the final guest leaves shortly after ten. I'd hoped he'd stay to eavesdrop a bit and relish in all the sung praise, but then again, that's never been Halcyon's style.

"Some of us are going to grab some drinks after this . . . You want to come?" Annette, one of our brokers, asks when we're locking up after the exhibit. "I think we're meeting at Hillsborough Tavern."

"Actually, I have plans. Thanks, though," I say, fighting like hell to keep a dopey grin from forming on my face. If they only knew I was on my way to spend the night with *the* Halcyon, they'd die. They would cease to exist.

I'm not quite certain how I'm still existing myself.

I'm pretty sure I've been floating on air since the moment I saw Roman's face tonight.

Waiting out front, I pull up my phone to order an Uber—just in time to spot a familiar black Escalade pulling up to the curb. The passenger-side window rolls down, and the driver leans over.

"Antonio," I say, approaching the car. "What are you doing here?"

"A little birdie told me the exhibit just got over, and I happened to be in the area," he says with a wink that tells me Roman arranged for all of this, down to the last detail of this evening.

"You know where we're going?" I ask when I climb in. Only I don't take the back seat this time. I sit beside him, up front. I'm not some princess needing to be driven around the city, and he doesn't work for me.

"What kinda question is that?" he asks, pretending to be offended.

"I'm Sloane, by the way."

"I know who you are," he says, before pointing. "I know all about you *and* your sister. I had one of those, you know."

"A sister?"

"A narcissist," he says.

"Margaux's not a . . ." My voice fades as I consider—for the first time ever—that there's an explanation for my sister and all her *ways.*

"They're sneaky little devils. Make you think everything wonderful is their idea and everything awful is your fault," he says. "I was married to one once. Worst nine years of my life. Thought I was going crazy by the end of it. But that's what they do. They get in your head and make you question everything. Anyway, sorry. I know it's your sister we're talking about. Don't want to offend you or anything. Just think it's shitty what she roped you into, that's all. Family shouldn't do that to family."

"I agree," I say. "Which is why I plan on setting some boundaries . . . eventually . . . we're not exactly on speaking terms right now."

"I heard."

"Yeah?" I'm not sure where he could have possibly heard that.

"Roman met up with your sister last Saturday."

"What?" I'm surprised, though I'm not surprised she didn't mention it to me. She'd have to break her silent treatment to do that, and she's not about to lose that war.

"He said ten minutes of talking to her and he knew all he needed to know." Antonio shrugs. "And now here you are."

Gazing out the clear glass, into a night-speckled Manhattan that looks like it belongs in a Halcyon painting, I release a dreamy exhalation. While exhaustion sinks into my bones, I know the odds of getting any real rest tonight are slim to none—not that I'm complaining.

Rupert's words from several weeks back pop into my mind: *Everything always works out. It always, always does. Even when we don't believe that it can. It just does. Life is funny that way.*

Antonio drops me off outside a chic hotel with a black awning, a tuxedo-wearing doorman, and a red carpet that stretches out to the sidewalk. Across the street is Central Park, and all along the facade of the building are Juliet balconies.

This is the hotel he wanted to take me to last weekend.

Heading to the door, I greet the doorman with a smile.

"Welcome to the Thornwood," he says as he opens the door for me. "Enjoy your evening."

"I plan to," I tell him as I make my way inside. I don't stop until I reach the elevator, and while it carries me to the twelfth floor, I swear I must be flying. Every part of me is lighter than the sweetly scented air I breathe.

I follow the signs to room 1217, swipe the key on the lock, and make my way in, where a small table for two is set up by the open balcony.

Roman steps into view, looking every bit as delicious as he did at the exhibit several hours ago. Same silky chocolate hair, shoulder-hugging navy suit coat, and mischievous smirk. Same glint in his eye, one that indicates he's seconds from devouring me.

"Thought you might be hungry," he says, motioning toward the covered dishes on the table. Between them is a flickering candle and a small arrangement with three red roses—a nod to our first date.

"I am," I say. "But it's a different kind of hunger."

The hunger of loss and uncertainty.

The hunger of second chances and redemption.

The hunger of desperately wanting to be with someone you never thought you'd see again.

Closing the distance between us, he places one hand on my hip and pulls me against him. The other lifts to my chin, tipping my face until our lips are in perfect alignment. My heart beats hard in my ears, and I drag his musky scent into my lungs until I'm drunk with anticipation.

Lowering his mouth onto mine, he gifts me a punishing kiss—one that indicates he's not going anywhere ever again.

"You were always meant for me, Sloane," he whispers, his lips grazing mine.

I kiss him hard, hooking my arms around his neck and holding on with everything I have.

"It's you," he says. "It's you or it's no one."

CHAPTER THIRTY-EIGHT

ROMAN

I watch her sleep—and not in any sort of creepy way, though I suppose the act of watching someone when they're passed out is inherently disconcerting. There's no romantic way to paint this picture, but I settle against my pillow and watch the sweet faces Sloane makes when she's dreaming. The twitch of her mouth. The subtle flutter of her eyelashes as she stirs. She even lets out a little chuckle. Whatever dream she's having, it must be a good one.

Sloane rolls to her back, and the sheet falls below her bare breasts. I pull it up. Not because I don't appreciate the view—I love the view—but because I don't want the chilled air-conditioned hotel air to wake her from her peaceful slumber.

The past week has been trying, telling, and a million other things for each of us.

But now we're here . . .

"Are you . . . watching me?" Sloane rustles, her eyes blinking slowly.

Busted.

"I can't sleep," I say.

She frowns, reaching to pull me closer. Settling under my arm, she rests her cheek on my chest.

"What's wrong?" she asks.

"Nothing." I kiss the top of her head, breathing in a waft of her vanilla shampoo. "I just want to enjoy this moment. Not ready for it to be over."

Sloane lifts her head, gazing at the alarm clock on my side table.

"It's four in the morning," she says as if I wasn't aware.

The second she showed up, I wasted no time making up for the week and a half we lost, and when it was over, we took a brief break, feasting on five-star room service food, before going back for round two.

"I love the way I feel when I'm with you," I say. It hasn't always been easy for me to talk about my feelings. I'm like an old book with pages glued together by time. But for some reason, whenever I'm with Sloane, it's as if someone is peeling apart those pages and giving them air for the first time in ages. "I wish I could bottle it up and take it with me everywhere."

Emma was the first person I ever felt I could be myself around. I was raised by a suit-and-tie self-made man who expected me to follow in his footsteps, a man who laughed at my artistic endeavors and interests, a man who wouldn't know a Monet from a Chagall if his life depended on it—fortunately for him it never did.

Emma spoke my language.

And now, so does Sloane.

I'm not sure what a man like me did to deserve to strike gold twice in one lifetime, but I'm not one to look a gift horse in the mouth.

The more I think about the way Sloane came into my life, the way she left an impression on me, the way she cracked my facade like it was nothing . . . the more I'm convinced this entire thing was orchestrated by Emma.

I would never admit that. Not out loud, anyway.

I'm self-aware enough to know that it sounds insane.

But it's a feeling.

A knowing.

And that's what Emma promised all those years ago . . . she'd give me a sign, and I'd simply know it was her.

"You should get some rest," Sloane says, adjusting her arm across my chest. She doesn't mention the girls, but we both know it's Saturday. I promised Harper I'd be home no later than eight, and Theodora will be rolling in around nine.

Someday soon, I'll have her meet the girls.

I'll merge my two worlds.

I have no doubt they'll love Sloane—I just have to make sure the time is right.

Until then, I'll soak up these early-morning moments with every waking breath.

"Go back to sleep," I tell her. "Don't worry about me."

I could easily sneak a nap in while Theodora takes the girls out, but the sheer adrenaline of last night's sold-out exhibit, combined with the fact that Sloane is back in my arms where she belongs, brings me far too much excitement to allow for that.

"If you stay up, I'm staying up," she says, peering up at me. A slow smile spreads across her lips—lips that are swollen from all the things I've done to them the past several hours.

All the things she's done to me too . . .

I'd suggest we watch the sunrise together, but there are far too many buildings in the way. We could order room service breakfast, dine on the balcony, and watch the city wake up. What I wouldn't give for a million more mornings just like this. Simple and serene.

"Close your eyes," I tell her. I won't have her sacrificing rest on my account. "I'll be here when you wake up."

CHAPTER THIRTY-NINE

SLOANE

"Oh," I say when I walk in the door to my apartment. "Hi."

Margaux is seated at the kitchen table, her hair sporting fresh curls and her eyes looking particularly restful, considering recent events.

A stack of plastic totes is shoved against one of the walls, containing what's left of her belongings.

"Hi," she says. "I texted you . . ."

My phone died. I was planning on coming straight home after work last night, so I didn't leave with a full charge.

"Do you have a minute?" She slides the chair out beside her and gifts me a hopeful stare.

"Yeah, of course." I take a seat, placing my bag on the table and facing her.

"I just want to start out by saying I hate when we fight," she says. "And I hate not talking to you."

I begin to remind her she's the one who went radio silent on me, then think better of it. I get the sense she's about to apologize . . . maybe?

"So I'm moving into that apartment," she says, eyeing the totes across the room.

"I gathered that."

"I put an envelope on your nightstand with my half of the next three months' rent," she says. I'd almost forgotten our lease is up in three months.

"Really?" I ask. "You're having babies, and weren't you fired?"

She lifts a finger. "I wasn't fired. I resigned."

I lift a brow. "Oh, okay."

"Theodora and I had a long talk. She apologized for pressuring me to date her nephew. She said she didn't realize I was equating that with getting that promotion," Margaux says, adding, "But then she went on to say she was very disappointed that I wasn't honest with her. She said she always saw me as the daughter she never had, that she only wanted the best for me. She said she wasn't going to fire me, but the next thing I knew, I was telling her I was resigning effective immediately." Margaux rolls her eyes. "This is going to sound silly, maybe, but it was the way she looked at me. It wasn't the same. I don't think it'll ever be the same again. And I didn't want to show up at the office every day and have her look at me. I didn't want that daily reminder of failure."

"Sweets, you didn't fail." I reach my hand across the table, covering hers.

"I messed up." She swipes a rare tear from her cheek. "I fumbled this whole thing."

"Hindsight is twenty-twenty."

"I get so focused, so obsessed sometimes, and it gives me this tunnel vision. It brings out the worst in me," she says. "I don't want to be that person anymore."

Watching my sister soften and fold is like watching a fiery comet fade into the night sky. Margaux isn't perfect, not by any stretch, but I'd hate for her to lose her light.

"When Ethan's mom looks at me," she continues, "there's so much love, so much hope, so much sweetness. And when I see how excited she is about the babies, about being a grandmother, it made me realize that I've been focused on the wrong things all this time."

"There's nothing wrong with being ambitious."

"There is if it costs you everything," she says. "I don't know how many relationships I threw away because their schedule didn't mesh with my work schedule, or my drive intimidated them, or they weren't on my level professionally. Perfectly good guys. Men who were crazy about me. Men who brought out better sides of me. And I threw them all away because they didn't fit into my perfect little box."

"I love that you're realizing this now and not when it's too late."

"Ethan," she says, her lower lip trembling. I brace myself for bad news. "Ethan is wild about me, and I don't know why."

"Wait, what? I thought you always said he was a playboy? That he refused to settle down?"

She shakes her head. "It was me. I was the one who refused to settle down. Ethan wanted more, he wanted all of me. And in this messed-up way, I saw that as a red flag. I mean, who in their right mind would want *me*? There's got to be something wrong with him. At least that's what I told myself."

She swipes at another tear.

"And I couldn't be more wrong," she says. "He's pretty much perfect. And his mom. She's the icing on the cake. I don't deserve them." Margaux's hand rests on her belly. "But they make me want to be a better person. The babies deserve the rest of me, not the scraps of me they'd get outside of my nine-to-five."

"I have no doubt you'll make that happen," I say. "You've always done anything you've ever set your mind to."

"Right." She offers a bittersweet smile. "That's the plan, anyway. Ethan and I are moving in together, and I'm going to spend the next few months reading every baby book I can get my hands on, going to therapy, and trying to figure out how to be someone who doesn't suck."

"For the record, you've done some sucky things, but you don't suck."

"You've always been kind to me, even when I didn't deserve it. I just want you to know that I'm sorry for all the trouble I've caused you. I'm sorry things didn't work out with you and Roman."

Sitting straight, I say, "Actually, on the contrary. I was with him last night."

Margaux cocks her head. "Wait, what?"

"Apparently the two of you met last weekend? Whatever you said made him see things differently, I guess?" I still don't quite know the full context of their conversation. All I know is what Antonio shared, which wasn't much. I'm sure Roman would fill me in if I asked, but we were a little too . . . busy . . . last night.

"Really." She sits back, staring off as if she's trying to remember what was said. "Well, that's awesome . . . I have no idea what I said, but I'm glad I said the right things for a change."

"He wants me to meet his daughters," I say. "Not soon, but soon-ish. Maybe in the coming month? I have no idea how that's going to go . . ."

I imagine if it doesn't go well, that could complicate things.

His girls are his entire world.

"They're going to love you," Margaux says, her voice warm as a smile claims her mouth. "I mean, how could they not? You're literally one of the nicest people in the world—and you know I rarely give compliments."

"Thanks." I chuckle.

"No, really. I mean that. Every word of it. They're going to love you," she says. "Remember when you told me everything always works out? I'm paraphrasing, but you told me that last month."

I nod. "I remember."

"Well, it's happening," she says. "It's happening right now. Everything is working out for both of us in their own ways."

"Yeah, you're right."

"I'd be lying if I said I wasn't terrified." She glances at her totes.

"I'd be worried if you weren't."

I never imagined in all my life that a single summer would send us on separate trajectories—though I suppose it was only a matter of time.

We can't live the next twenty-seven years of our lives the way we've lived the past twenty-seven of them.

"It's going to be weird," she says, "not coming home to you and your weird take-out cravings or listening to you ramble on about artists or having someone to vent about my day to."

"It's going to be good for you, this change," I say. The apartment has been eerily quiet the past week and a half as Margaux avoided me like the plague, and now that we're in a better place, I'm realizing just how much I'm going to miss her.

This change is going to be good for both of us, I know it.

And who knows, maybe it'll even bring us closer.

"Do you need help?" I point to the totes.

"Ethan's coming by in a little bit with one of his friends," she says. "He rented a truck, and they're going to load up my bedroom furniture."

"Wow," I say.

"What?"

"With Ethan's mom being so generous . . . I just figured she'd shell out for movers or something," I say before lifting an apologetic palm. "That's what I get for being presumptive."

"She's generous all right," Margaux says. "But Ethan's stubbornly independent. He likes to take charge and do everything himself."

"Well, well, well." I arch a brow. "That's going to be an interesting little dynamic for you."

She chuckles. "To say the least."

"That and your children are going to be a couple of control freaks," I say. "You realize that, don't you? It's in their DNA."

Margaux tosses her head back, laughing. "I don't even want to think about that. I'm still wrapping my head around the fact that I'm going to be a mom. It still doesn't feel real."

She rubs her palm against her belly.

"That sweater is clinging to your stomach within an inch of its life. It's practically see through," I say. "Let me know when you want to go maternity-clothes shopping . . ."

My sister rolls her eyes. "Yeah, I guess I should do that soon, huh."

Her phone vibrates on the table, a text filling her screen.

"They're here," she says, effectively putting a period on the end of this conversation.

Rising from our chairs, we hug.

I breathe in her Chanel perfume and the faint scent of hair spray and fabric softener, and she buries her face into my shoulder.

"I'm going to miss you," she says.

"You act like we're not going to be living in the same city anymore."

Ethan buzzes below, and Margaux exhales.

"I should let him in," she says.

"Yeah. You should." Everything's happening so fast, but I keep a brave face, knowing this is for the best. I imagine I'll shed some tears when she's gone, when her room is an empty echo chamber of Manhattan-size-bedroom proportions.

But just as Rupert once said, *Everything always works out. It always, always does. Even when we don't believe that it can. It just does. Life is funny that way.*

EPILOGUE
ROMAN

Three Years Later . . .

"Dad, I'm hungry." Marabel taps my shoulder. "You said we could get something after we got through security."

JFK Airport is crammed full of Thanksgiving travelers, a chaotic sea of unfamiliar faces, coffee, and luggage. Overhead speakers play gate changes and announcements every other minute, but it's so loud in here they all sound like garbled word salads. Thank goodness for texts, or we wouldn't have learned that our flight was delayed forty-five minutes. Nothing we can do about it, but at least it'll give us a little time to eat and relax before we cram onto an economy-size jet en route to Cincinnati.

"I'll take her," my wife says. She adjusts baby Eames on her hip. "Adeline, you want to come with us?"

Adeline glances up from some Disney show on her iPad. "Yeah, I'm starving. You guys rushed us out the door this morning, so I didn't get to eat."

Sloane tilts her head, giving her a stern but knowing look.

"Next time wake up when your alarm goes off," I tell her.

"You want to take the big guy?" Sloane hands Eames to me, along with his diaper bag. "You hungry? Want me to grab you something?"

"Yeah," I say. "Just surprise me. You know what I like."

Sloane smiles. "Of course."

I watch them walk off, hand in hand—three-fifths of the Bellisario family. Now it's just the two of us guys—a rare occurrence these days. It's crazy to think of how much things have changed in the three years since Sloane came into my life.

Sometimes it feels like a lifetime ago; other times it feels like I blinked and everything happened in an instant. From dating, to having Sloane meet the girls, to eventually moving Sloane in with us, then proposing to Sloane, marrying her by the sea in Marseille—with the girls and my mother by our side. Then came baby Eames—his name being a nod to Emma, who was clearly the architect behind the scenes of all this. I'm convinced none of this would have happened if it weren't for her "signs."

A year ago, we officially opened the Bellisario Gallery. I sold off my father's company, and Sloane quit her job, and between the two of us, the place has been a smashing success so far. It doesn't hurt that we managed to snag the exclusive Halcyon contract . . .

Either way, we're both living the dream in every way imaginable.

And at the end of the day, life is too short to spend it doing things you don't love with people you don't love.

Some days all this feels too good to be true, and I'm certain a rug will be pulled out from under me at any moment, but I try not to get too caught up in those thoughts. Sloane and the kids have a way of reminding me to focus on the present, and not the unpredictable, ever-changing future.

Life is fleeting.

And precious.

Sloane taught me this trick—if I'm ever feeling anxious about the future, stop and pretend like I've just traveled back in time with the sole purpose of living this day all over again. It forces me to stop and view my current situation as if I've been given the onetime gift of being able to reexperience or relive a good memory. It's a strange little exercise, but I find it never fails to bring me back to the present moment.

Taking out my phone, I tap the camera icon and pull up some photos for Eames. He's only ten months old, but he loves seeing his reflection in the screen and swiping through the various images of his favorite people. He squeals and claps when we get to one of him with his sisters at the Central Park Zoo last month.

"You have a beautiful little family," an older woman sitting across from me says with a wistful look in her eye. "I'd give anything to go back in time, relive the days when my kids were that young. It goes by so fast."

"Thank you," I say, leaving it at that. I'm not about to go into the past six years of my life with a kind stranger, but I appreciate her sentiments.

Sloane and the girls return a few minutes later, paper bags and drinks in hand. They sit down and divvy out the food, handing me a sandwich and a bottle of water.

"That was quick," I say.

Eames reaches for his mom—not surprisingly—and she scoops him into her lap.

"One day you'll be his favorite, you know," she says with a wink.

"I don't know about that," I tease.

"Oh, let me get that for you," Sloane says to Marabel when she spots her struggling to open the wrapper to her granola bar. We've both learned with the girls that there's a fine line between being too much and not enough. Sloane has never wanted to replace Emma and always makes a point to include her memory whenever it feels natural, but she also knows that sometimes the girls need her more than they realize. It's a balancing act, and I don't know how she does it, but she makes it look like a cakewalk.

"As soon as we land, it should be time to check into the Airbnb, and then I'll get the code," Sloane says. "I'm so excited . . . this'll be the first time we're all under one roof with our families."

I can't say that I'm over the moon about living in the same house with Margaux, Ethan, their twin terrors—I mean toddlers—and Sloane's mom, but it's one of those things you sign up for when you say "I do."

I've only met Sloane's mom a handful of times over the years, seeing how she doesn't like to travel, but she's always been kind. She's certainly no monster-in-law, and she's significantly less self-involved than Emma's parents were.

"Theodora wants us to FaceTime her Christmas morning," I remind Sloane.

"Where is she this month?" Sloane asks.

"Greece. I think . . ."

My aunt finally retired at the end of last year. At first she was worried about what she was going to do with all that extra time on her hands, but it didn't take her long to figure that out.

"What time does your mom land tomorrow?" Sloane bounces Eames on her knee as he giggles, gripping onto her hands for dear life. She's been so busy keeping him entertained that she hasn't even touched her food. I throw back the last couple of bites of my sandwich and take him so she can eat.

"Eight o'clock," I say. "Somewhere around there."

"I can't wait to see her again," Sloane says. "She hasn't seen Eames since he was two months old. She'll hardly recognize him, I bet."

"She said she's bringing something special for you . . . she wouldn't tell me what it is, though."

Sloane places her hand over her heart and tilts her head. "She's the sweetest. I love her."

When we initially invited my mom to Ohio for Christmas, we never expected her to say yes. We're glad she did—of course—but this will be the first time she'll be meeting Sloane's family, and with all of us staying in the same house, it's going to be interesting.

I have no doubt there'll be zero dull moments.

That's one of the best parts about having a family.

It's never boring.

When Sloane first found this rental, she was so excited she screamed. Literally. I heard her from the next room over and rushed down to find out what was wrong. It turns out, this old Victorian mansion in her hometown was always her favorite house growing up, and she always dreamed of living there as a little girl. With nine bedrooms, ten baths, a horse stable, and a million breakable antiques, I'm prepared for an expensive week.

Correction—a priceless week.

"Attention, Delta passengers, we're about to begin our boarding process for flight 5215 with nonstop service to Cincinnati . . . ," the gate attendant announces.

"Here we go," Sloane says. "Christmas in Ohio . . ."

I lean in and steal a kiss from my wife's smiling lips. While everyone around us gathers their bags and makes their way to the line forming outside our gate, I take a moment to appreciate how far we've come. It's been a pretty amazing ride so far, and I have no doubt things are only going to get better.

AFTERWORD

Dear Reader—

I was in the midst of penning this book when my brother's wife passed away. Valery was only thirty-five, and it was her second time battling the cruel and merciless monster that is breast cancer. While my brother and Val attended the same high school many moons ago, they didn't connect until a few years ago, when they found themselves working for the same employer.

I'm convinced the universe knew exactly what it was doing when it conspired their reunion.

From the instant Tim and Val met, they were inseparable. And from the moment I first saw them together, I knew I was witnessing the beginning of something special. Their connection wasn't fire and ice. It wasn't dramatic. They weren't caught up in the rush or blinded by the newness of a budding romance.

It was easy. It was sweet. It was genuine. It was tender.

It was as if they'd been waiting for one another their entire lives, and once they found each other, they slipped into their own soft and gentle bliss.

As someone who writes romance for a living, I'd never seen anything like the connection they shared—fictional or otherwise.

Within a year, Tim and Val were fast-tracking their own fairy tale. They'd bought a house in their hometown and were eagerly planning to marry, have babies, and live happily ever after.

Less than two months after moving into their new home, Val learned her cancer had returned . . . with a vengeance.

Her doctors told her she had two weeks to two months to live if she didn't start treatment immediately—which she did—and our family rallied together to throw them a wedding in the midst of a global pandemic.

The celebration miraculously came together in mere weeks. We hosted the nuptials in our home with only immediate family in attendance (we streamed it on Facebook for everyone else). My husband got ordained online so he could perform the ceremony. Our mom coordinated the flowers and cake. Our youngest brother handled the playlist. I did Val's makeup and took the photos. Our stepmom (Iowa's own Martha Stewart) made the most beautiful altar. Val's dad gave her away, walking her down a makeshift aisle in the middle of our living room.

It was a chilly February day amid a surreal and uncertain backdrop, but by the end of the night we were dancing to the Backstreet Boys, taking tequila shots, eating take-out pizza, and laughing so much we temporarily forgot the true reason behind their shotgun wedding.

Their earthly marriage lasted exactly one year and eight months.

Not nearly enough time with the love of your life, but that's the thing about cancer—it doesn't care.

But I digress.

Val fought like hell every step of the way, and my brother was by her side for every high and low moment of it. There were periods of good news and hope, and then there were periods of heartbreak and harsh reality. But throughout it all, they never stopped loving each other in a way that I can only describe as otherworldly.

We were fortunate enough to be by Val's side the moment she passed, and I'll never forget watching my brother seated at the foot of her hospital bed, massaging her swollen feet as he played one of her favorite songs from his phone ("Here on Out," by Dave Matthews Band, if you're wondering). He wore a smile for her sake, though his eyes were full of pain. In her final moments, all he wanted was for her to be comfortable, to be cared for, and to know how much she was loved.

While we all know there will never be another Val—not even close—I hope that my brother can someday find the courage to love again.

And if there's one thing I want my brother (and anyone else who has ever loved and lost) to know, it's this: loving someone new doesn't mean you love the one you lost any less.

Love is as simple as it is complex. There's seldom a direct path. It's an expedition for which there are no road maps—only detours, obstacles, delays, inevitable breakdowns, random roadside attractions, and the occasional lonely stretch of highway before you reach your final destination.

Embrace the journey—it's the only one we get.

And safe travels to all.

Love and only love—
Winter

ABOUT THE AUTHOR

Wall Street Journal and #1 Amazon bestselling author Winter Renshaw is a bona fide daydream believer. She lives somewhere in the middle of the USA and can rarely be seen without her notebook and laptop. When she's not writing, she's thinking about writing. And when she's not thinking about writing, she's living the American dream with her husband, three kids, and two extremely spoiled dogs.

Winter also writes psychological and domestic suspense under her Minka Kent pseudonym. Her first book, *The Memory Watcher*, hit #9 in the Kindle store, and her follow-up, *The Thinnest Air*, hit #1 in the Kindle store and spent five weeks as a *Washington Post* bestseller. Her work has been featured in *People* magazine and the *New York Post* as well as optioned for film and TV.

She is represented by Jill Marsal at Marsal Lyon Literary Agency.

Connect at www.facebook.com/authorwinterrenshaw or https://winterrenshaw.com, or follow her @winterrenshaw on Instagram or @winterrenshaw.minkakent on TikTok.